MW00333431

NOTES for a EULOGY

A Novel by

Eric J. Matluck

Publisher, Copyright, and Additional Information

Notes for a Eulogy by Eric J. Matluck
Published by Eric J. Matluck, Hackettstown, New Jersey.

ISBN- 978-0-578-73999-1

Cover design and interior design by Rafael Andres

ACKNOWLEDGMENTS

offer my heartfelt thanks to Rafael Andres, whose wonderful designs made his book what it is, and my journalism professor Tom Simonet, who inspired my passionate love of literature.

For Gretchen

"To come up with the right answer often takes little more than clever calculation, but to come up with the right question takes genius."
—Albert Einstein

NOTES for a EULOGY

PART ONE

To tell the TRUTH

Tonight, I decided, I would tell her the truth: that everything I'd told her until then was a lie. Everything. All twenty-three years of it. Of the time I'd introduced her to my mother, who was a lady from the neighborhood playing the role of a woman who'd passed away five years before. Of the time I'd taken her, many months later, to my mother's funeral, this time the role of my mother being played by a woman who'd married one of my father's cousins, so shared our last name. And why didn't she get suspicious when we hadn't gone back to anyone's house after the burial? Probably because she knew I had work to do at home, and that I'd never been close to my mother, or so I'd told her, so I wasn't interested in discussing her death with anybody just then. After all, I'd found my mother hard to get along with. I'd told her that, too, and that provided me with the luxury, for more than half a decade, of having someone to complain about.

But what about all the other stories, the other illusions? What purpose did they serve? They served many, but each will be explained in its own time. And why was I even doing this; telling her that I hadn't told the truth? I don't know. Maybe to understand and absolve myself or maybe just to rile her. As I said, everything in its own time. The first thing I should probably explain is how we met; she and I. We met at work. In fact, I hired her.

Please meet MS. TANZER

I'm a teacher of high school English, and the district in which I teach, Lake Quaintance, has again been voted to be academically the finest, most advanced district in our state. Which comforts and stimulates me because it means that the number of recalcitrant students who filter into my classes is kept to a minimum. No, not everybody spends all of his or her free time reading, and not everybody even reads what's been assigned, but the number of students with whom I can have a serious conversation about what makes literature great seems, to me, unusually high.

And hiring another English teacher, our fifth, would be gratifying, because it would provide me with one more person to converse with, and someone closer to my own age.

"Morley," my boss Leo, the head of the English department, said one cloudy early spring morning, when the world looked like it was being broadcast in black and white. "I'd like you to meet Ms. Tanzer."

"Hopelessly old-fashioned, Leo," I said, and turned to the woman standing in front of me. "We go by first names here. Or are you, Mr. Kubol, a student addressing his teacher?" I smiled at him. "Have we hired her already?"

"Why don't you decide?" Leo asked me, and winked.

"How are you?" I asked her, as Leo walked away.

She seemed relieved. "I'm doing well," she said. "You?"

"Fine," I told her. "Just fine."

The first thing that struck me about her, and I still didn't know her first name, because Leo had never shown me her résumé and always referred to her as "Ms. Tanzer" or "the Tanzer woman," was how tall and thin she was—at least six-foot-two or six-foot-three and likely not more than one hundred fifty pounds—and the fact that she wore her almost grayish blonde hair in a beehive, which only accentuated her slenderness and made her look like she'd just been dripped from the end of a long pipette or an astonishingly narrow paintbrush. The hairdo appealed because it was so unthreateningly old-fashioned. People said that I was old-fashioned, too, so having someone else who people thought of in the same way could take some of the onus off me.

Her face was pale, naturally pale, as she wasn't wearing makeup, and thin, though her eyes were wide and periwinkle blue, and her mouth, a mere dash, while not expressive, hinted at a pliability that I liked. Looking at that dash, I bet myself that I could make her smile. She was neatly attired in a turquoise pantsuit and white blouse, but no jewelry, and that outfit alone might have made me feel comfortable with her, something I rarely was around people, because turquoise was my favorite color. And although I couldn't have known it then, every time I would see her after that, she would be wearing something containing turquoise, even if it was just a solitary stripe on a sock or stocking or a single stone in a bracelet, necklace, or earring, all of which she took to adorning herself with after she was hired.

I walked her into the small office, a couple of doors down from Leo's, that was open to everyone in our department. It was long and narrow and had no windows, in contrast to most of the classrooms, which had six windows. And if it was oppressive, I was sure she realized that she wouldn't be spending much time there. We sat in two armless dark green leather chairs without a desk between us. I figured that the absence of anything signifying hierarchy would relax her.

"Please call me by my first name," she said. Which, of course, I was planning to. "It's Francine. And it's 'Mrs.,' not 'Ms.'"

Was she worried? She needn't have been.

"So you're married," I said.

"Happily enough," she said.

"Enough?"

"Happily."

That sounded better.

"May I call you Fran?" I asked.

"Please don't," she said. "Only my husband calls me that."

Well that was surprising. Who's so defensive about being called what her husband calls her? Something, I figured, wasn't right there.

"And you're Morley," she said quickly, then considered it.

"Yes," I said. "Morley Peck."

"That's a name you don't hear much anymore—"

"Ley," I said, completing it. "I know."

"It's from another time," she said.

I figured that she'd be smiling, but she wasn't, so I smiled for both of us.

"To be honest," she said, lowering her voice, "when I heard your name, I was expecting to meet someone much older. Do you mind my saying that?"

I looked at her, surprised by how personal her question was. She looked to be about my age—I was thirty-seven then—but I wasn't sure why she'd asked it. If it was meant as flattery, it was lost on me because I didn't have enough self-esteem to appreciate it. "Well not if you don't mind my being younger," I said, and laughed. Then I reminded myself that this was her interview, not her first day on the job and not someone else's cocktail party. "Would you like to talk about your previous places of employ?" I asked, half-jokingly.

She screwed her mouth into a pucker, and her eyeballs rushed toward each other so quickly that for a moment I thought she was cross-eyed. "Not really," she said. "You've read my résumé, right?"

No, I hadn't. Nor had I ever been asked to interview anyone, so I wasn't sure what I'd say and whether talking about a person's previous jobs was either necessary or appropriate. And Leo seemed so determined to hire her that I figured that any time I spent with her would be just for show; to give the impression that our decision had been based on careful thought. So "Of course," I said. "I was just curious."

But there was something about her reluctance that intrigued me and that I even found endearing. It made me want to hire her just so I could learn the answers to my questions. Maybe that was a deliberate ploy on her part, but I doubted it.

She placed her right leg over her left and pointed her foot toward me.

I leaned forward, then realized we'd both been sitting stock-still since we sat down. "I have to tell you," I said, "I took a course in nonverbal communication when I was in college, and there's a lot of meaning in what you just did."

"Nonverbal communication?" she asked, sounding like she didn't understand what I'd just told her, and looking a little stricken.

"Oh, it was weird. The professor didn't talk for the whole semester. He just gestured."

Her look of surprise turned to shock, then horror, and then, finally, she covered her mouth and laughed, but it was the laugh of somebody who wasn't used to laughing. Of course my story was made-up, but lies are often more entertaining than the truth.

"What a wonderful laugh," I said. It wasn't. "But seriously, they say that when somebody crosses his or her legs toward you, it means they're comfortable with you."

I expected her to uncross them then, but she didn't.

"All right," I said, and realized I was rolling my eyes, though I was trying not to. "If you could describe yourself in one word, what would it be?"

She slouched and said, "Good Lord, I don't know. Give me a minute. One word?"

"It's a trick question," I said.

"Not yet. Give me a second now."

"No," I said. "You don't have to answer it." I smiled limply. "The only reason I asked you that is because I wanted to tell you a story."

She looked confused. "What? Why?"

"It's not fair, but Leo asked me that when I came in for my interview. And I thought it was a stupid question. Except that I had a great answer. 'One word?' I asked him. 'One word,' he said. 'Okay,' I told him. 'If I had to describe myself in one word, I guess it would be "pathetic."' 'Pathetic?' he asked. 'Yes,' I said. 'If I could describe myself in one word, meaning that if my life were so simple that it could be described in only one word, that would be pretty pathetic.'"

She smiled wanly. "I like that," she said, but I wasn't convinced. Nor should I have been, since that was made-up, too. "I was actually thinking of the word *curious*," she said, "as you'd said just a few moments ago, because I like the double meaning. I'm a curious person because I've got a lot of curiosity...about other things and other people, and I'm also different. Unique. So, to most people, curious."

And I loved that. "That's a better answer than mine," I said, stunned, impressed, and terribly disappointed with my own cleverness, which suddenly felt very facile. And then, "Okay," I told her. "You passed." I stood up.

"Passed?" she asked.

"Yes," I said. "You're hired, if you want the job. And I'm assuming you do, or why else would you be here?"

And finally she smiled, more broadly than I thought she could, and in that smile I saw not just warmth but acceptance. I took that smile as an accomplishment, and felt good about myself. *Look at what I can do!*

"Don't take this the wrong way," she said, "but are you in a position to hire me? Isn't that up to Leo?"

"No," I said. "It's not up to Leo. It's up to me, and I want you to take the job. If you still want it, knowing that you'll be working with a bunch of loonies like Leo and me."

In fact I had no idea if I was in a position to hire her, and I could imagine Leo flying into a rage, even if he never had, finding out that I'd offered her the job, or even take legal action against me. Who knew?

But when we walked into Leo's office and I said, "She's ours," he beamed, got up, said, "I'm glad," and, extending his right hand to Francine, said, "Welcome."

Not-quite-immediate
CONSEQUENCES

Francine started teaching English at Lake Quaintance High School that fall. On Tuesday, September second, to be exact; the day after Labor Day. It was a short summer that year. I would never find out why she'd been interviewed in the early spring rather than closer to the start of the new school year, as was more common; perhaps she was going away for the warm months. Leo would later tell me that he'd talked to her again a few times after her interview but hadn't seen her until she came back to teach.

And that made me jealous, which surprised me. I'm not usually so possessive of people that sharing them with others is a bother. In fact, I'm not possessive at all. I enjoy my own company more than other people's, and if that isn't the way most people feel, I was always glad to have something that marked me as different. What really set me apart, though, was knowing what I loved, what made me happy, and, because of that, being able to keep myself happy. Most people didn't make me happy but, I think, most people didn't make themselves happy, either. They stumbled across happiness, didn't know how or where they found it, and then couldn't get it back. But by knowing what I enjoyed—listening to classical music, reading, and teaching—I was always lucky enough to charm myself.

Francine wasn't like me. Although I'd spoken with her for all of twenty minutes at that point, she struck me as unhappy and not so much someone who *needed* help but someone who would *appreciate* help. So I set myself the task of lightening her burden by befriending her. If she wanted it. And that, again, would make me feel like I'd accomplished something.

She taught five classes that year, typical of any new teacher. Those who were there for more than a year would teach six. Her five were *French Literature in English Translation, Elizabethan Poetry, Essay Writing, The Short Story,* and *Bestsellers.* Yes, they sounded more like college courses than high school courses, but each year more than ninety-six percent of our graduates went on to college, and we wanted them to feel comfortable with, and be prepared for that transition. Which was a nice way of acknowledging that people hated change.

Her favorite course was *Bestsellers*, though she privately referred to it as *Bestsellers: Genius or Crap?* But one of the advantages to it, she said, was that she never knew what books she'd be teaching until just before the semester began, because it depended on what was topping the *New York Times* best-seller list.

Her other favorite course, which she told me she was looking forward to teaching almost as much, was *French Literature in English Translation*, and she made a point of letting me know that she avoided Proust, not because she didn't like him, which, it turned out, was true enough, but because, especially as a new teacher, she didn't want to overwhelm her students.

Only later would I find out that she'd never read Proust because, she'd said, she found the thought of him too intimidating. I never had either, and for the same reason, so I couldn't criticize her for that, though intimidation could be hugely inspiring. Still, I wondered why she hadn't felt comfortable enough with me to be honest. And this was before I started lying to her as a way of life.

Take NOTES

There were eight periods to the school day. Everybody broke for lunch during fourth period, and Francine, who taught five classes, had two periods free. I, who taught six, had one. But it was second period, which was a nice respite after my early morning salvo, and it was one of Francine's free periods—the other was sixth, which meant that she had to teach only two classes back-to-back, at the end of the day—so we had time to talk every morning.

She was quiet for the first few weeks; quieter, even, than she'd been on her interview. She would come by the office where we'd originally sat, say good morning, smile, and then leave or, later, bring over a cup of coffee—I drank tea—and let me know what was on her mind. And I, in turn, would tell her about myself: that I enjoyed being alone, that I listened to classical music, and that I read a lot, and since I hadn't discovered literature until I was in college, I read with the zeal of the converted. That was true, but it ended there, because then I told her that my mother, a difficult, elderly woman, lived with me.

"Why?" she asked.

"Because she had no place else to go after my father died." I laughed affectedly. "And believe me, nobody else would take her in."

"What makes her so difficult?"

"Disapproval," I said. "She doesn't approve of anything I or anyone else does."

She smiled placidly. "I can understand that," she said, but then the bell rang and we were off to our next classes. And I couldn't quite dislodge the thought that she meant, I can understand somebody finding you at fault.

In very little time she told me that I was old-fashioned, primarily, she said, because of the way I dressed and, incongruously, because I always grabbed the handrail, though never tightly, when walking up or down the stairs. That, she thought, was more old-mannish than old-fashioned, but she believed it contributed to my quaintness or courtliness, as she called it. Clearly she was paying a lot of attention to me, and I was surprised, because I wasn't paying a lot to her. As to the way I dressed, I wore a sport jacket to work every day, but almost never a tie, most often a dress shirt, but sometimes a turtleneck, and dress slacks and leather shoes. And always a fedora: felt in the cool months, straw when it was warm. There was no dress code at our school, and Leo was fine with people dressing any way that made them comfortable.

"Very quaint," she said, almost laughing, when she walked in on me one morning. I was wearing a brown tweed sport jacket, one I rarely wore, with leather patches on the elbows, a cream crew-neck wool sweater, powder blue button-down shirt, chocolate brown flannel pants, and burgundy wingtips, but those, at least, she'd seen before.

"I have to tell you," I said, "I'm not really old-fashioned."

"No. You just look it."

"I'm actually very progressive."

Her smile fell, she held up her right hand, said, "I don't want to talk politics, if that's what you meant," and the conversation ended there. That, I thought, would require revisiting.

A week later she seemed more comfortable around me, if not happier.

"I walked into the local 7-Eleven this morning and was surprised to see that they sold mace," she said.

"Why?" I asked.

"I didn't think they'd sell that in a town this quiet."

"Hey," I said. "Even Oz had its Wicked Witches."

She shook her head. "No place is paradise."

And so it went as the first month dragged into the second.

"What do you think is the most important thing you can teach your students?" she asked me one day. I didn't have an answer, so she said, "Take notes. It helps. In fact, it's essential if you're going to remember anything. That's what I tell all of my classes. Not because they're good to go back to after you've sat through a forty-five minute lecture, but because the act of writing triggers a part of your brain that's connected to memory, so when you write something, the statement will bury itself much more deeply in your mind than if you just hear it."

"I'll have to remember that," I said. I'd actually heard it before, but I was still impressed, and happy that we at least shared that.

Finally, one Wednesday morning in mid-October, she came in and asked, "Would you like to have dinner tonight?"

"I'd like to have dinner every night," I said, but I knew what she meant, and what she wanted, only I didn't feel like extending our relationship outside of school just yet.

Steadily she said, "I meant with me."

"I'm sorry," I said, "perhaps my humor got lost. Actually, I can't make it tonight. I have plans." And then, to get her mind off the thought, if it was there, that I was dining with someone else, I said, "You know, papers to grade. I've been putting them off for the longest time and have to give them back tomorrow."

"No, that's all right," she said, though she sounded remarkably unconvinced. And why shouldn't she? I was lying to her again.

So I said, "But I can make it next Tuesday, if you'd like." I didn't want to disappoint or hurt her. Besides, it's one thing to sit home alone on a Saturday night because no one has asked you out, and very much another to sit home alone because you've turned down at least one good invitation.

She seemed pleased. "Really?" she asked, and smiled.

I nodded. "Really."

"Cool," she said, a word I didn't expect to hear from her, because it struck me as whimsical. "I'll pencil you in."

"Where would you like to go?" I asked.

"Come to my house," she said.

I was hoping any look of disappointment wasn't obvious. I much preferred dining in restaurants to dining in other people's homes. I was a terribly finnicky eater, avoiding all red meats, which didn't include veal, and in poultry I would eat only dark meat, and most people, simply put, weren't especially good cooks. I certainly wasn't. Besides, restaurants offered a variety of stimuli, other guests and waiters and waitresses to watch and listen to, and a large space to let my mind wander, in contrast to the forced intimacy of dinner between two people in someone's house.

But then she added, "And we can decide where to go when you get there."

"Where do you live?" I asked.

"In Oberlies," she said.

In the CATBIRD seat

Oberlies was a town of about fifteen thousand that was considered upscale by the people who lived around it but not by the people who lived in it. In fact it wasn't especially wealthy, its residents living more comfortably than extravagantly, but its main street had an unusual number of high-end shops and boutiques, and was often said to look like a picture postcard. It was twenty miles east of Lake Quaintance, where I lived, so it took me a little more than half an hour to get to Francine's house. To her credit, she'd given good directions.

She lived in a split-level on Schepper Avenue, which dead-ended, a few houses down, at a park, and wasn't even walking distance from the center of town. It looked large from the outside but surprisingly small and even claustrophobic once I got in, probably because all of the walls were dark. Her foyer and living room were painted burnt orange—there was no wallpaper, which might have added variety—her kitchen and dinette maroon, her dining room almost navy blue, and her hallway forest green. I couldn't tell what color the basement was. I was no lover of white walls but I kept wanting to ask her to turn on more lights.

"So this is home," she said when she met me at the door.

"Nice," I said.

"I don't think so, either, but Peter likes it."

It was a little disconcerting that she could pick up so easily on my fibs.

And Peter's—at least I assumed it was Peter's—presence filled the house, or what parts of it I could see, because there were pictures of him everywhere; in each room and along the hallway. Maybe she needed to remind herself what he looked like because he was away a lot, maybe he had died and she'd converted her home into a shrine, and maybe he'd never existed. I couldn't have been the only one who lied. Five framed shots of him sat in the living room, three much smaller pictures were pasted to the side-by-side refrigerator, which seemed unusually large, at least to someone who lived alone, and more were collected in the dining room breakfront. What struck me as odd was that every one of them showed Peter by himself.

He looked to be slightly older than she was, had a broad, flat face, a wide jaw, and teeth that also looked flattened in the middle, making him appear to be trapped under glass or emulsion and within four metal, wooden, or paper bars. His smile looked forced. His dark hair was combed back neatly and was graying, but what struck me most about all of the pictures was how incredibly pale his eyes were—almost colorless, so that in the color photographs I could barely tell that they were blue—and how each picture was cropped so tightly around his face that I had no idea what his body looked like. He may have been very thin, like Francine, but the face, or perhaps the face the way it was shown, made me expect a man of girth.

I pointed to one. "Peter?" I asked.

"Peter," she said. Then her look turned serious. "Sit down, I want to tell you something."

I was standing in front of the couch so I lowered myself onto it. The furniture, while nice, didn't seem to fit her at all. More grandiose than I expected, but also more dowdy. As though it had been passed down for at least two generations. I half-expected to see plastic slipcovers on the couch, club chair, and ladies' chairs, an insanity that was popular with our parents' generation. "All right," I said, matching her sobriety. "What's up?"

"I feel as though I owe you an explanation." She stood just to my right.

"For what?" I asked. "What did you do now?" I chuckled, but I did that often, especially when I was nervous.

She shook her head. "Oh, nothing," she said. "Except that I'd told you on my interview that only my husband calls me Fran."

"Yes," I said. "I was intrigued by that." Intrigued was too strong a word, but it was close enough.

"Well, okay, the truth of the matter is," she said, and paused to inhale deeply, "I never explained why I hate being called Fran. It's because there was a group of girls in high school who used to tease and taunt me by calling me Fran Tan. You know, short for Francine Tanzer. And I never got over that."

"But your husband calls you Fran," I said, though I was already shaking my head.

"Yes, but that's different."

"Why?" I asked. "Because he doesn't care?" I was surprised by my own question, but still wondered if theirs was a good marriage.

"Because," she said, "he's my husband."

Sad, I thought. And no, don't ask me if I'd like something to drink. But "That makes sense," I said. "Okay, then. Can I now ask you a terribly personal question?" I was kidding, but curious to see what her reaction would be.

"*Terribly* personal? I guess," she said. She always sounded more guarded than I thought she needed to.

"Your name. Tanzer. Is that German?" I knew it was, but the derivation of people's names always fascinated me because I was adopted, so I never knew what my original last name was or where my family came from.

"Yes," she said, "though I'm not a dancer, even if my name implies it. But my husband is."

"A dancer."

"Yes, but not German. He's Dutch. Ghell. Peter Ghell." Her voice had taken on a stammer, as though she were discussing something she didn't want to.

"So you go by your maiden name."

And even more morosely, she said, "I do."

"Can I ask you why?"

"No," she said. "Or yes, you can ask, but I just won't tell you. Let's just say it's easier this way."

The woman of a million unanswered questions.

"Where is your husband, by the way?" I asked, and as soon as I did I realized that I'd made a mistake. I knew he wouldn't be there, but the way I'd voiced it made it sound like I was disappointed that he wouldn't be joining us. And that threw Francine off her guard.

"He's out bowling with a friend of his."

"That's nice," I said.

"Why do you say that?" she asked.

Why did I say that? What was I supposed to say? "Why do you ask?"

"What's nice about it?" She seemed concerned, and possibly hurt.

"What's *nice*," I said, "is that it gives me the opportunity to have dinner with you. After all, you invited me."

"True that."

"Which, I'm thinking, we couldn't have done if he were here. You know, I would feel awkward being the proverbial third wheel."

She showed a look of surprise. "Oh. So you're not married, then," she said.

"You know my mother lives with me," I said.

"Yes, I knew that, but I didn't know if anyone else did, too."

"Look, with the way I described my life, did it really sound like I could be involved with anyone? Intimately?"

"You never know," she said.

A tuxedo cat wandered up to me, rubbed against both of my legs, and purred. "Nice outfit," I said, looking down at it. "What's her name?"

"His. Fisher."

I tended to think of cats as female and dogs as male. "Well good," I said. "I'd hate to think she was a cross-dresser."

He meowed then jumped on my lap.

"He likes you," she said, sounding pleased. Perhaps she used him to determine the inherent goodness of others, because animals were said to be good judges of people.

"Does he like sticking his paws in fish tanks?" I asked. He was pawing me, and I was surprised. In those days I thought that felines were expressive and affectionate only on cans of cat food and boxes of litter.

"I don't have any fish tanks so I can't answer that," she said impassively. "No, Fisher was my grandmother's maiden name. That's why I named him that."

"Oh. Did *she* like sticking her...hands in fish tanks?" I laughed and Francine ignored me. But when Fisher jumped down and I got up to follow him—for the moment, at least, he seemed more endearing company than she did—I saw that there was a bird cage holding two parakeets, one green and one blue, around the corner, in the dining room. "Cat food?" I asked.

"If I run out," she said.

"Well if you do, feed them both to him at the same time, or the other one is bound to blab to the police."

And finally she laughed.

"So where do you want to eat?" I asked her, glad to hear her laugh, and looking forward to being someplace where she might feel less inhibited.

We decided on Roscoe's Diner in Saloway, a town roughly midway between Oberlies and Lake Quaintance, and a little smaller than either. We both knew and liked the diner, and the menu was large, so it could satisfy whatever we were in the mood for, and we'd already rejected Chinese, Japanese, Mexican, Italian, seafood, and steak.

On the way there—I drove—I asked, "You know why dogs are more popular than cats?"

She shook her head.

"Think about it. When dogs open their mouths, which dogs often do, they look like they're smiling. But when cats keep their mouths closed, which is more usual for them, they look like they're frowning. So dogs look happier and cats look less happy. And we tend to be attracted to happiness. Make sense?"

God knows why I was attracted to her.

"I guess," she said.

Of course I knew that cats were more popular than dogs, but that interfered with the point I was trying to make.

FOOD for THOUGHT

Diners, when Francine and I were growing up, had been built to look, at least on the outside, like the railcars from which they evolved, and they prided themselves, or so it seemed, on their simplicity and efficiency. Nothing about them was fancy; not the food, not the décor, not the staff. Now diners were gaudy and glitzy, offering large dining rooms, faux-crystal chandeliers, marbled walls, fountains—ours did—and Greek statuary. And if it was all in horrendously bad taste, it was also great fun.

I was greeted by the hostess when we walked in; Francine was not. So I assumed I just came there more often than she did. We were shown to a booth in the long row of booths to the right of the entrance, and a waitress, Vicki, who'd taken care of me many times before, came by and asked, "The usual?"

I smiled and nodded. "The usual," I said.

"What's 'the usual'?" Francine asked.

"Iced tea."

"There's not a lot of variety in your life, is there?"

I was expecting that she'd at least be impressed by the fact that I *had* a "usual" somewhere. "There's plenty," I said. Which, of course, wasn't true, as there was virtually none, but my lie had a reason. What she was really saying was, Your life doesn't satisfy you, does it? It couldn't, because it would never satisfy me. And what I was saying was, My life satisfies me completely, at least as much as yours satisfies you. We just saw things differently and, possibly, heard them differently, too.

I'd often wondered about what people really hear. For instance, I could say to someone, "What's your favorite color?" and that person could hear, What does two plus two equal? That person could then say, "Four," but I would hear, Blue.

But that was an issue with the limits, or limitations of communicating and understanding. There were others. Take lamb. Some people love to eat it. I know that, but I like neither its taste nor its texture, so I don't eat it. And if someone were to ask me, "How could you not love lamb?" I would say, "I don't know how, I just don't." And, I'm sure, I never will. Understanding can extend only so far. But if someone were to describe it in terms of something I did love, for example, explain their attraction to it by saying, "I love lamb the way you love Brahms," I would instantly understand what they meant, and appreciate how much they enjoyed it. But most people, including Francine, or so it seemed, didn't or couldn't do that. They could see things only one way; the way that they were most familiar with.

It was time to change the subject. "So is Fisher your first cat?" I asked.

She pursed her lips. "Sadly, no," she said. "I lost Tomas nine years ago but never got another one until Fisher came along, and he was a stray, about three years back."

"Oh," I said. "If you don't mind my asking you," and here I shifted uncomfortably in my seat, "why did you wait so long? To get a new one."

Her eyes widened. "Why?" She must have minded. She pursed her lips again and said, "Because the time wasn't right. Don't get me wrong, a lot of strays crossed my path after Tomas passed, but I just wasn't ready for one." Then she said, "I can tell by the look on your face that you don't understand me."

She was right. And marvelously observant. Because I counted myself, too, among those people who couldn't see things in any way that wasn't familiar to them. "Well, I suppose it varies from person to person," I said. "I just remember that after my Aunt Doro died, my Uncle Olin remarried less than three months later, and even that seemed like a long time."

"Doro. Is that short for Dorothy?" she asked.

I had no idea, as I'd never heard her called anything else, so I said, "Of course."

"So why did he remarry so quickly?" She sounded thoughtful. "Did he not like your aunt?"

"Oh, he loved her," I said, "but I could tell that my uncle needed someone. To be there for him, to care for him. To do whatever it was that Doro had done for him."

"Three months?"

I raised my eyebrows. "She was actually a friend of my aunt's, his new wife, though not someone my uncle ever saw much. Just a friend outside the house, and that, I think, eased the pain. The fact that his second wife knew his first one."

*

My Aunt Doro died when I was seventeen, and my Uncle Olin followed her fifteen years later. He never remarried and, as far as I knew, never even considered remarrying. But he was my father's brother, and that side of the family, unlike my mother's side, was always quiet. So it wasn't that I couldn't read his moods so much as that I couldn't tell if he had any moods to begin with. But the impression I got was that, although he'd loved his wife, or so I'd assumed, he'd been satisfied enough with the relationship to be able to live off his memories for whatever time was left to him. He certainly never seemed to want for anything in the last decade and a half of his life, and that served as a profound inspiration to me.

But Francine's decision to not adopt another pet bothered me. Since pets, who lived shorter lives than we did, were replaced so much more frequently and easily, I came to believe that when a pet passes on, it does so to allow another pet's life to be saved, and that to *not* replace a pet in a timely manner is to disrespect the dead. So I chose to show my disapproval by lying.

*

"Are you ready to order?" Vicki asked.

We ordered and then felt unusually pleased with ourselves, as each of us found something that appealed and that, we said, we hadn't thought about: pot roast for her and chicken kabob for me.

After we were served, Francine said, "So tell me more about your mother."

I leaned back. "What would you like to know?" I was waiting for my chicken kabob to cool down before I tasted it. They were nice enough to make it with dark meat just for me, but I came there often and always tipped well.

"Is she seriously ill? Is that what makes her so bitter?"

I shook my head. "I don't think so. To both of your questions. Of course, if you ask her, she has *everything* wrong, but she'll probably outlive me. And I say that because spending that much time with a corrosive person really diminishes your quality of life." I always tasted my side dish first, in this case herbed rice. Then I said, "Look, we have this sort of weird definition of what's 'normal' when it comes to parent-child relationships. You live at home until you reach a certain age, say, eighteen or twenty-one, and then you move out on your own, and your parents become much less of an influence on you." I swallowed. "Until *they* move in with you. Or, more likely, one of them moves in with you. It's something people don't talk about or think about much. But they should. So they can be ready for it when it happens."

"It doesn't always happen, though," she said.

"No, of course it doesn't always happen. But it's good to always be ready for it."

"You don't sound like you were ready for it," she said. She seemed to be enjoying her pot roast.

"I couldn't have been. She was always like this. This isn't anything new. And I knew it would be hard after my father died. So I suppose *knowing* I wouldn't be able to deal with it was my way of getting ready." I put my knife and fork down. "You want me to give you an example?"

"Of what?" she asked, leaning toward me.

"Of her at her best?"

"Sure," Francine said. "I guess so."

"Okay. Once, when we were at a restaurant, my mother got livid because the people at the next table, who ordered after we did, were served before us. So she started yelling at the waitress."

"Well that must have been embarrassing."

"Exactly," I said. "It *should* have been embarrassing, for her, but she was sure she was right."

Francine sighed. "People often think that way."

"And maybe they just ordered something that didn't take as long. Besides, what control did the waitress have? She picks up the food when it's ready."

*

After my father died, my mother and I, who had always been close, became even closer. We both supposed that was natural. And to reinforce that closeness we set up a routine whereby we ate at particular restaurants on particular nights every week. On Tuesday nights we ate at the Greenwood Inn, a terribly fancy name for a terribly modest restaurant that served American food, and so was a glorified diner—glorified in the sense that it had only tables, no booths—that both my parents and I had enjoyed for years. One night, my mother looked at a loud family of four seated a few tables away from us, who were being served by the same waitress as we were, and said quietly, "Look at that. They're getting their food already, but they ordered after us."

"You should tell the waitress about that," I said.

"Why?" She looked surprised. "What can the waitress do? She serves the food when they hand it to her; it's not her decision."

"Yeah, but saying something to her might relieve the pressure."

"What pressure?" my mother asked.

"The pressure that's building up inside you."

She shook her head. "There's no pressure building up inside me. *You*, maybe; not me."

"Must you always criticize me?"

She rolled her eyes. "Yes," she said mechanically. "If you call that criticism, then I suppose I must." Then she laughed. "You take things much more seriously than you need to."

Displacement. It was always easier to attribute my worst habits to someone else.

*

As soon as I'd finished all of the grilled chicken and vegetables on my first skewer, Francine asked, "So have you lived in Lake Quaintance all your life?"

I shook my head. "I'm not that resistant to change. No, I grew up in Freeh's Corner." I'd never actually been there but I knew of it.

"Oh, nice town," she said.

"Yes, but it was small. And they don't have their own school district, as I'm sure you know."

"I know."

"So I went to school in West Ellis." I'd driven through there a couple of times.

"Great schools," she said. "I like West Ell."

And I forced a smile because I hated it when people spoke in abbreviations. Yes, almost everybody who lived in or was familiar with the town called it West Ell, but that drove me crazy, because it reeked of laziness. I can't even abbreviate the name of the month when I write a check or change "Street" to "St." when I'm filling out my home address.

"What about you?" I asked. "Where did you grow up?"

"Pelton," she said. "Now, as you know, I live in Oberlies, and I used to teach there, too."

"It's a nice town," I said. "A lot of old money. Or so they say."

She smiled. "Well, I'm neither old nor moneyed." She picked up a large forkful of meat.

"Yet," I said.

"Yes," she said. "Yet. It's always nice having what to look forward to." She ate it.

By the time we ordered dessert, Francine seemed much more relaxed. Perhaps that was because of how much time we'd already spent together that night or perhaps she was just looking forward to saying goodbye and, now being able to see that, laid down her defenses.

"So who do you enjoy teaching?" she asked. "Writers, I mean. Not students."

I looked out the window. "Right now my favorite course is *Modern American Literature*." It wasn't, but I enjoyed it.

"*Modern?* You?!"

"I'm sorry," I said. "I thought the air quotes around the word were implied."

She smiled.

"Anyway we're working our way through Flannery O'Connor and Saul Bellow."

"*Flannery* O'Connor and *Saul* Bellow," she said. "Did you think I wouldn't know who you meant if you just said, 'O'Connor and Bellow'?"

I opened my mouth.

"Morley, you do this all the time. Talk down to people. Or at least assume that they don't know what you do."

Again, perceptive.

"I rattle off the last names of composers without giving it a second thought," I said. I wished I had food in front of me to concentrate on.

"Yeah, because I've never heard of half of them."

And that made me realize something. "But don't you see the difference? You don't need to say '*Wolfgang Amadeus* Mozart' or '*Ludwig van* Beethoven,' because nobody's going to confuse them with Sam Mozart or Bruce Beethoven. It's just that music has become so much more deeply assimilated into our culture than literature has."

She nodded. "Maybe so. And O'Connor and Bellow? I find it odd that you should teach them. They're hardly leftists."

Had I told her that I was a leftist? "I'm teaching a course in literature," I said, "not politics."

"Fair enough," she said. Then, brightening, "Did I tell you that I met Saul Bellow once?"

"Really?!"

"Well, yeah. 'Met' might be the wrong term for it, but I went to a lecture he was giving at Harrowsgate a few years back, and after it was over I walked up to him, said hello, and shook his hand."

"How was it?"

She looked disappointed. "It was all right. Nothing special. Or not as special as I expected it would be."

"*Hoped* it would be," I said.

"He was a very dapper little man, beautifully dressed, but very frail and even a little effeminate. Not at all like his writing." She paused when I didn't say anything. Was she expecting me to criticize her for calling him effeminate? "Have you ever met anybody famous?"

Then Vicki brought the desserts: bread pudding for Francine and vanilla ice cream for me. She had a cup of coffee while I had a cup of tea. All of which gave me time to think.

"Mrs. Barish," I said.

"I know I'm jumping down the rabbit hole with this one—"

"Lewis Carrol?" I asked.

"Looney Tunes," she said. She had her moments. "Anyway, I know I'm jumping down the rabbit hole, but who is Mrs. Barish?"

"She was my sixth-grade teacher. And you know what's funny? I'd never met any of my teachers outside of class, really, to say nothing of outside of school, except this once. My mother went to the beauty parlor every Friday morning, and my father drove her there and then picked her up when she was done. Anyway, we had the day off, which was probably why Mrs. Barish was there, and when my father and I went to pick up my mother, who was just getting finished, I saw Mrs. Barish sitting next to her, under the dryer."

"Oh, cool," she said.

"It was. It was like meeting someone famous because the context was so unusual. Different. Not what you're used to."

"I know what 'unusual' means." She sipped her coffee.

"Like meeting an actor who you've seen only on the screen suddenly appear in real life."

"I can understand that."

"So yeah. It was really her. Nobody famous, but the way it made me feel, she might have been."

"Very cool," Francine said.

"And that was enough for me."

*

It was Wednesday morning and my mother was getting ready to leave for the beauty parlor. "I'm going now, sweetheart. Be back soon," she said, even though it was still ten minutes before she'd walk out the door. From the time I was six until the time I entered college, my mother drove herself to the beauty parlor at eleven o'clock every Wednesday morning and, when she was done, drove herself home. She always had her hair done on Wednesdays because she played mah-jongg with her friends every Wednesday night. My father was working and, aside from the summers and occasional vacations, I was always in class, so neither of us ever went with her, and she never went to the beauty parlor on a Friday because my parents rarely went anywhere on the weekends. And I never had a teacher named Mrs. Barish.

Yet I was so envious of Francine for having met and shaken hands with Saul Bellow—though who was to say that I couldn't?—that I had to make up something that would satisfy me.

BELIEVE it or NOT

When I was six years old, my parents bought a dog, a yellow Labrador retriever we named Ripley, and although the joke went that my father called him that so he could say to people, "We got a dog, believe it or not, and you'll never guess what his name is," I don't remember him ever saying that. In truth, I didn't like the name Ripley because it began with RIP, and I figured that would doom him to a short life, but he lived to be seventeen. Ripley was kind and affectionate, but had a peculiar habit. He would never bite anyone, but when I put my bald hand near his mouth, he would slowly start to sink his teeth into it and then, just as it was starting to hurt and I became afraid that he was going to draw blood, he would retract his jaws and lick me. As though to apologize for almost having gone too far.

And that was how Francine was. In the week that followed our first dinner together, she was quieter around me than she'd ever been, often not even showing up in the English office during second period. I had no idea where she was, probably on the front lawn or talking with someone else inside, but I never went to look for her. I told myself it was because I didn't want to seem desperate, which meant that I was but couldn't admit it, so I turned to Leo to take her place. And Leo did that in two ways. I would often sit and chat with him in the years before Francine showed up, so this was a return to normalcy, and he was just someone else to talk to, though the fact that I suddenly wanted company surprised and bothered me. But there was another advantage. I could ask him what he thought about Francine and, depending on his answer, either convince myself that she was a genuine find or convince myself that she was someone to avoid.

The door to Leo's office was open, as usual, and Leo was sitting at his desk, rifling through some sheets of notepaper. His desk faced the wall to the left, rather than the door, because he felt it was more welcoming, though he'd always have to twist his neck to see who was there.

I knocked.

"Hey, stranger," he said, smiling.

I shook my head. "No stranger than usual," I said, and we both laughed.

Leo was less than ten years older than me, but his dark brown hair was already thinning, his hairline was receding, and he was tending toward paunchiness. That said, the first thing you saw when you looked at him was a mustache that seemed to be pinned on, as it was never even. One side was always longer than the other; sometimes the left and sometimes the right. It must have grown so quickly that he had to trim it a lot, but couldn't match the two halves. For that reason I often thought he looked like Mr. Potato Head (or Oscar the Orange or Pete the Pepper, all of whom had mustaches; nineteen fifties machismo at its best), on which models I would always affix the mustache crookedly, though not deliberately. And I would frequently tell him, "Leo, you're a spud." Well, let him think I was punning on the word "stud."

"You haven't been around in a while," he said, "but I guess you've been busy with Francine."

I had no reason to feel defensive about that, but I did. The occasional dinner between coworkers couldn't have been frowned upon, especially as there was nothing romantic implied or involved, but I didn't know.

"And that's why I came here," I said. "To talk about Francine."

He rolled his chair toward me, pointed to a chair opposite him, and said, "Sit down. Please."

"If you don't mind," I said.

He smiled broadly. "Not at all."

I leaned back, trying to appear relaxed. "So what do you think of her?" I asked.

He shook his head. "I'm not going to tell you," he said, and I must have looked more surprised than I felt, because he quickly added, "and let me tell you why. I'll say this. I have very mixed feelings about our new hire." Was she really "new" anymore? "But I don't want to share them with you, because I don't want to influence your feelings." Perhaps he was attributing too much importance to his opinions.

"You seemed very excited when she came for her interview," I said.

He threw his hands back. "Oh, I was. But you know what they say, over-anticipation leads to ultimate disappointment. But no, I'm not disappointed in her, not at all. I would have spoken to her about that if I were, but I haven't. I just find her—"

And since he seemed so determined to not let me know what he thought, I finished his sentence for him. "Hard to read."

He grinned. "Exactly. And you know how important reading is to people like us." Again we laughed. "Let's just say that I'm not sure the woman who presented herself to us at her interview is the woman who's working with us now."

But there I disagreed. She wasn't forthcoming with me at her interview and was no more forthcoming with me then.

"Morley, do me a favor," he said.

"Sure," I said.

"Observe her for me and let me know what you think. I could be wrong."

"It sounds as if you're troubled."

He furrowed his brow. "I'm not," he said. "Why did you assume that I was? I could think she's the best hire we ever made and want to see if you agree. Why did you assume I didn't mean that?"

Leo could always understand me better than anyone else.

I shrugged to let him know I had no answer.

He exhaled loudly. "All right, then. Anything else?" he asked, and he suddenly sounded more officious than usual.

"No," I said, getting up. "That should do it."

"Okay," he said. "Then there is one more thing." He smiled lasciviously and winked. He rubbed the left side of his chin with his open left palm, and said, "I know that women have periods, but I wonder if men don't get them, too."

"Excuse me?!" I said. "Are we talking about Francine again?"

"Is Francine a man? No, I've just noticed that my beard comes in a little heavier at the same time every month."

I shook my head. "Locker room talk," I said, but I was trying to suppress a laugh.

"It's not locker room talk, Mr. Prim-and-Proper. I'm just wondering. Believe it or else."

FUNNY, you don't look it

Before another month had gone by, Francine and I were back to talking every day during second period. Now, finally, she seemed more relaxed, less guarded, and less afraid, if that's what she had been. And this time I decided to ask her if she'd like to go out to dinner again, so we picked a Wednesday evening and met at Roscoe's Diner. There were, of course, many other places where we could have eaten, in and between Lake Quaintance and Oberlies, but the diner had an element of familiarity, and it would be a short drive for both of us. Since I had extended the invitation, I didn't think it appropriate to suggest that we meet at her house, and I couldn't bring her back to mine, as she would then find out that my mother didn't live with me. My mother lived in a small apartment in Willemoes, about eighty miles north of Lake Quaintance. As a result, I visited her only every few weeks, but she never seemed anything but grateful when I showed up, and never asked me why I didn't visit her more often.

The hostess showed Francine and me to a booth, and placed down our menus, and Vicki, smiling, brought over an iced tea. I smiled back. "There's something I forgot to tell you the last time we were here," I said to Francine.

"Is that where we're picking up?" she asked flatly.

"I can't tell if you're being serious," I said.

"I am. So continue."

"Anyway, one of the advantages to having my mother live with me is that now I don't have to visit her anywhere, and I'm sure that she'd insist I see her every weekend if she did live somewhere else."

"Well, there's that."

"Relax," I said.

She looked annoyed. "I am relaxed."

"Could have fooled me." We opened our menus, and I asked, "So how are things going? You adjusting to everybody in the department? It takes time."

And after a few moments she asked, "Everybody? No." She sighed, and that seemed to relax her. "To be honest, I'm having issues with—"

"Let me guess. Pano?"

She nodded, still looking at her menu. I'd already closed mine. "Mm-hmm," she said.

"'A piece of work,' as Shakespeare put it."

"Shakespeare said, 'What a piece of work is man.' A piece of work, yes. A man? I'm not so sure."

I looked at her, disappointed.

She laughed frailly. "I'm being funny. You're just not used to that," she said.

"Are you?"

Pano Ledder was the drama teacher, drama coach—he staged and directed every play put on by the school—and resident Shakespeare maven and instructor. He never discussed his sexuality, but everyone thought he was gay. And in those days that was far more of an issue than it would later become. Not cause to remove someone from a job, or even not offer him a job if he was otherwise qualified, at least in a town that prided itself on being as progressive as ours did, but still an issue that others found worthy of discussion behind the poor man's back.

He was large of build, with a pear-shaped head and a pear-shaped torso: a narrow forehead, broadening face, and wide chin, and narrow shoulders, broadening chest, and bulging waist. He would sometimes give a sickly smile, the kind that cartoon characters put on before they fainted, and was prone to drop sexual innuendoes, which I found inappropriate and annoying, no matter how subtle they were. When we were first introduced I asked him, "How are you?" and he responded with, "That depends on who you ask." Perhaps I was reading too much into it, but I doubted it.

"And what do you think of Ron?" I asked Francine, anxious to change the subject. Ron Rubin was the principal of our school; like Francine, very tall, very thin, and very quiet, but blandly affable and always with a look of obeisance on his face.

"I like him," she said, if a bit reluctantly.

"But? Come on," I said. "I can tell there's something missing there. Something you're not telling me."

She sighed. "But I just feel like he has his hands in too many pockets."

"Meaning what?"

"That he's too beholden to people. That he'll do you a favor if—"

"If what?" I smiled. "If you pay him enough?"

She looked surprised. "No. I'm not saying that at all."

"Then let me tell *you* something," I said, opening my menu and turning it to page four, where it read:

Reuben $6.95

I pulled the black felt-tip pen from the inside pocket of my sport jacket, wrote "Ron" in front of "Reuben," and, sliding the menu toward her, proudly exclaimed, "Every man has his price."

She stopped laughing long enough to say, "You are the most manipulative thing on two legs. You were building me up for that, weren't you?"

"I was," I said, "but quite the build-up, wasn't it?"

"It was." She stopped smiling. "Can we get back to Pano for a moment?"

But Vicki came by and took our orders. Then we continued.

"Sure," I said.

"Maybe I shouldn't be saying this," Francine said, "but it's all right. Look. I know you're gay, too."

I never much cared for the taste of ashes in my mouth, and all I could think about was how quiet and standoffish she'd been when we'd first met, and then I wanted to know why she couldn't be like that again. I'd been waiting for her to come out of her shell but I wasn't expecting to see something discolored and spiny.

I stretched my arms in front of me and pushed myself against the back of the seat cushion. Looking at the counter, which was to my right, I asked, "What does this have to do with Pano?"

She looked surprised. "You see the connection, don't you? I think you're both gay."

"Pano, to be honest," I said, "I don't know about. But me? Well, all right. If you must know...yes, I am gay."

"See," she said, smiling. "That wasn't so hard."

"How did you know?" I asked.

She twisted her lips. "I'm not sure, but I could tell there was something different about you as soon as we met. I just hadn't figured out what it was."

Once more, perceptive.

"But when we got to talking about Pano," she said, "and don't get me wrong, it's not his sexuality that bothers me—"

"*Bothers* you?"

She shook her head. "'Bothers' is too strong a word. That gets to me, but something about him keeps me at a distance."

"Some people build walls around themselves," I said.

"Walls? He's got a moat around those walls," she said, and we both laughed. "And I just see you as hard to get close to, also."

I was. But I wasn't gay.

*

I'm asexual, neither gay nor straight. When I was growing up I never felt as though I were a part of things that most people enjoyed, and would always question why I enjoyed my solitude as much as I did. I never thought that my asexuality fully explained my lack of interest in romance and sex. It probably contributed to it, but it couldn't have been the only reason. To say that it was would be like making a diagnosis of exclusion, which is what happens when a doctor tells you that you must have condition D, because conditions A, B, and C have already been ruled out.

I think my *oneliness*, as I called it—jokingly, "loneliness without the 'ell"—bothered my parents at first, because they wondered whether I appreciated them (I did) and loved them (I did that, too, as much as I could). And if I didn't, it would have been especially painful to them, because I was adopted. So I began to question if they'd regretted choosing me over the other newborns who must have been up for adoption at the same time.

To their credit, they let me know, when I was only five, that I'd been adopted, and after they explained it, I envisioned them walking into a store where there were rows of babies sitting on shelves, and picking me because... well, I never could figure out what the reason was.

*

"And he seems very touchy-feely," she said.

"Pano. 'Touchy-feely,'" I repeated. "Not to put too fine a point on it, but has he touched or felt you?"

She looked disgusted and shook her head vigorously. "No," she said.

"Then if he's gay, I wouldn't worry about it."

"I'm not worried about me," she said. "But, you know, there are other, younger people at school—"

And now it was my turn to feel disgusted. "No one has ever reported improper activity from him, at least not that I'm aware of, so that's all you need to know." In fact, there had been rumors of illicit behavior, but they never amounted to anything. No charges had ever been brought against him and, obviously, he'd never been asked to leave.

She seemed complacent when she said, "You're right. I'm stereotyping again. Thinking that just because people are gay, and I'm not even saying that he is, I don't know him well enough, they have greater sex drives. Look, you must know more about gay people than I do—"

"Of course," I said. "We all hang out together."

"You know what I mean. You must have been to at least one or two bars, or joined a social group—"

"Or not," I said. "Ever."

*

I'd joined one gay social organization when I was twenty-two, and I did that for two reasons: to see if I was more attracted to men than I had been to women, and because I was pretty certain that I wasn't gay. Yes, I thought I might have been, as I obviously wasn't straight, and being asexual couldn't have occurred to me then—who either knew or talked about it in those days?— but ultimately knowing, on some level, that I wasn't gay, made it easy for me to sympathize with, and be around gay people. After all, I didn't have to go through the hardships that they must have endured.

One Saturday we had a daylong workshop at the Episcopal church where we used to meet. There were many classes and encounter groups offered, and I chose to attend one dealing with women's rights. I was surprised to realize that I was the only man there but, again, I went because it was easy to feel sympathetic, and it gratified me to be complimented on how sympathetic a man I was for going. Of course, when you came right down to it, I went only to inflate my own ego, but if the other people were happy to have me join them, we both profited, and profiting is often cheap.

*

Our dinners were served—I'd ordered sautéed filet of flounder amandine and Francine ordered meatloaf—and she said, "So let's get back to Ron," smiling awkwardly. "Geez, we seem to be circling back on people tonight, don't we? Is he Jewish?"

Inadvertently I stuck my right pinky into my right ear, and began shaking it, as I was sure I'd misheard her. And if I hadn't, I wondered who asked questions like that anymore, because even then it was unusual. Or so I thought. But maybe I just led too circumscribed a life. I was Jewish, but I would never tell her that until she came to my mother's—and it wasn't even my mother's—funeral, but that was because my father, who was a laboratory technician, had been fired from one job with a very small company, when I was still in my teens. They told him that they didn't need any Jews there. And, to quote Francine, I never got over that.

So "Yes, he is," I said suspiciously. "Why?"

"Just curious."

She must have seen that I was upset. "Why are you curious?" I asked.

"Because you'll often find large Jewish populations in towns with academically advanced schools."

I stared at her.

"Because...well, you know, they push their kids, the parents do, to achieve a lot. Like the Asians."

I felt my ears getting warm, which often happened when I was very irritated or felt especially vulnerable. "Well that must explain why so many Jews like Chinese food. That shared culture."

"What?"

I laughed. "Nothing," I said. "Inside joke."

It was a stereotype that Jewish parents pushed their children to be more successful or, God help me, *wealthier* than they were, and the same stereotype was applied to Asians. And also, though this was one that she obviously wasn't familiar with, a stereotype that Jews loved Chinese food. I just couldn't believe she was indulging in that, but, again, I normally surrounded myself with people who either were more open-minded or liked to think of themselves that way.

But finally I said, "I can't believe that you're resorting to stereotypes. Again."

"Oh, I didn't realize I was," she said, and seemingly honestly, but she wasn't stupid, so I didn't believe her. "But you know," she said, drawing out that last word, "stereotypes are based on some sort of reality. That's how they grow."

I rested my hands on the table. "Yes," I said. "Nurture those stereotypes, lest they be left to wither and die. Conversation over."

*

Bad joke: In the Jewish calendar the year is fifty-seven forty. In the Chinese calendar the year is forty-six seventy-seven. You know what that means? The Jews had to wait one thousand sixty-three years to get Chinese food.

*

But this seemed neither the time nor the place to be mad at Francine, if I even was. In truth, I could enjoy having her with me because she helped me be more forward with people. When I was out by myself, I never knew how the things I said might be interpreted, so I was more often cautious. But I knew what effect the things I said would have on her, so when we were together, I could show off, knowing that something that might offend somebody else might impress her. With time I would take it to mean that she made me feel good about myself, and she did, and maybe I was even proud to have her in my life, which would also enhance my forwardness around others. So I apologized. Not legitimately; just to keep the tension down.

"Don't worry about it," she said.

I wasn't.

Then dessert came and she asked, "You don't like the president, do you?"

And that was when I realized, or at least reasoned what she was trying to do, and what she had been trying to do all night: offend me. That way I would keep my distance. She'd just said that she saw me as difficult to get close to, but that put me in control. If I was difficult, there was nothing she could do to change it. But if she were the one being difficult, it would be her actions, not mine, that set a rift between us, and that would take the power away from me. So for the moment I indulged her, answering the way I knew she wanted me to, since she'd soured when I'd described myself as progressive on one of those first mornings we'd talked. "Sir Dickie?" I asked. "Can't stand him." The president's name was Richard Serdechy, but many of those who were not supporters referred to him the way I had. "And you know, only one in three Americans is reported to like him."

"So?"

"One in three Americans is also supposed to develop cancer this year. Interesting connection, don't you think?" I laughed, but she just shook her head, looking awfully serious, if not yet irritated.

"I know you're not a Republican," she said.

"Can you not be a Republican and dislike the president?" I asked. "But no, I'm not."

"You're a Democrat."

"But no, I'm not," I repeated.

"Then do you mind if I ask you what you are?"

"Not at all," I said. "I'm a member of the Communist Party, and have been since I was a teenager."

That shut her up.

"Would you like to see my card?" I asked, leaning toward her.

"You have a card?"

"Of course."

"No," she said, tight-lipped. Then, as soon as we finished dessert, she asked Vicki for the check and said, "Come. Let's go." She stood up.

The hostess, carrying two menus, showed a couple to the booth behind ours.

Then I stood up, too. "'Come,'" I said, imitating her, "and 'go.' That's all life is, isn't it? Coming and going?"

"Shut up!" she finally yelled. "Is everything a joke to you?"

"I don't know," I said. "Is it? I mean, come on. You seem to know who I am. Why don't you tell me?"

I could see that I'd hurt her, and I was glad.

"No, I don't. I don't know who you are. Not at all. How can you even say that?"

Glad because I could tell that our political sentiments didn't agree, and glad because she didn't know who I was, and now must have believed that she never would. But one thing I wouldn't do was give her the pleasure of setting a rift between us.

*

The extent of my involvement with communism was this: when I was seven years old, my mother said to me, "Morley, I want to tell you something. Do you know what communism is?" Of course I didn't, so I shook my head. "Anyway, it's the political system that they have in Russia. It differs from ours and, well, it isn't any good. Or isn't very good. But I've heard that they've planted spies in the schools, maybe even in your school, who will call you out of your classroom and talk to you in private, trying to convert you to their way of life. If anybody tries to do that, don't go with him. Tell your teacher and tell me, okay?" My mother was hardly narrow-minded, but it was the height of the Cold War.

And two years later, when I'd learned a lot more about it, I asked my father, "Why doesn't communism work?" And he said, "It does work, but only in theory. Maybe if it were followed the way it's supposed to be, it would work, but in practice it just turns into fascism."

My political beliefs were mixed, neither strongly conservative nor strongly liberal, but I was a registered Democrat, likely because many of the people I'd met at my gay social organization drifted leftward, and I could understand their reasons.

*

"Did you leave a tip?" Francine asked me, just before we walked out.

"Of course," I said.

"How much?" she asked. Things were quieting down between us.

"Well, if it really matters," I said, "enough."

She walked back to the table to check, and I followed her to make sure she wouldn't remove the large tip I'd left and replace it with something smaller.

"Ten dollars?!"

"Vicki is good," I said.

"Yeah, but that's thirty percent. That's ridiculous. The usual amount is half that much."

"Look," I said, "they work hard, they don't make much money, and they deserve it."

"No wonder you're so popular here."

"Perhaps," I said.

*

I always relished leaving large tips, but I did so for one reason: to remind myself of, and delight in the fact that I made a lot more money than the people who served me did.

Happy Holidays

That year, for the first and what would prove to be the only time, Leo decided to throw a holiday party, although back then they were still referred to as Christmas parties, as Leo himself called it, even though Leo and his wife were Jewish. The guest list was simple: me; Francine and Peter; Pano; Alice Millar, who also taught English, though mostly poetry, and her husband Jared; and Brendan Loor, who taught English, too, though his concentration was on grammar and medieval English, and his wife Callie. Simple but not necessarily harmonious, as our department could be a testy bunch when turned on itself. For all the years Leo and I worked at Lake Quaintance High School, this would never bother him, as each was an excellent teacher and, Leo argued, extremely bright people often disagreed with each other, just more cleverly than most.

The party was to be held on the last Saturday before Christmas, and that year it was December twentieth. I wondered if a lot of the people who celebrated Christmas, basically the rest of our department, would be otherwise involved, but all of them said they would come.

On the Monday morning before the party I asked Francine if she and Peter would be there, and she said, "Yes and no. Meaning that I will but Peter won't."

I wasn't surprised. But "Why not?" I asked.

She shrugged. "Because he has things he has to do. But actually," she said, "he doesn't feel comfortable around strangers." That sounded like the first honest thing she'd told me about him since we'd met, so I didn't question it because I didn't want her to start lying again. Assuming she had been.

Leo lived in Saloway, "at the end of Vale Road," he'd told us, which wasn't far from Roscoe's Diner, though the routes that Francine and I would travel to get to the restaurant didn't bring either of us near Leo's house. I'd asked her if she'd like us to go together, but she demurred, hinting that she likely wouldn't stay long. Of course, that could have been a perfect excuse for me to leave early as well, as I had no more desire for such social interactions than

Peter must have, but I also thought that it would look bad if I didn't stay, so I was fine with her decision.

I was surprised, and I couldn't say whether it was pleasantly, to realize that Leo's house was hardly larger than mine. I suppose that, conventionally, I always expected a boss' house to be larger, grander, and more opulent, giving me something to look forward to, should I ever decide to ascend to whatever position he or she held, but, to be honest, I never wanted to do what Leo did. I loved my job, and I'd been doing it in Lake Quaintance for thirteen years, my whole professional life, so when I entered his house I smiled, nodded to Leo and his wife Maline—as so often happened, I was the first one there because I hated walking into crowds—and said nothing.

Maline, a stocky, even masculine woman with a crown of chestnut brown hair and a pouty smile featuring thick lips and surprisingly square teeth, said, "Let me take your coat, Morley." She had a husky voice, and I thought I'd detected a hint of a Russian accent. I was impressed that she knew who I was and relieved to not have to introduce myself. There would be enough of that later. "Come," she said. "We're all going to sit in the living room." And she pointed me there, where there was a sofa, a loveseat, a club chair, which I imagined was for Leo, and three folding chairs, not comfortable but functional. "I'm going to bring around hors d'oeuvres in a little while, then later we'll eat."

The next person to show up was Francine, which made sense because if she was planning to leave early, she wouldn't want to show up late, and I was glad because now Francine and I could talk. And as soon as she sat down I nodded to her and asked, "Can I see you for a moment?"

She got up from her chair and asked, "Where?"

That was a problem with the party being held in a very defined space. There was no place to talk privately. So I wandered into the dining room, with Francine following, hoping Leo and Maline wouldn't mind. I asked, "Do you get it? Do you see the irony?" I smiled archly.

"What irony?" Francine asked, and she looked suddenly tired. "Should I sit down? I'm going to." And she settled onto one of the dining room chairs.

"Leo's address. Remember, he said that he lived at the end of Vale Road."

"So?"

"So...It's *Don Quixote*! The famous last word of the novel, the *end*, is 'Vale,' though it's pronounced 'vah-lay.'"

"Which means?"

"'Okay.' Or 'everything is fine.' Or, what's probably more accurate, 'And so it goes.' So I'm just wondering if that's why Leo bought this house."

She looked thoughtful for a moment, then said, "Well, yes, when you get rid of all the other nonsense, like What's available?, Where's it located? How much does it cost?, and How good are the schools?, I guess literary allusions are all that's left." And we both laughed.

And I thought, Only to people like us.

"So you've read *Don Quixote*, I take it," she said.

"Of course," I said.

"Of course."

*

I hadn't read *Don Quixote* at that time, but what I had read once, in the *New York Times Book Review*, was a quiz in which they presented the titles, opening lines, and closing lines of about a dozen novels, with instructions to the reader to match them. That was in the days before I'd discovered literature, but the word "Vale," which I'd pronounced like the name of Leo's street, haunted me.

*

When we walked back into the living room, Leo, looking concerned, asked me if everything was all right, and I told him that yes, everything was fine. I had no idea what ran through Leo's mind about my relationship with Francine. He knew that she was married, and I'd told him long ago that I was asexual, but I could imagine him thinking that she and I were becoming more than friends. Or maybe I just wanted to believe that we were.

Then the doorbell rang, the door opened, and Alice walked in. She didn't wait for anyone to answer it, she simply entered, but Alice was never one to stand on ceremony. What made her endearing, though, was the fact that, while she seemingly had no patience for anything that she wanted, she was extremely supportive of others, which was one of the things that made her an extraordinary teacher. And she knew how to laugh at herself.

Alice was one of those solidly middle-aged women about whom others say, "She must have been beautiful once," because the beauty is so faint now. She had a droopy, baggy face, short gray hair that she seemed never to comb, and small, deep-set, green eyes. But when she smiled, curling her upper lip inward, she gave off an aura of irresistible witchery, which I found beguiling.

"Oh, look," Leo said, without enthusiasm. "It's Alice Millar." He must have invited her out of a sense of obligation and hoped she wouldn't show, even though she'd accepted his invitation. He admired her professionally, not so much personally.

"It's Alice Mill*ar*," she said, kicking her left leg in front of her and spreading her arms as though she were swimming, nearly scratching Leo on the cheek, like a cat who's forgotten to retract its claws. She always pronounced her name the way it was spelled—M-I-L-L-A-R—and with the emphasis on the second syllable, while Leo pronounced it "Miller," with the emphasis on the first. She doted on that, I think, because she was Romanian and believed that her Waspy married name gave her clout. I could tell from the look on Leo's face that he was thinking the same thing I was: Somebody is already soused tonight.

"Jared is parking the car," she said.

"Oh, he came too," Leo said, sounding relieved. He must have forgotten that her husband was coming with her, but that often happens when you don't look forward to seeing someone: not realizing that there will be someone else there to take your mind off the person in question or keep that person otherwise occupied.

"Of course," she said. "As you can see, I can't drive."

Of course.

Leo said, "Drinks are over at the—," but she'd already started walking toward the bar, so he muttered, "But you know that already."

Brendan and Callie were the next to arrive, although they waited for the door to be answered because Brendan adored propriety. He was the oldest member of our department, by age, and I'd been waiting for him to retire since I'd met him. I didn't like him and he didn't like me, not because we hadn't found anything on which to agree—the books we read, the people we admired, the ways we occupied ourselves outside of school—but because we didn't, or couldn't respect each other's opinions. Like Francine he knew I was different, but rather than try to figure out why, he just dismissed it as an affectation, difference for the sake of being different, and rejected it. So I returned the favor. Leo once described him as "a brilliant man who can never let you forget it," and while I could admire his intellect, his arrogance and what he called his "focus," which, to me, was simple narrow-mindedness, made him a trial.

He was tall, balding, surprisingly gaunt, which made him look much older than his fifty-seven years, and had irregular teeth, which must have been one reason why he didn't smile, but couldn't have been the only one. However, his verbal articulation was faultless.

Now I was curious to see what his wife looked like. That was one of the minor delights of gatherings such as this: seeing who familiar people chose to spend their time, if not their lives with, though that could sustain my interest only so much. Callie had short blonde hair, which she wore straight down on her forehead; blonde almost to the point of whiteness, and her upper lip looked puffy. Perhaps it had been hit recently. I then realized that she was the only person in the room who was wearing glasses. Bright orange and far too large, they looked like something she'd been talked into buying by an over-zealous salesperson at an optical boutique, and that gave her a look of terrible vulnerability. That and the fact that glasses are as much a corrective device as an esthetic one.

Then Brendan reached into the inside pocket of his sport jacket—he and I would be the only men there to be so dressed—and pulled out a pair of half-glasses.

"Et tu, Brendan?" I asked.

He didn't seem impressed. "'Et tu' *what*?" he asked. "I thought you knew I wore glasses."

"I've never seen them on you."

He considered that then gave a grudging smile. "Well, no, I suppose you haven't. I usually wear contacts at work." Then he turned his attention elsewhere, as Maline was standing over us with a tray of pigs in a blanket, a small dish of yellow mustard, and a glass of wooden toothpicks with colored cellophane frills. Brendan selected a toothpick, skewered an hors d'oeuvre, dipped it into the mustard, then popped it into his mouth. "Extraordinary," he said. Fortunately, Maline had walked away by then.

When Pano finally arrived, tripping so busily over his own apologies that I was surprised he could still stand, I wanted to say, "Bringing up the rear?" but was afraid he'd answer that with a smile and the question "Whose?" No, I wasn't self-loathing. Really. What bothered me most about him was his theatricality, though that would bother me in anybody. The way his voice would swoop and soar made me think of milk curdling; thin and piercing but remarkably monotone.

I noticed then that Brendan seemed to be directing Callie by her elbows, which he was gripping tightly while walking immediately behind her. My first thought was that she must have been handicapped, but then I wondered if she, too, had had too much to drink, but who comes to a party drunk?

Aside from Alice. Surely Leo's reputation as a host couldn't have been that bad. But a little while later she was moving around fine by herself, and I would never find out, nor did I care to ask why.

Now that everyone except Jared, who seemed to be taking an awfully long time to park the car, was there, I walked into Leo's bathroom to adjust my shirt, pants, and sport jacket, and comb my hair. I was surprised and then disappointed to see that all four walls were covered in mirrors. I don't like mirrored walls because, ironically, they make a small room feel even smaller by drawing attention to the need for more space. And does one really have to watch oneself use the bathroom? Besides, it was gaudy, which was something I'd never associated with Leo, and the mirrors were tinted and the lights were dim, so I couldn't see myself very well. Maybe that was why his mustache never looked straight. Either that or the numerous reflections that all the mirrors produced yielded one where his mustache appeared perfectly even.

Jared must have slipped in while I was composing myself, because there he was on the couch, sitting next to Alice when I walked out.

"Morley," Leo said, walking over, "let me introduce you. Jared, this is Morley Peck, Morley, this is Jared Millar." He didn't bother to pronounce it the way Alice did.

"*Mor*ley," Jared said. "Do you have a sister named *Les*lie?"

Every party needs a boor to crash it, but this one was invited.

He held out his hand, and I shook it, trying hard not to roll my eyes, in case that was what he wanted. Jared looked to be at least two decades younger than Alice, in part because his chin was so smooth that I wondered if he'd started shaving yet. He had extremely thick eyebrows and a smile that seemed so artificial in its effortlessness that it might have been pasted onto his face like a label. He struck me as smug.

In time Maline stopped bringing over hors d'oeuvres individually and simply piled dish after dish on the cocktail table, the end tables, and finally the stack table on which Leo had set up his makeshift bar where, by his own admission, he was serving makeshift drinks.

"Is it just me?" Alice asked, "Or—"

"It's just you," Pano said, "because nobody else thinks the way you do."

She laughed. She might even have been impressed, but she said, "Shut up. Anyway, is it just me, or is there something sexist about the Academy Awards?"

"Sexist?" Brendan asked.

"Yes," Alice said. "Okay. They have Best Actor awards and Best Actress awards, right? Why don't they have just Best Actor awards, covering both men and women? So what I'm saying is, why do they separate them? Why don't they just vote on who gave the best performance, whether it was a man or a woman?"

Brendan, looking suddenly animated, stuck his right index finger up and said, "Because...if a man wins, the women are going to claim it's because the Academy thinks men are better actors than women are, and if a woman wins, the men are going to claim it's because the Academy felt sorry for them."

"Bullshit!" Alice yelled, and took a big swallow of whatever it was she was drinking. "And you know that, Brendan. You're just reverting to old stereotypes." Just as Francine had.

"They probably do it to make an already interminable evening even longer," Pano said.

"No, I don't think you understand," Brendan said.

And I could see Alice, usually the most bubbly of people, getting angry. "Just because I don't agree with you doesn't mean I don't understand."

"I'm not reverting to stereotypes," Brendan said. "I'm speaking the truth."

But he was wrong; it was his truth, not hers.

"Brendan, have you not noticed that I don't speak to you at work?" Alice asked. "Why should I speak to you here?"

Time to get more hors d'oeuvres.

"Does everybody have a drink?" Leo asked. He could see that everybody did, in fact, have one (some had more), but he wanted to sound caring and involved. And notably he didn't ask if anyone had food, because he knew that this crowd didn't need to be well-fed, they needed to be numbed.

There were advantages and disadvantages to small gatherings, just as there were to everything. And, just as there was to everything, the advantages and disadvantages were often the same. In this case, the party, meaning the group of people involved, was small, so while one could feel comfortable knowing almost everyone who was there, one could also feel uncomfortable having no place to disappear. And that, I could see, would become an increasing concern. I'd spoken to many friends who'd worked for large companies, and each always said that, at their office parties, people simply didn't mingle. They stuck with who they knew; the people they were most comfortable and most familiar with. Most people are a lot less sociable than they think they are.

"You know what I can't understand?" Alice asked.

"Much?" Pano asked, and everybody laughed.

"Remind me to clobber you," she said, smiling. She loved using what she called lonely words; words that other people didn't use anymore. "No, what I can't understand is why, when they examine your eyes, and yes, I just went to my eye doctor, and my vision is twenty-twenty—"

"Oh," Pano said. "I thought that was your IQ twice," and again we all laughed.

"Stop it," she said, trying to control her own laughter. "No, what I can't understand is why they put a black disc in front of each eye and ask you to read the smallest line of letters you can with the other eye, so they can determine how good your vision is. Because that's not the way you see. Why don't they just keep both eyes uncovered and test them that way? I mean, I don't know about you, but I don't walk around with a black disc in front of one eye."

"Yes," Leo said, "but then they let you read with both eyes. Don't they? My eye doctor does."

"Oh. Maybe he forgot," Alice said, sounding sad.

"Or maybe you forgot," Pano said, but I didn't think he was trying to be funny.

After we'd been back to the bar a couple of times for more drinks and more food, Alice pulled back the right sleeve on her dress and showed her right wrist to Pano. "What do you think it is?" she asked. She pointed to what was presumably a small mole toward the top of her hand.

"Probably a mole or a birthmark," he said.

Alice shook her head. "It hasn't always been there. Do you think it's skin cancer?"

"You're asking the wrong person," Pano said, suddenly surprised, "but probably not. I would get it checked out, but the odds of it being malignant are, what, maybe one in fifty thousand?"

"Or you could look at it another way," Brendan said. "It's either yes or no, so really the odds are one in two." When he smiled, his crooked upper teeth rested against his lower lip so forcibly that I was surprised they didn't make his lip bleed.

"That's not nice," someone said, but I couldn't tell whose voice it was.

"You ever in the army?" Jared asked Pano.

Pano shook his head. "Four-F," he said.

"Fuck, fuck, fuck, and fuck."

"Diabetes, actually."

"Oh, I'm sorry," Jared said.

"Don't be," Pano said. "I'm sure I take better care of myself than you do."

Leo walked into the living room. "Look," he said. "I don't want to embarrass anybody," and he stared straight ahead to avoid making eye contact with any of us, as we were all seated, "but who was the last person here to use the bathroom? Before me." Everyone looked at everyone else, and Leo looked down, grinding the tip of his right shoe into the carpet and smiling. I could tell he was smiling not because I could see his mouth but because I could see that his mustache was raised. "I ask because," and he picked up his head, "somebody left the first piece of toilet paper folded into a triangle. I'm just curious," he said quickly. "I've never seen that done anywhere except in fancy hotels."

Alice looked around the room, gave a slight nod, and said, "Well, all right. It was me." She sat up straight. "I did it because every time I go somewhere, anywhere away from home, I like to feel like I'm on vacation."

I could see Leo thinking, Please tell me she isn't spending the night.

"Even if it's just for a few hours," she said, and Leo exhaled maybe too loudly.

"I mean, come on," Alice said. "We all love to travel, right? So why not? Take Jared and me. We've now traveled to sixteen countries."

"Seventeen," he said, affecting boredom. "We've just been to Portugal."

But the whole scene seemed staged; scripted. She folded back the corners of the first sheet of toilet paper so that somebody would ask about it, and when she confessed, she could show herself off by commenting on how well-traveled she was. I didn't know; maybe growing up in a relatively poor country made travel seem more special to her than it did to a lot of other people, but the whole episode annoyed me. So I said, "I don't."

"You don't what?" she asked.

"Love to travel. I don't even like it. So I don't even do it." And I was being honest.

Alice looked hurt. "Why not?" she asked. Maybe she was bothered to realize that not everybody thought the way she did.

"Because I love what I have at home. It satisfies me completely. So I don't feel a need to look for satisfaction elsewhere. Simple."

"Everybody wants something more," she said.

"Alice, if you don't mind my telling you this, if you're going to say something, at least say something original, don't repeat what's already been said a million times, and that obviously isn't right."

Jared, who I could see becoming annoyed, said, "Well, not right in your case. But right in the case of most people."

Alice shook her head.

"Are you afraid of flying?" Jared asked, and I was sure I could see him snicker.

"No," I said. "I'm afraid of boredom."

Maline walked around the living room with another tray of canapés that she'd picked up off the table where all of the hors d'oeuvres were sitting. She seemed to have a great sensitivity to people's moods, and knew how to redirect others' attention.

I was hoping Jared wasn't going to show us pictures of their vacation. Very many things bored me, so I couldn't say that this bored me more than most, but pictures of other people's vacations were right up there. The reason, simply, was that I had no point of reference. Seeing photographs of places I'd never been and had no desire to go to couldn't elicit the comforting reaction of "Oh, yes. I remember that." So I had no interest in them.

After a while, Leo leaned toward the dining room and asked, "Why don't we go in and eat?"

The dining room table, covered with a good white linen cloth, had a large bowl of salad; two platters of freshly carved turkey, white meat and dark; gravy; mashed potatoes; Brussels sprouts; stuffing; and cranberry sauce, and to the left of those there were nine salad plates and nine dinner plates stacked up, as well as forks, knives, and spoons wrapped in white linen napkins. Yes, it looked like Thanksgiving dinner a month too late, but Maline might not have known what else to make. I got the impression that they didn't entertain much.

"You'll want to grab a spoon for the gravy," Leo said.

"Of course," Maline said. She ran into the kitchen, quickly removed a large silver serving spoon from a drawer, came back, and scooped it into the gravy bowl.

But when I stirred the gravy, clotted and gelatinous, and pulled out the spoon, I laughed.

"What is it now?" Pano asked.

"She gave us a slotted spoon."

"But look," he said, stirring the gravy and picking up a spoonful.

"It's not dripping through," I said.

"Right," Pano said. "You want to pass me a piece of gravy?" We both laughed then, but I was bothered by the overfamiliarity of his question,

"What is it *now*?" I didn't recall having laughed more than anyone else at the party, and I was sure I virtually never laughed while talking to him, so his coming across as a familiar acquaintance who observed too much bothered me. But then, I had to attribute that to the fact that I really didn't want to be there and wasn't especially enjoying myself. Under such circumstances, I couldn't let myself relax enough to have fun. If I could have had fun there to begin with.

"So tell me," Callie said. "What kind of name is Maline?" She opened her pocketbook, removed a roll of breath mints, unwrapped one, and put it in her mouth.

Maline turned around, looking surprised to have been asked, and said, "Ashkenazi. Jewish."

Callie looked confused for a moment and then said, "Oh. I thought it sounded black." She laughed.

"She's obviously not black," Leo said.

Callie, still laughing, shook her head and said, "No, she's fine."

And that was when I realized things were not going well.

"'Fine' in what way?" Leo asked. He was raising his voice, and Leo was someone I'd never seen get angry. "What do you mean by 'fine'?"

"She means it in the Italian way," Pano said. "You know, 'F-I-N-E' is Italian for 'end,' so we're ending this conversation."

For a moment nobody spoke, and then we all returned to whatever inanity had occupied us before. Why hadn't I said anything? I prided myself, however modestly, on my progressive beliefs, and as a solitary asexual Jewish male I certainly belonged to my own share of minority groups. But I tried never to label myself, so it didn't bother me when such abstractions were attacked. Besides, music. literature and teaching were the only things that really mattered to me. Attack my favorite composers or my favorite writers and you would hear about it. And attack my students and you would probably hear about it, too. But a group that I didn't belong to? Not so much. In the meantime everyone else's silence both bothered and pacified me. Bothered me because I hated thinking that no one else was as offended as I was, but pacified me because it convinced me that it wasn't my place to say anything just then. And let people think my silence was motivated by fear: fear of being disagreed with, fear of being told my opinions were wrong, fear of being rejected. It wasn't. It was motivated by indifference, which is at least as strong a motivator as fear, so that argument could be dismissed.

"Callie must be short for Calcium," I said to Pano. "Her mind is ossified."

"Don't be so optimistic," Pano said. "Some people never learn how to reason."

"You like light meat or dark?" Maline asked.

"I like dark meat," Callie said.

Brendan laughed and asked, "Since when?!"

"I mean to eat," she said. "Not to live with."

Ah, the sound of paint drying.

Pano turned to Callie and said, "Would you mind explaining that, please?"

"She doesn't need to," Brendan said. "If she doesn't want to."

"Oh, I'll explain it," Callie said, and placed another breath mint in her mouth. "We had a black family living in our town—"

"In your *town*. Not on your *block*." Pano said.

"Good God, no," she said, laughing mirthlessly. "But close enough." She shrugged. "And I just didn't like it."

"Then you interacted with them often."

"I saw them a couple of times, yes."

"Are you sure it was them? You sure it wasn't *another* black family? Because, you know, they all look alike." Then Pano muttered, "Not to mention reproduce like rabbits."

Everyone was quiet again. I wondered, at first, if they knew that Pano was kidding, that he was trying to bait her, but then I wondered if he really was kidding or if he was just using what seemed like kidding as an excuse to exercise his own feelings. If he wasn't kidding, I found his expression more offensive than hers, because she was at least being honest. And that got me to wonder what my own feelings toward minorities—and notice how broadly I use the term—were. I didn't encounter them much, so maybe my comfort was artificial: there because they weren't.

When our plates were filled we walked back to the living room, only to discover that small stack tables had been set out in front of each of our seats, a nice touch, though I imagined a sudden loud argument breaking out, laying waste to whatever care Leo and Maline had put into the planning of their party.

"Look," Callie said, "I'm sorry if I'm not as politically correct as you are, but I have my likes and my dislikes, as we all do." She stopped, then she started again with, "Well, it's just that black people...you know," she said and smiled with her teeth clenched. She swallowed loudly. "Smell. Or maybe I should say that they have a peculiar odor about them."

It's cum, because you know how oversexed they are. That was what I'd wanted to say, but I had visions of a fistfight breaking out and me being fired, so I resisted that cleverness, if that's what it was.

"Okay, can I talk?" she asked, already looking like she'd had far too much to drink.

"Sure," Pano said, "because nobody else is."

"One thing I can't understand is political correctness. Okay?"

Several people's mouths opened, but nobody said anything.

Again she took the roll of breath mints out of her pocketbook, but this time I could see that her hands were shaking. She put one in her mouth. "Take minorities. Why do they want to be treated the way everyone else is? They're not *like* everyone else. They're *different*. They're *minorities*. So they should be *treated* differently. It flies in the face of logic to treat them the way you would treat—"

"*Ordinary* people?" Pano asked.

"Is 'ordinary' anything to brag about?" Leo asked.

"And while we're at it," Pano said, "what does logic's face look like? Is he *handsome?*"

I could imagine Brendan about to explode.

"Look," she said, "I'm not saying it's their fault that they're a minority. They can't help it. They just are, and should be treated as such."

"She sounds like a white supremacist," Leo said to me, under his breath.

So I decided I would think of her as Blanche.

"I'm going to go back for more stuffing," I said, maybe too loudly, and nodded to Pano. He followed me into the dining room, and I said to him something I'd wanted to say to Callie. "Well *blanc* is the French word for 'white.' But if you take out the 'n' and add a 'k' you have 'black.' Ironic, don't you think?"

"'N' as in 'nigger' and 'k' as in 'kike,'" Pano said. "They're both the same to people like her. The original Semites weren't exactly what today's people would call 'white.'"

"Ah, if only she could patent those stupid ideas of hers, nobody would be able steal them and pollute the world more than she already has."

"You're too hopeful," Pano said.

After returning my newly filled plate to my table, I stepped into the bathroom for a moment, not because I needed to use it but because I had to get away, and when I came back I heard Callie laugh, though not heartily, and saw her put her glass down too hard on the side table, missing the coaster.

And then she said, "Well what can you expect from people whose skin is the color of shit?"

And that was the last thing I heard. It wasn't the roaring in my ears, something that happened beyond their getting warm because of muscle tightness when I suddenly got very anxious, but the fact that I stopped listening to her and walked away again. Leo had already left the living room so I followed him.

He stood in front of me in the hallway, staring at the floor, looking very sad, and didn't say anything.

"Leo," I said. "Leo."

"I don't know why," he said.

"You have to get rid of her."

He scowled at me. "I can't."

"Why not?!"

"Shh," he said. "Morley, please. Lower your voice."

"She's been drinking," I said.

He shook his head and smiled shrewdly. "She hasn't been drinking."

"I just saw her put her glass on the table and miss the coaster—"

"And did you see all of the breath mints she was stuffing into her mouth, so no one would smell the alcohol?" he asked. "The alcohol that isn't there?" He lost his smile somewhere. "Look, it's an act. It's all an act. That's just the way she is. She doesn't drink. Not alcohol. Ever. But she figures that if she can get people to believe that she does, they'll give her a pass on some of the things she says."

I couldn't believe what he was telling me. "This is a joke, right?"

"Morley," he said, "she's trying to offend people so they'll leave her alone."

And that chilled me, because that was the way I dealt with people.

"Then you've met her before," I said.

"I've never seen her until tonight," he said.

"Then how do you know?"

He gave a wavering smile. "Let's just say I'm a good judge of character," he said. But he might just as easily have said, I've known you long enough.

So back to the living room I went. I wouldn't sit next to her, both because she offended me and because I wanted to stare straight at her. I knew that attacking the wife of a colleague could have serious ramifications, the likes of which I couldn't even fathom, but I felt buoyed by what Leo had told me. Leo, who had to have found Callie every bit as insufferable as I did. "Well you know what I can't understand," I said. "The neo-Nazis who deny the Holocaust ever happened." She must have known I was Jewish. People like her had, I was sure, a highly developed sense for picking up on such things. There was silence, but then Pano smiled. He knew what I was doing. "I mean, come on. If you're going to indulge in mass homicide, especially mass homicide that's both *very* well thought-out and *very* successful, why pretend it didn't happen? Step up. Take credit for it." I tilted my head. "Don't you agree, Callie?"

She stared straight ahead, didn't let down her smile, but this time when she tried to set down her glass, I could tell that she genuinely did miss the coaster. "I have no opinion on that," she said.

"Oh, come now," I said caressingly. "I'm sure you do. Okay, let's take it away from the Holocaust. Answer me this. You do something that you're proud of. Complete a project that's taken a lot of time and effort. Are you now suddenly *not* proud of it?"

"Okay," she said, more keenly, "yes, I'm sure I would be, but those neo-Nazis that you're talking about weren't actually involved in whatever might have happened during the Second World War."

"*Might* have happened," I said. And I could see Leo first roll his eyes, then smile. "Well let's just say it did. And the people who did it were proud. But the people who followed them are not." I raised my voice. "What kind of sense does that make? They say they're following in the footsteps of their forebears, so why aren't they proud?"

"I'm sure they are proud," Callie said, but I could see she was getting confused.

"Just not proud enough to say it in public. Which means acknowledging that it happened. Or are they simply neo-Nazis who are proud of other things the Führer did, like building the Autobahn and introducing the Volkswagen?"

Then Pano and Alice laughed, and I thought that was the perfect reaction, because I was sure Callie didn't want to be laughed at.

"Okay," Brendan said, forcing the slightest smile. I was wondering when he was going to speak up. "We can end this discussion right now."

"No," I said. "We can't."

But then Callie looked down and over at Brendan and they nodded to each other.

"Come," he said. "It's getting late." And, damn it, for a moment I thought he sounded compassionate.

But the party was over. There was no desert and no coffee and tea, which I was sure Leo and Maline had planned to serve. I felt sorry for both of them, because I, at least, hated it when my plans didn't work out.

"Is Francine still here?" Leo asked me.

"Leo, she left over three hours ago; didn't you realize that? There aren't that many of us here."

He smiled apologetically. "I must have gotten so involved in—" he said, but let his sentence trail off. "Is everything all right with her?"

I perked up, proud to be asked that, as though I were her confidant. "I'm sure. She just had other things to do."

"I'm surprised her husband didn't come with her," Leo said, and I'd rather he hadn't, as that suddenly made me feel less close to her.

"He's a quiet man, not given much to parties," I said, and had no idea if I knew what I was talking about, so I shook my head. For a moment I wished Francine and I had come together. Then, at least, I could have left early, too, but look at what I would have missed. And that, I knew, would make my next night at home, alone, that much sweeter.

With that in mind, a few minutes later I put on my coat, hat, and gloves, shook hands with or nodded to everyone else, most of whom were also getting ready to leave, and said my goodbyes.

The AFTERMATH

Leo's party came at the beginning of winter break, so I didn't see or speak with Francine again until we got back to school on Friday, January second. A silly day; they should have just kept the school closed that entire week, but I knew there was a set number of days that students had to attend classes, and it was better to attend them then than after summer began.

"You didn't say two words at Leo's party," I said when I saw her in the English office during second period that morning. "Two weeks ago."

"I said three," she said. "I said, 'No, thank you' to Maline when she offered me those hideous pigs in a blanket."

"They weren't hideous," I said, but they were. Thawed and popped into the oven, tasteless and unoriginal. But I was sensitive to criticism against anything, unless it was criticism against something I really disliked, and I reasoned that if Francine could criticize something as ultimately meaningless as that, she could criticize me just as easily. Clearly, I didn't trust her yet.

"So how did the rest of the party go?" she asked. "After I left."

"Yeah, about that. Did you actually say goodbye to anyone when you took off?"

She stiffened. "I said goodbye to Leo and Maline. That seemed like enough. You know what I mean?"

Of course I did. She felt as out of place there as I had, though for entirely different reasons. So I said, "Not at all. Everyone was sorry that you'd left, and Maline even asked if she'd somehow offended you." I was still smarting over her comment about the hors d'oeuvre.

Francine looked sheepish. "She did?"

"Mm-hmm, but I wouldn't worry about it. She's not the type to hold a grudge, I don't think."

"But how did things go after that?"

"Eh. Boring," I said. "Nothing out of the ordinary."

"Really?" she asked. "Why do I not believe you?"

I laughed. "I don't know. Why don't you?"

"Probably because I asked Leo and—"

"And—?" I smiled because I couldn't let her see how anxious I was.

Her face relaxed. "He said the same thing. And I didn't believe him, either."

Another laugh. "Why not?"

"Because of Callie. If you don't mind my saying so, she just bothered me. Something about her didn't sit well. She was actually one of the reasons I left as early as I did."

"Interesting," I said. "She didn't bother me at all. I just looked the other way."

But Francine knew what she was talking about, so she must have known that I was lying. She'd foreseen trouble and did what I'd wanted to do, *leave*, but felt I couldn't. Still, things worked out well enough. There was no yelling, no fighting, and nobody was threatened. And as far as Brendan was concerned, I would never know if any words had passed between him and Leo. I hoped not, because I could imagine Leo apologizing for himself or for one or another of us, but he didn't mention it, so I assumed we'd gotten off safely. Now it was just one more thing to forget.

TIME PASSES and
SOMETIMES people grow

Then several months fell behind us; Francine and me. We met for dinner about once every four weeks, and still looked forward to seeing each other every second period. One morning, though, she didn't show up, and I found out from Leo that she'd taken the day off, suddenly, he said, because something was wrong.

The next day I said to her, "You were out yesterday. Is everything okay?" I knew it wasn't.

She looked unusually serious. "Didn't Leo tell you? My uncle died. So I had to go to the funeral."

I shook my head. "Oh, I'm sorry to hear that, but no, he didn't tell me. He just said that you'd be out, but not why."

"Well now you know," she said. "That's why."

I could tell she was tense. "Older? Younger? Expected? Unexpected?"

"He was in his mid-nineties, so very much expected."

"Nice man?" I asked.

She looked at me suspiciously, as she often would, but this time she wasn't smiling. "He was all right. Why do you ask?"

"Oh, nothing," I said coyly. "I was just wondering. Because, you know, some people believe that everybody gets what they deserve."

Suddenly she yelled, "What the fuck is wrong with you?! No. My uncle was a very nice man. He didn't deserve to die. He was just old."

"Interesting," I said. "First you said he was 'all right,' then you said he was 'very nice.'" I smiled wryly. "Which one was it?"

"You know what?" she asked. "You should work in a hospice. You know why? Because that way people who have spoken with you will realize they're not going to miss anything by dying."

She walked out.

"I'm not saying I believe it," I said. But she didn't hear me, or pretended not to. So yes, what the fuck *was* wrong with me? Why did I say that? Probably because I was surprised and then hurt that she hadn't told me herself why she'd been out. Which would mean that I was expecting a greater degree of intimacy between us by that point. But then, just as easily, I asked myself if I didn't say it because I was simply getting tired of her and was looking to push her away. We might have been seeing each other too often: every morning, except the previous one, when we were at school, and once a month for dinner. And that may not sound like much to most people, but to me it was a lot. Again, change of any kind was going to seem entirely disruptive to someone who led as orderly a life as I did. But beyond that, for somebody who relished his solitude, and the absolute control that comes with it, relinquishing that control was hard and, at least until that time, simply not worth it. I would never quite understand my feelings for Francine, except to acknowledge that they weren't sexual and weren't romantic, but maybe I was just afraid to realize that I'd finally found someone I did want in my life, but knew I couldn't have. Because she was married. Because we worked together. Because we really didn't respect or possibly even much like each other. Because, ultimately, people didn't matter to me as much as I'd wanted them to, or wished they could. I could come up with a dozen good reasons, but it all boiled down to one thing: I didn't want to find out that the happiness that had seemed so real up to that time, the happiness that always attached itself to my being alone, had all been an illusion; something that hadn't really satisfied me. Or, perhaps I should say, something that couldn't satisfy me anymore. Because maybe my life was changing. And nothing could have scared me more.

Thinking about that, I began to wonder if I shouldn't ask Francine to make our dinner trips routine, which is to say, something we could schedule for every four weeks on the same night each time. Usually it was Wednesdays, and that was nice because it intersected my five days of teaching classes and gave me almost as much time to be with myself before we met that week as after. Logically, such a plan was unnecessary. We were already seeing each other regularly, so why was there a need to codify it? In the end, then, I chose to say nothing, and I would never be sure if that was because I really didn't want to keep going out for dinner with her every month or because I didn't want to hear her say no.

FAUST and the ANTI-FAUST

Three weeks later we met at Roscoe's Diner, but that night there was a surprise for us. Since we never drove there together anymore, whoever got there first would ask to be seated and would wave to the other when he or she walked in. It made more sense than waiting in the vestibule, where there was no seating anyway, or in our cars. But when I opened the inside door, I realized that Francine hadn't shown up yet, and then I saw Pano sitting at the counter. To be honest, I didn't want to say hello because I wasn't in the mood for his theatrics that night, but I knew that he'd be bound to see me, so I tried to lay low by stepping toward my booth as quickly and quietly as possible, and sitting stock-still until Francine arrived. Which she did a few minutes later, and as soon as we were together I felt more comfortable letting him know that we were there, because I figured he'd be less likely to talk at length to both of us than he would to either of us alone.

I waved toward the counter to attract Pano's attention. There was another row of booths between us and him, and my gesticulations attracted the attention of a lot of other people, who laughed or smiled, before they attracted his, but eventually he swiveled around and said, "Hey Morley! Hey Francine!" He walked over to us, and I invited him to sit down, but he said, "I can't just now. I'm waiting for my soup."

I wanted to ask him to eat with us, but then decided against it, rationalizing that Francine wouldn't have liked it, but really I was thinking only about myself. Still, Pano, that man of girth, would look better seated in a booth than on a stool, as the stool made him seem to spill over the small round seat on all sides, and that simply became off-putting. So I asked, "Why don't you come back for dessert then?" He said he would, and I was very surprised by the look that Francine gave me; something between pity and disgust. I had to laugh.

"Oh, you're hopeless," she said as soon as he walked back to the counter.

"What?! I'm trying to be nice."

"Feeling sorry for someone isn't being nice."

And, as usual, she was right. I did feel sorry for him; terribly sorry. He lived alone, just the way I did, and likely, if not probably, led every bit as full and rich a life as I lived, but I just didn't think so. And yet, I was sure there were a lot of people who felt the same way about me. That my life was bereft. The problem is that we become so devoted to the very specific things that make us happy that we can't quite believe that other things can make other people just as happy.

Francine laughed. "And, seriously, I was going to say that we don't really talk about work outside of school anymore."

"You know why that is?" I asked. "Because we don't want to. Eight, nine hours a day of the grind, and you just want to go someplace else and think about something else. Let me tell you something. Else." I laughed. "At my first job I worked at a school that was almost an hour from where I lived. But I did that because I didn't want to see, on the weekends, what I had to see every other day of the week."

"I can understand that," she said, but she sounded completely unconvinced. Perhaps she was thinking about Pano.

*

I'd never worked anywhere but Lake Quaintance, where I'd already lived for over thirteen years, so notably I didn't mention the name of the town where my imaginary first job was. It would have been easy enough to think of one, but Francine was paying scant attention to me anyway, and saying too much would have made it sound like I was lying, which I was.

And the reason I'd stopped talking about school after hours was that I was perfectly satisfied with the time I spent there. There were no issues that needed debate or resolution, and I was sure that Francine felt differently, so I didn't say anything, both to not hurt her, by coming across as somebody who had attained a quality of comfort that she hadn't, and so that I wouldn't end up questioning my own contentment.

*

Unusually, I wasn't particularly hungry that evening, so I ordered just a cup of vegetable soup and a Greek salad, without anchovies, while Francine ordered one of my old favorites, the chicken kabob, which I found touching, whether I should have or not.

"You don't like anchovies?" she asked.

"No, I think they're evil. Like sardines."

"Then you don't like fish," she said.

"Fish is all right," I said. I loved fish.

"You don't like salt, then."

I rolled my eyes. "Who doesn't like salt? No, I just don't like the taste of anchovies and sardines. Don't ask me why."

*

"Morley," my doctor said, "your pressure is a little high again; one forty-five over ninety-one. Are you cutting back on your salt?"

"I'm not cutting back on it because there's nothing to cut back on," I said. "I don't salt my food and I never eat salty food because I just don't like the taste of it. Don't ask me why; I never did."

"Really?" he asked, sounding surprised. "Who doesn't like salt? I'm sure I've never met anyone who—"

"Just different, I guess."

The reason was that my father had fought high blood pressure, mostly unsuccessfully, for much of the time I'd known him, so salt was never a condiment in our house. And when I ate out or ate someone's cooking other than my mother's, I'd find the sensation of salt unpleasantly sharp.

*

Francine stared at me. "You know what I wanted to ask you about? Vacation."

And for a moment I wondered if she was going to ask if I'd want to join her on one. Then, of course, I reminded myself that she was married and that I couldn't imagine her and me having a good time for an extended stay anywhere, under any circumstances. So "Go ahead," I said. "Shoot."

"Do you ever take them?"

"Sometimes," I said, though I made it sound obvious enough that my answer was no.

"Why only sometimes?"

"How many reasons do you want? I can't afford it—"

"You don't have to go anywhere expensive."

"When you spend as little money as I do, *everywhere* is expensive. And—"

"And?" she asked. "And I remember what you told Alice when we were at Leo's party. You told her that you never take vacations."

I shook my head and laid my right palm on the table. I'd wanted to slam it down but decided against it. "In the first place," I said, "why are you bringing up that God-awful party again? And in the second place, and much more importantly, why are you trying to back me into a corner?!" My voice was raised; I was angrier than I'd realized.

"What are you talking about?" she asked, suddenly contrite. "I'm not."

"No, I think you are," I said. "You don't want to ask me anything about vacation or if I ever take them, because you already know the answer. You know that I don't, so why couldn't you have just asked me why, and cut out all the crap before it?"

Clearly I didn't like being caught in a lie.

"I'm sorry," she said, "I didn't want to offend you."

And that got me even angrier. "Why?! Because you think there's something wrong with my decision to stay home and stay by myself? Is that why you're afraid you were going to offend me?"

Artificially she said, "I don't think there's anything wrong with that at all."

"Bullshit, Francine. If you didn't think there was anything wrong with it, and maybe you don't even realize that you do, you just would have asked me why."

"Would you have told me?" she asked.

And then I laughed, because I could see that my lying hadn't really bothered her. "No," I said. "I don't think I would." Then we both laughed.

Vicki brought the food, serving my soup and salad at the same time, because I liked to eat them together, which was something I never did when I ordered soup and a full entrée.

"Morley," Francine said, "you are one interesting man."

And again I thought that her husband, if he was real, must not have been.

"So you want to hear a funny story?" I asked, folding my napkin neatly in my lap.

"Sure," Francine said. "We might as well enjoy ourselves before dessert."

"Oh, come on," I said. "Pano isn't all that bad. What have you got against him?"

She rolled her eyes, a habit, I was convinced, she'd picked up from me, and asked, "You have half a lifetime?"

"Okay," I said, leaning back and smiling, to set the mood. "I was walking down the hall; you know, the big hallway on the first floor, the one that heads toward Montague Street, and one of the kids in front of me was a student from one of my classes. I won't bother to mention his name. Anyway, he's... what? Maybe fifteen. Sixteen. But he's already very noticeably going bald."

"Oh, okay," she said. "I know who you mean."

I glared at her. "And a few feet behind him were these two other students from the same class. And one said to the other, 'Poor guy. He's going bald. He must get that from his father.' To which the other replied, 'Nah, he gets it from his mother. She gets balled every night.'"

She forced a smile but didn't laugh.

I did. "I guess you had to be there," I said. "Or be a guy to appreciate it." And she said, "Even then."

But her reaction was very unsettling. Because...

*

When I was in my biology class in my sophomore year of high school, I sat a few seats away from a kid named Arthur Six. He was a nice guy, and we were friendly but never friends. He was very popular; an excellent athlete who played center back for the soccer team, but was very self-effacing. The thing about Arthur, though, was that he looked like he was aging more rapidly than he should have. So a lot of the students would refer to him as Arthur *Sixty*, but never to his face, most likely because he was well-respected, rather than because anybody was afraid he would get mad, to say nothing of being hurt, because I never saw him demonstrate a temper and couldn't imagine him feeling sorry for himself. But at fifteen he already had a full beard, which he would shave off from time to time, leaving a very heavy stubble, and was going bald. One day, while walking to my English class, I saw him a few feet in front of me, and heard two of our fellow students talking to each other. "Geez, poor Arthur," the first one said, sounding genuinely sympathetic. "I can't believe he's going bald. He must get that from his father." To which the second one replied, "Nah, he gets it from his mother. She gets balled every night." And they both laughed, and so did I, because I admired their cleverness.

But in Lake Quaintance I had no bald students, and had never even seen one at our high school. So either I didn't know who Francine thought I was talking about or I didn't know why she'd decided to lie to me. On one hand I liked it, because it made me feel less self-conscious about lying to her, but on the other hand I was bothered, because I wondered if it was one more reason that I couldn't trust her. Which is to say, maybe my distrust was motivated more by fact than by fear.

We were almost finished with our entrées when Francine asked, "So can we get back to our conversation now? And I promise I won't be judgmental."

"If you can swing it, sure," I said.

"Okay. I just don't understand why you never look for anything more than what you have."

I opened my mouth, but Pano said, "Because he's the anti-Faust."

And both of us jumped. Not because of what he said, but because he was standing right next to us. We'd both been staring at the counter, both saw him get up and walk to the cashier, and, presumably, both assumed he was leaving, making his word to join us for dessert an unfulfilled promise or an unfulfilled threat, but no, there he was.

"Come," I said, patting the empty space next to me, and moving closer to the partition. I was sure that Francine wouldn't want him sitting next to her, though now she'd be facing him.

"Where's your dessert?" I asked.

"Vicki is bringing it," he said.

"Oh," I said, unsmiling. "You have Vicki, too." She brought him a bowl of sugar-free Jell-O and a cup of green tea, and Francine and I both ordered slices of cherry pie, and coffee for her and tea for me, which Vicki brought over hurriedly.

"What are you talking about?" Francine asked.

Pano laughed. "Faust's shortcoming wasn't that he made a pact with the Devil, it was that he couldn't be satisfied. He wanted more. Always more. More of everything; nothing was ever enough. So he dealt with the Devil to get everything he wanted, and," he said and laughed, "we all know how that turned out."

"She never read *Faust*," I said.

In fact, I had no idea if Francine ever had. I hadn't, so I'd just assumed that she hadn't, either.

Pano looked disappointed, but then said, "So what? Even people who've never read it know what it's about." He turned back to Francine and asked, "So what, exactly, is wrong with it? Do you believe that you should always want more than you have and never be satisfied?"

"I think you're confusing two very different things," she said. "You can want more and be satisfied."

"How?" Pano asked. He was eating his Jell-O quickly.

"By getting it."

"Then you don't want it anymore because you don't *need* it anymore because you already have it. So no, my dearest, I'm not confusing two very different things."

"That's right," I said. "Faust's real damnation was his never being able to appreciate what he had. That was his hell."

"His mistake," Pano said, "was that he asked for worldly pleasures, when he should have asked for satisfaction. It's not a question of how much you have. It's a question of how much you can appreciate it. And those, dear heart, are two very different things."

Francine, too obviously disgusted, shook her head. "Morley," she said, as though Pano weren't there, "I need to go."

"Yes," I said. "Pano, we're going to leave, so if you'll excuse us—"

He put his palms up and said, "But of course." He smiled blandly. "I already paid"—that was why we'd both thought he'd left earlier—"so you don't have to pick up my tab." He laughed and stood up. "Okay," he said. "See you both tomorrow." And he sauntered away.

If there was anything satisfying about that encounter, it was that it gave me some closure on Leo's party, which had been held so many months before. We hadn't had dessert then, because the people involved weren't getting along with each other, but at the diner we got through dessert just fine.

But as soon as Francine and I stood up, she said, "I didn't appreciate that."

I sighed. "Appreciate what?"

"His attitude toward me and your siding with him. And now your disinterest in the way I feel."

I extended my chin, rested it in my right palm and said, "My *studied* disinterest, you mean."

"Stop it, Morley! Be serious for a moment. Can you do that? He put me down. He always makes me feel like I don't know as much as he does, so I'm unworthy."

"Unworthy of what? His friendship? It's something you don't want anyway, so why the hell should you care?"

"Respect," she said.

"Oh, he makes you feel as though you're unworthy of respect. How? Why?"

I could see her starting to tear up, but that struck me as manipulative.

"He just does."

"That doesn't answer my question, though. Do you want to sit down?"

"No!"

"But more importantly," I said, "it doesn't answer yours."

"What's my question?"

"Why does he upset you so much?"

"I can't stand the way he talks. The affectation. The 'My dear' and 'dear heart.' I hate it when people talk to me like that."

"That's just his way."

"No, Morley. That's not a good enough excuse. That doesn't satisfy."

"It's not an excuse, because I'm not trying to apologize for him," I said, but I could feel myself becoming too honest with her, so I stopped.

"Let's not come here anymore," she said. "I don't want to run into him again. Okay?"

At that point we'd been going to Roscoe's Diner for the better part of a year and had never run into him before. Of course, I hated reshaping our routine because I associated that with reshaping our friendship, which must have meant that I was finally getting used to it, but I was delighted to hear that at least she wanted, or so she implied, to continue having dinners out with me.

Some things CAN'T be taught

One morning, during second period, Francine walked into the English office. "Can I ask you a stupid question?" she asked.

"Again?"

"I like to be consistent," she said. "Anyway, why is Drews Avenue called Drews Avenue, without an apostrophe? Or why isn't it called Drew Avenue?"

Drews Avenue was the street on which most of the high school stood, and if its front yard actually faced the corner of Drews Avenue and Montague Street, the address was One-O-Five Drews Avenue.

"Ever the English teacher, aren't you?" I asked. "Actually, that's a good question. Which means I have a good answer. The founder of this town was a man named Drew Quaintance Senior, but they named the avenue, which isn't quite the main street, but is one of them, Drews, to commemorate both the founder and his son, who was Drew Quaintance Junior."

"Oh, I see," she said, smiling. "Interesting."

"It is," I said. "You live here long enough and you begin to pick up on these things."

*

"Leo, who was the founder of this town?" I asked, when I walked into his office.

"Robert Quaintance," he said. "Why?"

I shook my head. "Just curious." I loved inventing my own realities.

*

On another morning Francine came in looking much more serious. "We need to talk," she said, standing still and looking down at me.

"Is this something I'm not going to want to hear?" I asked.

"It shouldn't be," she said. She put her cup of coffee on the table.

"Sit down," I said. I almost never had to ask her to sit; she usually sat right next to me or, less often, across from me, but the fact that she'd been standing made me think she had a lot on her mind and was afraid that any relaxation might diminish it.

She sat, inhaled deeply, and said, "I'd like to teach a course in novel writing."

I looked at her expressionlessly.

"Of course I know I need to talk this over with Leo, but I wanted to run it by you first. What do you think?" She smiled uncertainly.

So I inhaled deeply, too, and said, "You want to know something? I don't know what I think."

Her expression deflated.

"Oh, come on," I said. "It's not that bad. In fact it's not bad at all. It's just that, well, I'm not sure that novel writing, or writing of any kind, really, can be taught."

"That's ridiculous," she said.

"No, it's not," I said. "Either you *can* write, or you *can't*—"

"I don't believe that."

"You don't have to. It's an innate talent. You can *perfect* it, you can *develop* it, but you can't *teach* it. Do you see what I'm saying?"

"No, I don't," she said. "Not at all." She sipped her coffee, then said, "Look. What about playing the piano? People teach *that*."

"It's a mechanical action," I said. "You can teach somebody how to read the notes, how to strike the keys, how to depress the pedals, but you can't teach somebody how to express himself or herself musically. It's two different things."

She shook her head.

I laughed. "You know, there's a famous, or infamous story about Sviatoslav Richter, who was pretty inarguably one of the greatest pianists of the twentieth century. Anyway, he'd been called on to judge a number of piano competitions, where each performer would be graded on a scale of one to ten. And you know what he said? 'I give only two scores, one and ten, because either the person *can* play or he *can't*.'"

"Your point being—"

"My point being that either you *can* write or you *can't*."

"But what about people who *can* write, then. Can't they be taught how to write a novel?" She shifted in her chair.

"Yes, of course they can. But you know how? Tell them to read. Because anyone who has the seed in him, or her, will feel inspired and liberated by reading great literature. Look, I'm sorry to tell you this but—" I let my words trail off, then decided to approach the topic in another way. "Let me ask you something. What kind of books do you think you're going to inspire these people to create? Mass-market pulp fiction? Because that's about the best you're going to get. Novels that read the way a paint-by-numbers picture looks."

"There's nothing wrong with pulp fiction," she said.

I leaned back. "No. It makes money. It pays the bills. But does it bring artistic satisfaction?" I shrugged. "I don't know. Maybe, maybe not. It wouldn't to me, but I don't have to depend on it to make my living."

At that point I expected her to get up and leave, but she said, "I don't know. Maybe you're right."

"Entertain all the possibilities," I said. But I hated the fact that maybe she agreed with me, because once I'd had the same idea myself.

*

Until two years before Francine joined us, we used to have department meetings with Leo every Monday afternoon. Our schedules were arranged so that no one had class during seventh period. We could have met after classes were dismissed, but we all wanted to be available to our students then, and a lot of us had extracurricular activities that involved them.

The department then was me, Leo, Brendan, Alice, and Pano, and invariably those meetings would go exactly the way Leo's holiday party had gone, though we'd been even more stupidly obstinate in those days. At one of those meetings I said, "I'd like to teach a course in novel writing."

And Brendan snorted.

"What?!"

"You want to teach novel writing? I can teach it in one word. *Read.* That's the only way you learn how to write. People who are good enough will absorb what they need to, or some of what they need to, from reading books, all books, not just great literature, even bestsellers, and if they're good enough they'll produce something worthy."

I rolled my eyes.

"The thing I like most about *Faulkner*," Brendan said, mentioning one of my favorite writers, on whom I taught a class, and teasing out his name, "is that he'll never be popular. When someone becomes popular, run," he said, "because most people don't have the ability to appreciate what's really good."

"And that's what we're here for," I said. "To help them develop that ability. And if *that*'s what you like most about Faulkner, you've obviously never read him with any understanding."

Brendan shook his head and laughed. "You're an asshole, you know."

And I said, "I would say the same thing about you, except that assholes serve a purpose." Childish, of course, but accurate and true, and everyone knows how brutally honest children can be.

"Too funny, you old sumbitch," he said, and poked me in my ribs, an act that was far more defensible then than it would later become. But Brendan was being serious. We never got along, but in front of others he'd try to disguise his distaste comedically, as though he meant his jibes as jokes.

"Brendan," Alice said, "is there any way to shut you up?"

Brendan laughed. "Me? No." But then I could see the delight in his eyes from suddenly discovering something new over which to verbally masturbate. He even raised his right index finger. "You want to get people to shut up," he said, "ask them to talk about themselves. And all of a sudden it's, 'What? Who? Oh, I'm sorry, no, thank you. I think I'll pass.'"

"I'll have to visit your planet someday," I said. "Will you be selling tickets soon?"

Leo grunted. "He doesn't agree with you."

"Of course I don't," I said. "You ask people to talk about themselves and they go off on all sorts of tangents and can't stop. Just the way we are now."

"Not with me," Brendan said.

"Of course not with you," Pano said, "because you judge everyone, so nobody wants to tell you about themselves."

"I do not," Brendan said, but he could barely suppress a smile, so I knew he understood the effect he had on others and how uncomfortable he could make them feel.

Pano asked, "How did you ever become a teacher?"

"And why?" Alice asked.

For a moment then I saw Leo as a weak leader. I'd assumed he'd hired Brendan and, because of that, wouldn't get involved in any arguments over him. In fact, I was wrong. He hadn't hired Brendan; Brendan was there long before Leo was. But Leo never sought unanimity or comfort in the department, and seemingly had no issues whatsoever with people arguing against one another. He would tell me that he liked people to feel comfortable with themselves, and that only by expressing their feelings unchecked could they do that. I'd argued that the constant slights tossed around had to erode those feelings of comfort, but he disagreed. And, to his credit, our department was often praised and had once been called the best high school English department in the state.

Presenting Brendan's views as my own had a few advantages, the primary one being to find out what it felt like to say what he'd said to me. I was still undecided on whether writing, especially novel writing, could be taught, so I didn't hold that view strongly, but as long as I could attribute it to someone else, I didn't need to.

*

"Can we talk about Walter Bailey?" I asked Francine.

"Who's Walter Bailey?"

"He's a student of mine. Anyway, he's looking to write a novel."

"Really," she said, her expression brightening. "On what?"

"Life after death. Or, as he's planning to say in the book, 'What they called life.' So the idea is that after this man dies, and he's the protagonist, he wakes up, basically, in an alternate reality—"

"Or what they called reality," she said, and laughed. I was annoyed by her sounding dismissive, even if she hadn't meant to, but I was glad she was listening.

"And that's all he's got so far. He needs to flesh it out a lot. Like deciding on what this alternate reality is like. How people communicate. *If* they communicate. *If* they're people."

"Well that's the problem," she said, leaning back and looking surprisingly serious. She sipped her coffee. "There are too many variables. And how do you describe them?"

"Well that's just it," I said. "You can't. Not really."

She shook her head. "I don't know," she said. "I like the concept a lot, but I don't know if it can be carried through, especially by somebody so young."

"I'll spread along the encouraging word."

She looked disappointed, maybe thinking that I was mocking her, but I wasn't sure if I was.

*

A few years earlier I'd had an idea for a novel I'd wanted to write, about a man who dies and then wakes up, basically, in an alternate reality. I even had the first lines selected. "So how was it?" one character would ask. "What?" the protagonist would ask in return. "That thing they called life." But how would the other character know what *life* was called or even what it was? Maybe alternate realities were so alien that they couldn't be described. So the questions began to mount. Are there, or could there be any commonalities between the two realities? Can you describe one reality in terms of another? Are you not defeating the purpose by even trying to? So I gave up. Still, I found myself drawn back to it every now and again.

Now, had I introduced that to Francine as my own idea, her reaction might have been, and probably would have been very different, either much more supportive or much less supportive, but I think that by distancing myself from it and presenting it as someone else's, I got a more objective response. And I was glad to hear her give at least her grudging approval, but, like Escher trying to draw his *Magic Mirror*, at least at first, I figured it was beyond me.

Walter Bailey was a student of mine, though, as far as I knew, he'd never tried to write a novel. But I knew Francine would have more tact than to approach him, unless he ended up in one of her classes, so I didn't mind mentioning his name.

LIEBESTOD for ONE

I was sitting in Leo's office one Monday morning, and we were talking about nothing in particular. "Do you mind if I ask you a personal question?" he asked.

"Not at all," I said. "Go right ahead. I love talking about myself."

He grimaced. "I know. Okay," he said.

"So what is it?"

"What's what?"

"What's your question?"

"Oh, I don't have one," he said. "I just wanted to know if I could ask you anything personal. Now I know, so that's fine." He broke into laughter.

I shook my head. "Leo, you know how to keep yourself entertained," I said, then started laughing myself.

"You too, obviously," he said, and we both laughed again.

But then we saw Francine standing at the doorway, looking stricken, so we stopped.

Leo stood up. "Are you all right?" he asked. "Come, sit down." He pushed his chair toward her. A nice gesture, but did it mean that he didn't want to talk to her? Because then he could have just walked away.

Her expression neutralized. "Oh...sorry," she said. "I'm fine. I just need to ask Morley a question, if you don't mind."

"Be my guest," he said, and stepped into the hallway.

"I could hear your laughter halfway down the hall," she said.

"It might do you some good, too," I said. "You look terrible." She really didn't, but bad enough.

"I've been through a lot." She shook her head. "Not recently, so don't worry. Anyway, dinner this week? Wednesday night?"

"Of course," I said, "We'll just have to find a different place to go."

"Parisi's," she said.

"Parisi's will be fine," I said. It was more than fine; I loved Italian food.

"Morley, there are a couple of things I want to talk to you about. But don't worry, they can wait. And they're nothing bad."

I used to have a friend—*used to* being the operative term—who, back in the day of answering machines, would leave me messages saying, "Hey, it's Elliott. And"—*pause*—"well"—*pause*—"we need to talk." And that would be it. No explanation of what he wanted to talk about or whether I should call him or he would call me, and it drove me crazy. Now Francine was indulging in that, and by then she had to have known how annoying I found it. But when we met in the English office the following two mornings, she seemed and sounded perfectly relaxed, though maybe that relief came from letting me know that she wanted to talk, or that we had Parisi's to look forward to.

Parisi's was in Janesboro, about ten miles north of Oberlies, so it was much more convenient for her than it was for me, and yet *convenient*, in that context, was a relative term, because while it meant I would have to drive farther to see her than I was used to, it gave me that much more time to mentally prepare myself, which could mean an increase in anticipation or a waning of dread.

Unlike Roscoe's Diner, Parisi's was dark inside, and remembering what Francine's house looked like, I could imagine her being attracted to it, even if she said it was Peter who preferred such an ambience. And, unlike Roscoe's Diner, it smelled wonderfully appetizing. I always loved the aroma of Italian food and often wanted to say to whoever was taking my order, "I'll have whatever it is that smells so good," but I knew it was many things that I was smelling.

She was sitting on a petite sofa, upholstered in a faded burgundy and white–striped fabric, just to the left of the entrance, when I walked in.

"You could have taken a table," I said, "like you usually do. I'm sure I would have found you." In fact, it would have been almost impossible not to, as there was only one other table occupied, but there was the dark. "Power failure?" I asked.

She laughed. "No, it's just like home."

"You sure Peter isn't a coal miner?" I asked.

She ignored me.

We were seated, looked at the menu, looked at the people at the one other table that was occupied, and then our waiter, a young man who introduced himself as Danté, leaned over our table to light a candle. We ordered a large antipasto that we would share, then she ordered veal marsala and I ordered shrimp oreganata.

"So, you're probably wondering why I asked you here," she said.

"The thought crossed my mind."

"There are things I want to tell you. But not just yet." She stretched her arms.

I frowned. "I've never known you to be so manipulative. Have I been missing something? Have I not been paying attention? Have you always been like this?"

She twisted her lips and sat back straight. "No," she said. "I just don't feel like I'm ready to say it yet."

"Why? Are you afraid I'm going to get angry?"

"It's not something that's going to make you angry," she said. "At least I don't think it is."

"Okay, then let's relax and talk about other things until you feel comfortable enough to talk about that." I unfolded the napkin in my lap, then removed it and leaned over the table, toward her.

"What are you doing?" she asked.

"You're not pregnant, are you? I just want to make sure."

She laughed—one point for me—and said, "Actually yes, I am. And it's yours."

"Well, talk about an alternate reality," I said, and we both laughed, but her laughter was sad in the sense that it made me realize how little of it I heard.

She smiled cunningly. "Um. On the subject of which. Okay. This is going to sound a little strange, but...do you find any of your students attractive?"

Make-believe anger: "What kind of question is that?"

"I don't know," she said. "The kind that deserves an answer?"

"Well, yes, there are plenty that don't." I looked around but there was nothing to stare at, and my eyes seemed to be taking unusually long to adjust to the dark.

"So do you?" she asked.

I smiled and said, "Of course I do." But, of course, I didn't. But she couldn't have known that. I'd spent my maturity learning how to come across as somebody who was just like everyone else, and I hated it, but sometimes it had its place. So I asked, "Do you mean 'Do I find attractive' or 'Do I find myself attracted to'?" I was sure she meant the latter, even if she didn't realize it, or wouldn't admit it—after all, the people we were talking about were minors and at least twenty years younger than we were—so I was letting myself have some fun. And since she'd insisted that we talk outside of school, as this was not the sort of conversation we could have had there, I chose to take advantage of it.

"Good question," she said.

"Are you blushing?" I asked. "I can't tell, it's too dark in here. But you must be, because I am."

"Do you want to know who I'm attracted to?" she asked.

"Yes."

She laughed caressingly. "I bet you do. I just wanted to make sure. I'm not going to tell you," she said.

"Why?" I asked. "Afraid I'm going to steal him away from you?"

"You might."

We were laughing a lot then, but by the time Danté brought our appetizer and then our entrées we'd quieted down.

"This is delicious," I said, tasting my shrimp. "Want a taste?"

"Okay," she said, and, tasting it, agreed. Then I tasted her veal, we agreed that it, too, was delicious, and that left me with only one thing to do: wait for the proverbial other shoe to drop, because this wasn't the Francine I was used to, and couldn't have been the Francine she was used to.

"Great place," I said.

And then she went silent. And then she said, "I've got a serious question for you, Morley."

I raised my eyebrows. Was this it? Was this what she'd wanted to talk to me about? Maybe all of the frivolity was necessary because she couldn't have faced it any other way.

"Okay," I said.

"Do you ever get lonely?"

That was a difficult question for me to answer, and I say that as someone who's been asked it very many times. We carry around loneliness like a badge of dishonor; something to be ashamed of. If you're lonely, people think, it's because you made the wrong decisions in life. You didn't find the right people; you didn't meet the best friends. Maybe people *do* end up getting what they deserve.

"What do you think?" I asked.

"I don't know," she said.

"All right, then I'll tell you honestly. I don't." Which was a lie. I do get lonely sometimes. Not often but sometimes. But only when I'm around other people; never when I'm with myself. (And notice, I say "with," not "by.") To me, loneliness has always been a result of not liking yourself. If you like yourself unconditionally, meaning, if you accept who you are, you'll enjoy your own company and never be left wanting, so never be lonely. But I couldn't explain that to her because she wouldn't understand it, because she was lonely in a different way. She didn't like herself much, I was sure of that, so she was lonely for other people.

"You?" I asked, less because I was interested than because I didn't want to explain myself.

"All the time," she said.

"Is that why you brought me here?" I asked.

She smiled wistfully and shook her head. "No," she said. "That's coming."

"Do you want something to drink?" I asked, then thought that was a stupid question, because she had to drive home.

"I've had enough already," she said. Her answer surprised me, but it might have explained what had gone on before.

"Does that take away the loneliness?"

"No," she said. "Not at all."

I then expected to hear, Sometimes it just adds to it, but I didn't.

There were two windows to look out, but one faced a row of pine trees and the other faced a concrete wall. Not even a parking lot where I could stare at people getting in and out of their cars, but there were no such people there.

"So what makes you happy?" she asked.

"I should be asking that of you," I said.

"Why?" she asked. "You'd just get a short answer."

"Which would be what?"

"I don't know," she said.

The people at the one occupied table were getting ready to leave, which would make us the only customers there. So I couldn't even stare at them.

"Don't you find this strange?" I asked. "The fact that, in a few moments, we're going to be the only people here. I mean, it's not late or anything."

"It must just be an off night," she said. "Usually it's pretty crowded when I'm here, but I've never been here on a Wednesday night."

Why did she say "When *I'm* here"? Why didn't she say "When *we're* here," meaning her and her husband? I was finding it impossible to believe that he was real anymore or had ever existed. It was anybody's guess who the pictures showed.

"So are you going to answer?" she asked. "What makes you happy?"

I rested my shoulders against the chairback. "We've had this discussion before," I said. "Music and literature make me happy, and teaching makes me happy." I was surprised, at first, at the hard tone of my voice, but then I realized I was expecting an argument. To be honest, I could sometimes enjoy feeling angry, because it gave me a sad illusion of power.

"What are you afraid of?" she asked.

"Meaning what? Like ghosts and spiders?"

"No." She shook her head, looking suddenly serious. "What are you so afraid of that makes you such a solitary person?"

"Fear isn't the only motivating factor in life," I said. "At least not in mine. *Yours* maybe; not mine." But if she had to know the truth, I was afraid of wasting my time with people whose company I enjoyed less than my own.

"If you don't mind my saying so," she said, "I don't buy that."

The perfect rationale for lying: no one believes the truth anyway.

"Buy what?"

"That that's what makes you happy. That that *can* make you happy."

I stretched my shoulders. "Well it's true, whether you 'buy' it or not. Your acceptance or lack of acceptance of the facts doesn't influence the way they turned out. That's not how truth works." I placed a forkful of shrimp in my mouth. "Come on. Eat," I said.

"You don't have to tell *me* how truth works!" she said loudly.

"Shh. Lower your voice, please."

"I'm not a child," she said. "You don't tell me to lower my voice."

I wanted to get up and walk away, but I didn't, both because I thought that would show me as weak—obviously I did care what she thought of me—and because my morbid curiosity wouldn't let me. I had to find out what was coming next.

"So what makes you happy?" I asked.

"I. Don't. Know. I told you that already. Didn't you hear me?" She was almost yelling, but leaning farther back in her chair rather than toward me.

"I thought you were answering a different question."

"You don't listen to people very well," she said. "But why do you need to? You don't spend any time with them." She smiled glibly.

"I teach six goddamned classes every fucking day and right now I'm talking to you, so how do you have the goddamned fucking gall to tell me—"

"Morley, I've tried to kill myself."

And she was laughing so hard, just as she'd been before, that there were tears running down her cheeks. And that was how I would remember that moment for so many years afterward, her laughing, because I couldn't face, couldn't wrap my mind around, couldn't accept the fact that she was crying, and that there was nothing I could do about it because I didn't know how.

"When?!"

She collected herself. "Not too recently," she said. "Not recently at all."

"How many times?"

"Two and a half."

"Two and a half?!" I asked, and, I had to admit, felt like laughing. And that seemed to relieve her.

"The first time was just a test. A trial run. To see what it felt like."

"How old were you?" I asked.

"Seventeen."

"In high school, then. This couldn't have been because of those girls who taunted you—"

"You remember that." She smiled again, but genuinely.

"I don't remember it. I remember you telling me about it. See? I do listen."

She shook her head. "No, it wasn't them. It was a lot of things. Other things."

"Like what?"

"I don't want to talk about them."

To a point I could understand that. Maybe it would trigger some memory that she couldn't or didn't want to deal with just then. But to a point I wondered if I wasn't being played for a fool.

"How?"

"Cutting. With a razor blade," she said.

I blanched, because blood was something I could never quite deal with. When I'd gotten blood drawn from my arm during my precollege physical, I passed out as soon as I saw the tube fill, and the very mention of it often made me feel faint. "Thank God you're not a woman," my friend Matt had said when I'd told him that.

"How did it feel?"

"How do you think it felt? It hurt. But don't you see? That was the point. Exchange one pain for another." She clasped her hands. "Or compare them, decide which is worse, and go with whichever one is going to be cheaper."

"All right, important question. You're not thinking of killing yourself now, are you?"

She cast me a sidelong glance. "You're asking that just so you can feel good about yourself. Trying to sound like you care."

But I did care, and much more than she could have realized. Well, okay. That would be her loss. My Faust.

Then, for no apparent reason, I shrugged and said, "I'm surprised." But I wasn't. She was starting to strike me, or maybe, really, she always had, as somebody who was depressed. But then, even more stupidly, and stupidly because it was so obviously untrue and condescending, I said, "You didn't strike me as the type."

"Well if you don't mind my asking," she said quietly, then yelled, "How dare you? How fucking *dare* you?!"

"How fucking dare I what?"

"Tell me that I don't strike you as 'the type.' What *type* is that? Are we all the same? Are all people who try to kill themselves alike? Do we all do it for the same reason, in the same way? How incredibly, unbelievably stupid you are."

But I wouldn't apologize. I leaned forward again. "It seems to me that if you did it because you were in pain, or *thought* you were in pain"—I really wanted to antagonize her—"that's the worst reason you or anyone could think of. If you're going to kill yourself, do it when you feel wonderful. Complete. When you realize that things can't get any better than they already are, that they can only decay."

"Well that would explain a lot," she said, and smiled malignantly. Then her smile began to glaze over.

"Like what?"

"Like why you've never attempted suicide."

"And why is that?" I asked.

"Because you've never been happy enough."

"Danté," I said, when, after I signaled him, he came by. "Please bring us the check."

Then I turned to her and said, "This is my treat."

And she was crying again, but she needed it. "You know something?" she asked. "I don't understand you."

I was glad.

Greetings from
YOKNAPATAWPHA COUNTY

And before anyone knew it, it was finals time. Of the six classes I taught that year—*Modern American Literature; Science Fiction,* which was wildly popular; *The Literature of Adolescence,* which Leo thought should have been called, more comprehensibly, *Adolescent Literature,* except that it was literature about adolescents, not for adolescents; *Irish Literature; The Victorian Novel;* and *Understanding Faulkner*—*Understanding Faulkner* was unquestionably my favorite, because I loved his writing so much. That said, a lot of my students argued that the title of the course was misleading because Faulkner was too difficult to understand, but really, I said, I could teach them that he wasn't. That it was just a matter of shifting one's perspective enough to allow him to captivate. And if that didn't work I'd ask them, "But how important is understanding anyway?" completely contradicting myself. "All great art communicates and touches us before we can understand the first thing about it, and understanding it might deprive us of its mystique." Classic bullshit, but it won me a lot of admirers, which is to say, students who didn't feel stupid for not being able to grasp something completely.

And something that all of my students seemed to love was the final in that class. For years I'd focused on the novels that were set in Yoknapatawpha County, which meant that I'd never taught *Pylon, The Wild Palms* (later *If I forget Thee, Jerusalem*), or *A Fable,* and that year we'd focused on the three novels of the so-called Snopes Trilogy: *The Hamlet, The Town,* and *The Mansion.* For the final, as I did every year, I asked my students to dress up as their favorite character from any (or all) of the books, and talk about himself or herself. So while, on the surface, it felt as much like a costume party as an exam, it helped them understand and relate to the characters much better than they could have otherwise. And after each brief presentation, I allowed five questions to be asked of each of the characters, but the students had to answer those questions as they believed the characters would have answered them, not the way they themselves would have answered them.

That year, I knew, would be particularly heady, because the Snopes clan, which appeared in all three of the novels, was notorious for seeking respectability when, pretty much down to the last of them, they were anything but respectable, so I was expecting a lot of creativity. And a lot of the class dressed up as one or another of the Snopeses, but two of my students came dressed as Gavin Stevens, who was a lawyer, and three, including one girl, came dressed as the itinerant sewing machine salesman, V. K. Ratliff, which thrilled me, because he was my favorite of Faulkner's characters.

"Lisa," I said, walking over to Lisa Rapisardi, the girl who'd come dressed as Ratliff, wearing a light blue button-down shirt and khakis, and with her hair slicked back. She was even holding onto a small dog kennel painted to look like a house—I had no idea where she'd gotten it—just like the one in which Ratliff carried his sewing machines. "I have to tell you, I'm impressed. That's really going the proverbial extra mile with props and your coming dressed as a man."

She smiled, then said, "Not really. I'm flat-chested anyway."

Then Walter Bailey walked in. Walter, who might have been my favorite student that year, was tall and thin, pale of complexion, and had very stiff, wiry brown hair. He also had a painful smile, which is to say that every time he smiled, and he smiled often, he seemed to be exerting an awful lot of effort. But when I saw him that time my jaw dropped, because he was dressed as Colonel Sanders. White hair, white mustache and beard, much padding under a white suit, white shirt, black bolo tie, and a walking stick. He'd even stuffed cotton into his cheeks to make his face appear rounder, though I imagined that would make it difficult for him to talk. Everyone burst out laughing, but he just smiled his painful smile. He walked up to the front of the class, posed for a moment in front of the blackboard, by resting his chin on his walking stick, then took his seat.

I deliberately wanted to save him for last, because I thought it would be a great way to conclude the exam, and because I was trying to get over feeling sorry for him. Clearly, I thought, he must have had the costume to hand, possibly from the previous Halloween, when he must have gone to a party, and simply didn't know what else to put on.

So many Snopeses took their turn, then one Ratliff, one Gavin Stevens, then a few more Snopeses, another Ratliff, the other Gavin Stevens, and I laughed uproariously at Margie Landis, who came as the deaf Linda Snopes Kohl, because she asked the rest of the class to write out their questions on notepaper so she could answer them.

And just before it was Walter's turn, I walked over to him, put my hands on his shoulders, and said, with fake solemnity, "Walter. Walter, I hate to tell you this, but Yoknapatawpha County is in Mississippi, not Kentucky."

"Missippi," he said. "That's how they pronounce it down there." Then added, "Some."

He'd read his Faulkner well.

"Well," he said, "you told us to come dressed as our favorite character from Yoknapatawpha County, so I came as the *forgotten* Snopes." He half-smiled his painful smile, making it only half-painful.

"The forgotten Snopes?" I asked.

"Yeah," he said. "You know how they name their offspring after commercial icons, like Montgomery Ward Snopes and, well, sort of, Wallstreet Panic Snopes. So I decided to come as the forgotten Snopes: Kentucky Fried Chicken Snopes."

I stared at him for a moment, then patted him on the shoulder and said, "Walter, you're a genius." And immediately I turned away because I didn't want to see his reaction. I complimented my students for reasons at least as selfish as they were selfless. To make them feel good about themselves and validated, of course, though only when I felt they deserved it, and that made my accolades precise and meaningful. "Old Mr. Peck can be hard to impress," I'd heard somebody say once, and I'd liked that, even though I wasn't even forty. But when my students felt good that I complimented them, I, too, would feel validated, because it meant that they respected me, that my opinions mattered and meant something to them, so I would always look away, in case I was wrong and was holding myself up meaninglessly.

But Walter's act was exceptional; he ended the period brilliantly, and he would go on to get an "A" on the exam and an "A" for the course. My dream student.

LIFE on the EDGE

During the last few days of that semester I made myself scarce during second period. I didn't look for Francine because I had nothing to say, and if I wasn't sure that I didn't want to hear what she might be thinking or doing, or thinking *of* doing, I wasn't sure that I did, either. So I'd walk up and down Main Street those mornings and stop at and look in the store windows, but that frankly bored me, and three days later I was back in the English office during second period, waiting for her.

Leo stuck his head in. "She's not coming, you know."

I suddenly felt very worried, though about myself, not her. Had she reported me to Leo? Was that why she wasn't around? Of course I couldn't even articulate what "reported" meant. Certainly nothing untoward, at least as far as the school would be concerned, had happened between us, and what did it matter what occurred outside, in our private lives?

"Did she say something?" I asked.

He flattened his lips and shook his head. "No. Or not about that, anyway."

I got suspicious. "Not about *what?*"

"Not about you. She said nothing about you. But yes, we did talk."

"Leo, what's going on?"

"Why don't you ask her yourself?"

"I haven't seen her."

"Have you been looking?" The fact that he was still standing in the doorway made me uncomfortable in much the same way she'd made me uncomfortable that morning she'd stood in Leo's doorway and we could both see that something was wrong. Now I knew that something different, something else was amiss.

I sighed. "No, Leo, I haven't. I haven't sat here for three days now. I guess my timing is just off."

He looked at me sympathetically. "Room One-O-Two," he said. "That's where her last class was. And that's where she is now."

Abashedly I asked, "Does she even want to see me?" And I thought about how angry I was that night at Parisi's, when, it then occurred to me, angry was both the last thing I should have been and the last thing she needed me to be. Yes, I'd paid for dinner, but in retrospect that seemed like a slap in the face, implying that she couldn't even manage to support herself.

So I walked down to room One-O-Two and saw her sitting at her desk with her right arm bent in front of her and her head resting on it. She might have been sleeping and she might have been crying, or she might have been acting, but this time, I thought, I would be better off assuming that whatever caused her to take up that pose was genuine.

I knocked on the doorframe.

"Come in," she said, not lifting her head.

"What's wrong?" I asked.

She picked up her head and looked at me dispassionately. "What makes you think anything is wrong?" she asked, but so overemphatically that I knew that any conversation between us was going to be difficult. So I seated myself directly in front of her, in one of the students' chairs, to give her a feeling of superiority, or at least control. No, ideally a good teacher will never feel superior to his or her students; one taught and learned from the other. But in this case I was hoping it would open a vein of empathy.

"Well, until now," I said, "nothing, but judging by the tone of your voice, I'm sure something is. Sarcasm isn't a good fit for you."

"It's a good fit," she said, "just not a usual one. Okay. Morley, I'm leaving."

"Why?"

"Um...because I got a better job elsewhere?" Sarcastic again.

"I gathered that. But why were you looking? Or did somebody find you?"

She shook her head. "Nobody found me. I'm just tired. Do you know what it means to be tired?"

I nodded.

"No you don't. Don't lie to me." She laughed, then let her face fall back. "Not tired the way I am. I've been here for a year already and feel like I need a change."

"I've been here for—"

"Morley, I know how many years you've been here." She raised her eyebrows. "And bully for you, but I want to get out. But look at who I'm talking to. You can't understand that."

I looked at the sun coming in from under the shades. "Or *can* but choose not to," I said.

"Exactly."

"Does it have anything to do with me?" I asked. I was sure it did.

"Of course it does," she said. "Don't you realize that everyone's life re-volves around you?"

Not everyone's, I thought. Only mine. And that was the only one I cared about, but I didn't say anything, because I couldn't make her feel worse than she already did, and her suffering didn't matter to me unless I could cause it. Clearly I was getting angry again, and realizing, remarkably quickly, that ours wasn't a good friendship and never would be.

"I can't stand it here. Don't get me wrong; it's a great school, and a great staff, and great students—"

"Wait a minute," I said, "let me check." I got up and walked behind her chair. "Nope. Nobody's holding a gun to your head. Continue." I sat down.

"But I'm climbing the walls because I do the same goddamned thing and see the same goddamned people every day."

I waited for her to ask me how I enjoyed a lack of variety as much as I did, but I knew she wouldn't, so I said, "You're right. I don't understand it." And I got up again, that time to leave.

"You're leaving?" she asked, sounding suddenly hurt.

"No," I said. "You are. But I'd rather be the one to pull away first."

Unbelievably—there was no other way to describe it—we had dinner the following Wednesday night. By then school was over, the faculty and students had cleared everything out, but she called me at home to ask if I wanted to join her. We decided we'd go back to Parisi's. It would be familiar, of course, but even familiarity carried its disadvantages.

We were seated across the room from where we'd been placed the first time, close to where the other customers had been seated then, and had a different waiter, an older man named Neil, who came to light our candle and hand us our menus.

"Well, I guess Dante isn't going to become the new Vicki," I said.

"Change is afoot," Francine said expressionlessly. "Can you deal with that?"

I couldn't tell whether she was trying to mock me or be playful. "Well you're leaving, so obviously it is. And what choice do I have but to deal with it?"

"That's just like you, isn't it?" she asked. "Not realizing that there are many choices. There always are. Your choices don't always have to be the same."

"If you like them they do." And when she waved her hand dismissively, I said, "Believe me, it helps."

We looked at our menus and she asked, "What are you having?"

And suddenly I realized that I didn't want to be there at all, that ordering would be a waste of time at worst or just me going through the motions at best, though once those motions were gone through I would be free to move on. "Shrimp Fra Diavolo," I said. "You?"

"Chicken francaise."

Neither of us ordered an appetizer.

Then I wondered if she was really being bristly, or if I was just expecting it and interpreting perfectly neutral statements as more barbed than they were. Still, I could just imagine where the conversation would go:

ME: So why, exactly, did you call and ask me to come out with you?

HER: (Laughing) You know what's funny? Now I can't remember. I must have had some reason at the time, but now it's not coming to me.

But instead it went like this:

ME: So why, exactly, did you call and ask me to come out with you?

HER: Because I wanted to see you again. Why do you think?

I hated it when people didn't follow the script.

Our food was served much more quickly than I'd expected. Were they looking to rush us out after what happened the last time? But this time we had no reason to quiet down when Neil came.

"So how's your mother?" she asked, leaning back and staring at me.

"Oh, driving me crazy, as usual," I said.

She flicked her right wrist, turning her palm upward. "Tell me about it," she said. "If you don't mind."

"No," I said. "I don't mind at all. Here's her latest. Just the other day she told me, 'I have a life, but I don't have a life.'"

"Meaning what?"

"Meaning that I'm not there enough for her. And here's the thing. She'd spent her entire life, well, really *my* entire life, pushing me to get out more, to be more social, to make more friends and be more active."

Francine nodded. "I can understand that."

"So now that I do get out, now that I am more social, I mean than I was when I was a child, she resents it, and blames me for ignoring her. Or maybe I should say abandoning her."

*

"Hi, sweetheart," my mother said.

We kissed. "How are you?" I asked.

"Fine," she said. "Just fine."

"You know what grandpa used to say when people asked him that?"

My mother laughed. "Of course I do," she said, and imitated an old man's voice. "'I'm still alive; draw your own conclusions.'" Then we both laughed, but laughter came often and easily to us.

"I'm sorry I haven't been by in so long," I said.

"What are you talking about? You were here three weeks ago."

"Five."

"You have a job, you have a life, and you have things you need to do," she said. "That's good."

"I'm lucky," I said.

She put her arm around my waist and said, "So am I."

*

And in that moment I realized that what I'd been doing all along was transferring Francine's most hurtful qualities to my mother, because that was the only way I could accept her friendship.

"Look, I hate to say this," I said, "but the truth of the matter is, I have to get rid of her before I can be happy."

"Get rid of her?!"

"Oh, you know what I mean. I'm not going to kill her or anything."

"Or anything."

"Maybe just stuff her into a broom closet somewhere." I laughed.

"Sometimes you frighten me," Francine said.

"Really? Only sometimes? What I'm saying is that this relationship is so deformed and demented that it can't be salvaged. And as long as she's alive she's going to exert this malign influence over me."

Her look hardened. "If you let her."

I picked up a shrimp with my fork. "So now it's my fault?"

"You can just walk away."

"Yes, but don't you see the problem with walking away? Guilt. Taking on too much responsibility. Thinking that maybe, if I hadn't walked away, things could have gotten better." I chewed the shrimp, swallowed it, and twisted some linguine on my fork. "Things can't get better; I know that. Don't get me wrong, the damage is done and the rift between us is too deep for that, but if I'm the one who chooses to leave, I'll be left forever questioning whether that was the better thing to do."

And then I realized something else. I'd initially walked out on Francine when she'd told me she was leaving Lake Quaintance, because I wanted to be the one to pull away rather than her. I wanted the control, and remember, as a solitary individual I constantly crave control. But then I saw that the only way I could get that control was, perversely, to let her pull away, because that would absolve me of any responsibility for having done something wrong. So now I knew what I had to do and, fortunately, I'd come prepared to do it.

After a while I said, "So I guess the big question now is, and you'll forgive me for not having asked you this earlier—"

"Or not," she said, but she was smiling.

"Where will you be teaching?"

"Two blocks down and one block over."

"In Janesboro?!"

"Shh. Not so loud. Not here, at least. People here feel possessive of their town."

I rolled my eyes. "People anywhere can feel possessive of their town, especially in as sparsely populated an area as this. But why Janesboro?"

"I don't know," she said, and leaned back. "I liked it. I came to interview, met with a few people, and realized immediately that it was going to be very different from Lake Quaintance."

"Different in what way?"

"In what way?! Come on," she said. "You've never worked anywhere else... or have you? I forget."

I hadn't, but I couldn't remember what I'd told her, so I said, "It doesn't matter."

"So maybe you can't see how dysfunctional your department is."

Now it was *my* department. No longer *ours*.

"I mean, absolutely nobody gets along with anybody else there, nobody talks. It's very wearying and, to be honest, very depressing. I don't need that."

"Who does?" I asked, but I was deliberately baiting her.

"You do, obviously."

Not bad, I thought.

"It works for you, but it doesn't, never did, and never could work for me."

"Is everything going to be sunshine and roses in Janesboro?"

"You can say 'here.'"

"Francine, you're not teaching in this restaurant."

She didn't laugh. "No," she said, "but—"

"But what? The school district isn't nearly as good as *ours*, and you're going to get a whole different kind of student there."

She leaned toward me. "I can teach them more than I could teach in Lake Quaintance."

Now I thought she was attacking me and the job I loved, and I couldn't tolerate that because, again, it could make me question whether I'd made the right decision. "The students in Lake Quaintance are smarter," I said. "Does that intimidate you? Are you afraid that there's nothing you can teach them? Or that they have nothing left to learn?"

"We all have a lot to learn," she said. "Especially you."

If that sounded threatening, and it did, it was because that was something that I would have said and, ultimately, nobody could scare me more than I could.

I bit into another one of my shrimp and said, "You know, I don't like it. I think the quality of the food is slipping here." I thought it was delicious, but I knew what I was doing.

"How can you say that?" she asked. "You've eaten here once before."

"So I can make a comparison then. This time isn't as good as the last time. If this were my first time I couldn't make a comparison."

"In case you can't tell, I'm ignoring you," she said, and she wasn't smiling.

A few minutes later we were both finished and, when Neil came by, we ordered tiramisu and espresso for her and tortoni and tea for me.

"Okay, look," she said, "I know you lie to me, but were you being honest when you said that you enjoyed being alone?"

"I was."

"Do you have any friends?"

Interesting, I thought; she didn't say "any *other* friends." But that's what I assumed she'd meant. "I do," I said.

"Then how come I never hear about them?"

"For the same reason that they never hear about you." Which was another lie, because I talked a lot about Francine to my other friends. How could I not? She'd slipped beyond my ability to comprehend her, if I'd ever had that ability to begin with, and I welcomed their insights.

"Which is what?" she asked.

I looked around the room. "I just think it's unfair. When you're with somebody, you owe it to that person to make him or her feel that he or she is the only person who matters just then."

"But *just* then," she said.

"Yes. *Just* then. As soon as the person leaves you can forget all about her." I deliberately said "her."

And here I was trying to be genuinely funny, but she said, "Do you ever think about me when I'm not around?"

I laughed. "Oh, I see where this is going," I said. "You're wondering if we're still going to keep in touch after you leave."

But much to my surprise, she said, "No, I'm not." Which might have meant that yes, of course, we would, or no, of course, we wouldn't.

"So the loneliness," she said, just as Neil was bringing our desserts and beverages. "How do you deal with the loneliness?"

And that was a perfectly apt question because, for reasons I'd already explained, at that moment, with her sitting directly across from me, I felt incredibly lonely.

"I don't deal with it because I don't feel it. Can you stretch your mind to think outside of yourself for just a little while? I derive deep, profound satisfaction from doing what I do when I'm alone. Listening to music, reading books, even eating in good restaurants."

"You eat alone, too?"

I enjoy good food, but can't concentrate on it if I'm talking to somebody. So "Of course," I said. "You want to know something? I walked into a restaurant once, many years ago, and the hostess said to me, 'Just one?' And I told her, 'Naturally. Any more would be superfluous.'" Crap, of course, but I loved the story.

"Then you're saying that you're the only person you like. Or the only person who likes you. That doesn't seem like something to brag about."

I wondered what effect it would have if I lifted my side of the table and let the cups of hot coffee and tea spill into her lap, but I didn't need to get the authorities, whoever they were, involved.

"You're not listening to me. I have friends!" I said a lot more loudly.

"You know something?" she asked. "I don't believe you. You're lying to me again because, really, who'd want to be friends with you?"

I stuck my right pinky into my cup of tea to see how hot it was.

"And the fact of the matter is, and maybe you just don't realize this yet because you're not nearly as bright or insightful as you think you are, you can't be happy being alone. It's not that easy."

And that was what I was waiting to hear, the old message, warped and corroded, that I used to feed myself when I was trying to understand how and why I was different. Then I couldn't tell her voice from mine, so I said, as I'd said then, "You're just scared."

"Of what?!"

"Of realizing that everything you've done in this life is wrong. So you're not happy because you *can't* be happy, because you don't know *how* to be happy."

"Fuck you!" she said.

And that was when I reached into my left pants pocket and pulled out my wallet.

"What are you doing? Going to pay and leave?!"

"No," I said, and, after fingering through the card holders behind the one credit card I kept, I extracted a razor blade. Smooth and gleamingly polished, I'd been keeping it there just for the occasion, because I knew this would happen. "Here," I said, placing it on the table and pushing it delicately across the linen toward her. "Cut your wrists, die, and satisfy both of us." And before she could say anything else, I said, "See? It isn't hard to make me happy at all."

We didn't talk for five years after that.

PART TWO

REAL friends

A *real* friend, somebody once told me, was a friend who you could go for years without seeing, but feel as though you'd been with just the other day when you saw him or her again. Somebody with whom the thread of thought or conversation never quite dies. And in that regard, I suppose, Francine and I would finally become real friends because, after five years, she called me one Monday night, and from that point on, we could go for months, and sometimes years without seeing or talking to each other, but we would always feel close. I couldn't say why she felt that way, but I felt that way because, given the distance that time would put between us, I would be less bothered by the facets of her personality that offended me. I wouldn't be exposed to them as often and, when I was, know that it would be a long time until I had to endure them again, so I could find forgiveness. But then I realized that even those bothers had disappeared.

Still, hearing from her again *at all* surprised me. We'd left each other amid such ugliness that I was sure she'd never forgive me. And if our becoming friends again—*again*?!—was dependent on that forgiveness, it wasn't a concern of mine because I'd come to enjoy the years we'd spent apart more than the year we'd spent together. And yet, the concept of forgiveness appealed, because I hadn't forgiven myself for what I'd done, and if she was ready to forgive me, I could forgive myself, too, and feel vindicated.

"Hello?" I said when I picked up the phone. I always phrased my greetings as a question because I was apprehensive enough about speaking to people to begin with, and especially so when they called. On the telephone I couldn't read their facial expressions or gestures, and I never knew who I would be talking to. This was back in the day before caller ID and cell phones became popular.

"You'll never guess who this is," she said. But, of course, I recognized her voice, as she knew I would.

Still I paused. "Sylvia?" I asked. "Sylvia, look, I'm sorry about last night, honey. But I will get you the money, I promise. I'm getting paid this week."

Then she paused. Let her think I'd mistaken her for a prostitute, and a female one at that. And I'd listened to Delibes' ballet *Sylvia* a couple of nights before, so that was the first name that came to my mind. "What?" she asked tentatively.

"I'm *kidding*!" I said.

"I *know* it!" she said, and we both laughed.

"My God, how the hell are you?" I asked.

"Well," she said, "funny you should ask."

"Is everything okay, or is that a funny question, too?"

"Oh," she said, followed by a deep sigh. "I got a divorce."

I shook my head. "Why?!"

"Why?" She sounded surprised, as though I should have known the answer, as though the answer were obvious. But she didn't seem to mind. "Because he was seeing someone else."

"Peter," I said.

"Yes, Peter."

Okay, I thought. At least she was still trying to convince me that he was real, and really was, or really had been her husband. And after what felt like a respectable time I asked, "So did you leave him or did he leave you?"

Silence.

So I said, "It goes both ways, you know. You could have left him for his infidelity, or he could have left you because he had other things he wanted to do." I spoke slowly, so I wouldn't miss the sound of her hanging up. But she didn't.

"I left him," she said, and sounded almost guilty. "I thought I deserved better."

"I'm sure you do, but do you remember what you said the first time you met me? On your interview?"

She laughed. "Oh God, no. Who remembers that? I can't even remember the last time I saw you."

"I do," I said. "I asked you if you were married, and you said, oddly, I thought, 'Happily enough.'"

"Yeah," she said, "well, it's not enough anymore, is it?"

"I guess not," I said. "But was it ever?"

She sighed. "Morley," she said, "I don't know. And you know what this does? It makes me think about the past and wonder if we were ever happy together."

"You and me? Hint. We weren't."

She laughed more voraciously than I expected. "God, how I missed you."

"Missed?" I asked. "Past tense? Are you over it now?"

She laughed again. "Tell you what," she said. "Let's get together next week. And this time, if you don't mind, it'll be my treat."

"Don't be ridiculous," I said. "I can pay for myself." I didn't mind being treated, but if she was planning on bringing up the last time one of us had treated the other, when I'd treated her that first night we'd gone to Parisi's, I didn't want to be reminded.

"Okay," she said. "Your choice. But don't say I didn't offer."

My God, I thought. She actually sounds happy.

"And don't worry," she said, as though she were reading my mind, "Parisi's closed down."

So we agreed to meet the following Wednesday night at a new seafood restaurant called Allie's in West Ellis, which she still called West Ell, picking up where we left off. And I was excited.

One of the things I'd enjoyed about our hiatus was that it allowed me to relax, to drop the act I'd played for almost a year. When you play a role, you have to define yourself more narrowly than you do when you're acting naturally, but the illusion of naturalness has to remain. Nothing should rile, nothing should provoke the question, Why are you acting like that? That isn't like you. They say that if you never lie, you never have to worry about slipping. And I was always worried about slipping, until, suddenly, I wasn't. But then, perhaps surprisingly, knowing that I'd be seeing her again soon, I was looking forward once more to being somebody I wasn't. It wasn't that I didn't like myself, I did absolutely, I just thought it would be fun to broaden (or narrow) my repertoire, especially as she was the only person to whom I lied routinely.

The EX and the "X"

Allie's was, cleverly enough, located on an alley in the southernmost reach of West Ellis, which is to say, far from the hustle of downtown, but unlike Roscoe's Diner and, even more so, Parisi's, this restaurant was busy and noisy. Part of the reason was that the kitchen, which was surrounded by glass walls that were clouded on their bottom halves, sat in the middle, with the tables arranged around it. And while I found it admirable that they let people see everything that the staff was doing, I also found it boisterous and distracting.

We actually pulled into the parking lot at the same time, and as soon as we saw each other and got close enough, we hugged, something we'd never done.

"Race you to the door," I said.

"You're on," she said.

And we both walked to the entrance as slowly as we could, laughing the whole way and when we got there. How did each know what the other was thinking?

We were shown to a table that was, as we'd requested, as far from the kitchen as we could get, and it sat beneath a large picture window, which was pretty, but views could also be distracting. That said, distraction, I thought, might have been beneficial under the circumstances, but, as it turned out, I needn't have worried.

After we ordered, she initiated the conversation. "So I guess the important question is, How's your mother?"

"No," I said. "The important question is, How are you? But thank you for asking." I unfolded my napkin and placed it on my lap.

She smiled. "Why don't we talk about your mother first?" she asked, but this time, rather than make me think she simply didn't want to discuss Peter, or her "new" job, or anything else that had happened in the past five years, I got the impression that she had a lot to say but wanted to save it up.

"My mother?" I asked, arranging my silverware, a habit I'd picked up to emphasize a point. "Not well at all. She's given up on her health."

"Meaning what?" Francine looked disappointed and concerned.

I sighed deeply. "She has lung cancer."

"Oh, my God, Morley. I'm so sorry." Then she paused, let a smile flicker across her lips, and said, "At least I think I am."

I smiled too, and nodded. "I know what you mean," I said. "She's been difficult."

"Is she any less difficult now?" Francine asked, reaching for her glass of water, and drinking. I assumed she didn't want to say or ask anything more, and was giving me time to answer.

"Still difficult, just in a different way," I said, raising my forehead and nodding. "You see, she doesn't complain as much or criticize, at least about me." I laughed, then said, "But she's in and out of the hospital now, so I need to be with her when she's there. Because, as I must have mentioned already, nobody else is going to visit her."

"That's terrible," Francine said, looking angry. Then, "Did she smoke?"

I smiled morosely. "She still does," I said. "And has been since she was a teenager. Look, she knows she doesn't have much time left...or maybe she does. Who knows? And she's determined to enjoy herself to the no-doubt bitter end."

*

My mother and I stepped into the restaurant, the Greenwood Inn, as it was a Tuesday night.

"Smoking or nonsmoking?" the hostess asked. Didn't she know already?

"Nonsmoking," my mother said. And after we were seated, she shook her head sadly and said, "I don't understand why they put the smoking section up front, because that means you have to walk through it to get to the nonsmoking section."

"Which, let's be honest, isn't even that fresh," I said.

"No. The smoke drifts over anyway. I'm just glad I never took up smoking."

"Were you ever tempted to?"

"Of course," she said. "Plenty of times. All of my friends smoked, and one of my friends used to brag that she could go through five packs a day. Think about it. That's a hundred cigarettes. Who even has the time to smoke that much? And she was just a teenager when she said that."

"Is she still alive?

My mother shook her head. "I don't know," she said. Then added more consolingly, "Probably not. How could she be?"

*

"Well, as you said," Francine said, looking resolute, "who knows how things will work out? Maybe she'll get better. They do sometimes, you know."

"I know," I said.

*

But my mother wouldn't, because she'd died five years earlier, about two months after Francine and I stopped talking. Still, I kept the thought of her alive, as it were, in case Francine's former habits resurfaced and I needed to attribute them to someone else. But then, given how easy the flow of conversation was between us, and had even seemed that night she'd called the week before, I figured I could put my mother to rest, or start to.

The actual cause of death was heart failure. "She went to sleep one night and forgot to wake up," her friend and neighbor Selma told me.

To which I replied, "She must have been losing her memory, too."

We smiled dolefully, but we both loved her. She and Selma spent almost all of their free time together—in that way I was much more my father's child than hers—and they were supposed to go out for lunch the day she died, but when Selma knocked on her door and there was no answer, Selma, who had a key to my mother's apartment, let herself in and found my mother in bed. Her skin hadn't discolored yet.

"She was sick, you know," Selma said.

"No," I said. "I didn't know."

Selma nodded. "Oh, yes," she said. "She'd had two heart attacks the year before, but didn't want to tell you about them because she didn't want to upset you."

"Selma," I said, "what would have upset me was the heart attacks, not her telling me about them. And since the heart attacks couldn't be debated; I mean, either they happened or they didn't—"

"No, you're right," Selma said. "She made the wrong decision. That's what I told her, but—"

But at that point, did it really matter?

*

I took a sip of my water, ordered a glass of cranberry juice, which, strangely, perhaps, I always thought went well with seafood, and asked, "Do you want to talk about it?"

Francine frowned. She knew what I meant. "Peter?" she asked. "Let's." Then added, "Might as well."

"How long had this been going on?"

"His cheating on me?" she asked, just as our waitress, whose name I didn't catch, brought over our appetizers—six baked clams for Francine and a dozen raw oysters for me—and a stack of paper napkins, but it remained so noisy that I couldn't imagine she'd heard us. "Evidently a few years." She shrugged. "More than two."

I widened my eyes. "When did you find out?"

She sank back in her seat. "Good question. And I say that because after he told me," and she smiled, "I felt as though I'd known about it all along." Then she looked more serious. "But the actual discussion came just over five months ago, and the divorce was finalized...oh...two weeks back."

"Fast," I said.

She dug her fork into her first clam, lifted the food to her mouth, then moved it away, and said, "It couldn't have happened quickly enough."

So I'd been right. Theirs hadn't been a good marriage. And that could have explained a lot of her moodiness, but that seemed too simple, too pat.

"And you know how he told me?" she asked. "He called to let me know. On the phone. I was at home, he was out, somewhere, I don't even remember where, and he said, very matter-of-factly, 'Look, I'm sorry to tell you this, but I'm seeing someone else. We'll talk when I get home.' So at first I thought he had to be kidding, but the fact that I was crying so much made me realize that I hadn't thought that at all."

This was a dangerous thing for me to say, but I said it anyway: "Maybe he was just playing it safe. Thinking that if he told you in person, you'd just walk out, or yell—"

She shook her head quickly. "No," she said, took a bite of her clam, and swallowed it. "He couldn't have, because he didn't *think* that much. He never made elaborate plans for anything. Unlike you."

I wondered then, and not for the first time, if Francine found me sexually, or at least romantically attractive. If she did, she might have felt more comfortable with those feelings because she knew I couldn't have felt the same way about her, so she could fantasize all she wanted, knowing it was safe. Which could also have explained her moodiness. And while it was objectively flattering, it didn't make me feel either happy or disappointed, at least not then.

"I'm sorry," I said.

"Oh, please," she said and waved her right hand. "I'm not. But you know something? This might be the first time that I actually believe you are."

But I wasn't, because I liked her better that way, and she seemed to like herself better that way. So we ate for the next several minutes in relative but comfortable silence. Then I asked, "Where are you living now?"

She tightened her lips. "At home. Still on Schepper Avenue in Oberlies."

"Oh," I said.

Our waitress brought the entrées: baked haddock in butter sauce for Francine, and pan-seared cod for me.

"Look," she said, "he pulled out of the relationship, he pulls out of the house." She ordered a martini.

"That's fair," I said, turning my head to look out the window.

"Do you really think so?" she asked. But the question wasn't combative. "Because...honestly...I don't know. Maybe it's not."

I didn't want to say anything about that because I didn't know enough to judge, or perhaps I just knew better than to judge. So I asked, "And where is he living now?"

She tightened her lips. "I don't know and I don't care," she said, maybe a little too loudly.

"Really?"

"Yes, really," she said, still more loudly than she needed to, and then she put her fork down and said, "because if I did know, I could always go there and forgive him."

And then I wondered if that was why we'd been getting along so well that night. I'd done something the last time we'd met that would have been considered unforgivable by most people. But maybe, compared with what Peter had done, what I did seemed entirely forgivable, so she chose not to be angry with me anymore. But I could tell that she didn't want to talk more about it.

Still, I was going to miss something. I'd found her troubled relationship with Peter one of the most endearing things about her, and I always believed she knew that. She might have thought it was because I was possessive: the less she was possessed by him, the more she could be possessed by me. But it was much simpler than that. It was because I'd never bought into the idea that any two people could genuinely *love* one another romantically. Which, I knew, was just a lazy way of saying, I can't, so how can anyone else?

"How is school?" she asked. Then she laughed and said, "Did they replace me?" She rolled her eyes. "They must have. It's been five years."

I put my utensils down and shook my head. "They didn't."

"No?!"

"Francine," I said, "it's a whole different place. All the old people are still there, but the classes have all changed. There's nothing special anymore, nothing elaborate. No courses that sound like they should be taught in a college rather than at a high school. We all concentrate on basic English, though I still teach my Faulkner class, and that's it."

*

Not quite true, but closer than usual. At least some of it. After Francine left, we hired a man named Ian Baines, who I instinctively disliked, maybe because he'd taken over Francine's position, though his course list was different than hers, or maybe because I didn't like people whose last names repeated all of the letters in their first names. But he brought no more humanity to the department than anyone else did. Happily, he lasted only one year, just as Francine had, and after that, Leo decided to not try out any more English teachers, at least for a time.

Ian was about Francine's and my age, maybe a year or two older, but had red hair that he was losing quickly, a widow's peak, a high forehead, a long, sharp nose, and a mustache and beard, both pointed, and both of which he would run his fingers along excessively. All of which led Leo to refer to him as "Brother Devil." And yes, we still taught the same wide, if not wild variety of courses we always had.

*

But I told her, "You're lucky that you don't teach there anymore. It's become too conventional." I supposed I just wanted to make her feel better about herself after her mention of Peter.

"Yes. Still," she said, and smiled, "it was so exhausting. Having to learn so many different things."

And in that moment I expected her to reach halfway across the table and take my resting hands in hers, but she didn't, and after feeling disappointed I felt relieved.

"And how's work been going with you?" I asked. "You still teaching in Janesboro?"

She seemed to take an awfully long time to chew what was in her mouth, and suggested a laugh because of that, but then said, "Oh, yes."

"Wow," I said. "Five years already. You must really like it."

She turned her face toward the window. "You would think so, wouldn't you?" she asked.

"But you don't."

"I feel like I'm in a groove," she said. "It's comfortable, it pays the bills, I actually get along with the people there—"

We both smiled, but then I said, "Francine, please understand something. Nobody ever had a hard time getting along with you."

"And that would be wonderful to hear, except that it eliminates my feelings. I was the one who didn't really get along with them, except you and Leo. You know that. I just needed to make myself happier." She frowned. "Does that make any sense?

I told her it did.

We were almost finished with our entrées when she said, "So tell me about you. Anything new happening in your life?"

And it didn't sound like a taunt, so I said, "I'm seeing someone."

Much to her credit, she didn't act surprised. "Oh," she said, "tell me about him."

Had she not noticed that I'd waited until almost the end of our meal to mention it? I didn't want to go into much detail, not because I didn't have a lot to provide—I'd thought it all through after I'd spoken to her the week before—but because I wanted to say as little as possible to maybe let her know I was making the whole story up. Given how nicely the evening had gone, I figured I owed her that much.

"His name is Corey," I said. "Corey Gilliam."

"Morley and Corey," she said.

"Yes." I smiled. "It doesn't quite rhyme, but it's nice. Anyway, we met online about four months ago."

The waitress asked us if we wanted dessert, and we both ordered bread pudding, which they topped with caramel sauce and whipped cream, and, as usual, coffee for Francine and tea for me. That way, I thought, if I wanted to extend the conversation, I could just order refills on my beverage.

"And I guess that was around the time I realized that my mother had cancer," I said. "So you can understand the timing, right?"

"Of course," she said. "You didn't want to be left with no one." Then she looked contemplative and added, "At least not then."

So why was I telling her this? There were a couple of reasons. After she told me that she was divorcing Peter, I figured I should announce something at least as big, but I wasn't looking to one-up her, I was looking to make my life seem less staid and placid—what she might have thought of as boring—than it was. And I'd believed, for the longest time, that that was one of the biggest sources of dissatisfaction between us. Maybe now she would be more comfortable with me. But there was also the fact that, even then, I didn't quite believe that Peter really existed, so why shouldn't I come up with a companion who didn't exist, either?

"So how did you two meet?" she asked.

"On a gay dating site," I said, though I could hear myself sounding far more uncertain than I wanted to.

"Hmm," she said and smiled. "Why do I not believe you?"

I had no idea what she'd expected me to say, so I thought I'd have some fun and let her know that I was, in fact, lying. "Well that's the sanitized version. The truth of the matter is that the man's a prostitute. I hired him for a night, and we just kind of hit it off. And yes, there are sites devoted to that, too."

Her expression fell. "I don't know what to say," she said.

"Then don't say anything," I said. "It's a good rule of thumb." But I laughed and, after a moment, she did, too.

"I just never saw you as the type—"

And that reminded me of what I'd said when she'd told me that she'd attempted suicide, so I avoided alluding to anything that was said then. "It's easy, you know? I mean, hiring a prostitute. Or, I'm sorry, a rent boy, as the Brits would say."

"How old is he?!"

"Twenty-five; eighteen years younger than me. And you know what they say; eighteen is legal."

She laughed. "Okay. True that," she said, "but how is dating a prostitute easy?"

"Well you remember what Aldous Huxley said about paying your money."

"No, I don't," she said.

"In *Brave New World*," I said. "Did you know the title comes from Shake-speare? But seriously, not that that isn't, I just thought it would be guaranteed time spent together. I didn't feel like exchanging emails, then meeting up with a guy who probably didn't look anything like his picture."

"Did Corey?"

"He did. Does. And maybe because there was no big build-up to it, I was expecting less. Remember, overanticipation leads to ultimate disappoint-ment."

Francine was busily eating her bread pudding, absorbing the caramel sauce. "Doesn't it, though? So how often do you get together?"

I laughed loudly. "Every other week or so. More often than *we* did." I winked, or tried to.

She cleared her throat. "We saw each other every day."

"I mean away from work."

Now it was her turn to laugh. "Yeah, but if he's a prostitute, he's not see-ing you away from work."

"Touché," I said, "but I don't pay him anymore."

She put her spoon down. "Well that's good," she said. "Then I'm really happy for you. You deserve it."

And there was that problem again. I'd always, or for longer than not, been happy, but she never seemed to appreciate that because my happiness came to me so differently than hers came to her. Or than she expected hers would come to her. But maybe then, with Peter out of the way, she was learning to appreciate solitude more than she could have before.

"You know what's fascinating?" I asked. "Our lives are following the course of an 'X'."

"An 'X'?" she asked.

"Yes," I said, "the letter X. Here, let me show you." I took out the black felt-tip pen from the inside pocket of my sport jacket, then reached for and laid down one of the paper napkins that the waitress had brought. On it I drew a large X. "Okay," I said. "Let's look at the two points on the left side of the letter. One is low and one is high. Let's just say you're at the bottom, the low point, because you were with somebody, but not happy. And I'll put myself at the high point"—I didn't want to say "the top"—"because I was not with somebody but was happy. So, opposites. But now, notice this. We've slid"—and I moved my pen along the napkin from the lower left-hand point to the upper right-hand point, and from the upper left-hand point to the lower right-hand point—"to the exact opposite positions. You're up here now, represented by the top of the letter on the other side, because you're happy, but alone, and I'm down here now," I said, pointing to the bottom right-hand point of the letter, "because I'm with someone."

"Which begs the question," she said, "'but not happy?' Does being with Corey not make you happy?"

In fact, it probably wouldn't have, so my analogy would have proved accurate, but I said, "No. Just happy in a completely different way."

"A better way?"

"A different way," I said. I ordered more tea, but Francine passed on the offer of more coffee because she hadn't finished what was in her cup yet. Then I laughed, and that almost scared her. "But you know what question this *really* begs?"

She shook her head.

"How come I don't remember running into you at the apex of the 'X'?"

Checking IN

Then three months went by before I heard from Francine again, but they were three months of quiet and comfort, similar to those moments that had passed between us during our dinner at Allie's, when we'd been discussing Peter. If her imagined sexual or romantic attraction to me didn't, because it couldn't, please or flatter me overmuch, the fact that she was always the one to initiate a conversation did.

"Just checking in," she said one Friday night, when she called.

"I'm sorry," I said. "Check-in time was three o'clock. You're late."

She laughed, but there was a specific reason for my pun. I figured that since I'd invented a relationship with a prostitute, an allusion to checking in, perhaps to a motel for an hour, would be entirely appropriate.

"Are you busy?" she asked.

"I'm not," I said.

"Oh, good. Corey over?"

"He isn't."

"Is that usual?" she asked. I was glad she hadn't used the words "normal" or "natural," because they would have implied judgment, at least to me.

I laughed. "Usual enough. We don't have any set schedule of when we see each other. Just whenever the time seems right."

"Okay," she said, her voice suddenly darkening. "I've been thinking about this, and I want to talk to you."

"You want to meet for dinner?" I asked.

"We will," she said, "just not now. I mean, we can talk over the phone if that's all right."

"Fire away," I said.

"Okay. Morley," she said. "I'm worried about you."

She couldn't have realized how little she had to worry about, but I was ready to play along. This was a big lie, the story about Corey (and Corey, incidentally, was a name I'd always liked, and often wished were mine, rather than Morley, while Gilliam came from Rosa Gilliam, my second-grade teacher). It was nothing like the small, specific lies in which I used to indulge, but from that point on, maybe because we no longer saw each other every day, the lies would have to expand to take up the available space.

"Why?" I asked.

"I just want to make sure he's not taking advantage of you."

And there she could have been, and probably was speaking from her experience with Peter, real or imagined.

"Look, I understand what you're saying," I said, and was surprised that my voice didn't imply more gratitude or affection. "But, as I'd explained to you, I'm not paying him anymore."

"That's not what I mean," she said, sounding even more serious than she had before. "Taking advantage isn't just a matter of money, of one paying for the other's services, or favors, or whatever you want to call them. Do you see what I'm getting at?"

Of course I did. And that was one reason why, I then realized, I'd made up the story of a prostitute: because I would never and could never get involved with one, and not just because I was asexual. I couldn't get involved with one because I thought of them as needy. Yes, we're *all* needy, but needy in different ways, and a prostitute's ways, I thought, were ways that I couldn't satisfy. I'd long believed that prostitutes were more interested in companionship than sex, but sex was easier to come by, a simple matter of meeting someone about whom you knew nothing and, importantly, from whom you expected nothing, except payment. There was no interrogation—What are your interests? What do you do for a living? Would you like to raise a family?—the results of which could lead to the involved parties not getting together. Just a quick, often anonymous encounter, and if things worked out, wonderful; marvelous. And if they didn't, neither could claim to be disappointed. But what I couldn't provide, and this became clearer to me with each passing year, was emotional support. And, of course, I could never rationalize a relationship by saying, "but at least the sex was good."

"I do," I said, feigning irritation. "Look, I appreciate that you're concerned, and I'm sure you believe that you have every right to be." At that point I expected to hear "Excuse me?!" But I didn't, so I continued. "But trust me, it's all right."

"Well, if you say so," she said, but, as she used to so often, she sounded unconvinced. Then, more brightly, "Dinner again soon?"

"Not if you're going to lecture me," I said.

She clicked her tongue. "Well isn't that just like you? Taking away all of my fun." Then she laughed. "I promise," she said.

So we made a date to meet the Wednesday after next, but at someplace quieter.

Table MANNERS

I had to hand it to Francine. She knew a lot more restaurants in the area than I did, but that didn't surprise me. I had my favorites, and stuck to them, and she might have been more likely to eat out then than she had when she was married, because she wasn't used to, or didn't like cooking for herself.

We met at Takahashi's, a Japanese restaurant that had just opened on Canter Street, the main thoroughfare in West Ellis. And if it was noisy on the outside, which it had to be, given its location, it was tranquil and serene inside, so the exact opposite of Allie's.

The bamboo walls, shoji screens, faux-jade fountain, and harp music that was too obviously not live left one in no doubt that it was a Japanese restaurant, but I wondered if the food would taste less good if the décor were less authentic. Of course, since I'd never been to Japan, I had no idea how authentic the décor even was. Maybe it was all a parody designed to please Western tastes. But no, I thought, it likely enhanced rather than distracted from one's dining experience, unlike conversation.

We were seated by a compact woman in a taupe kimono—I never saw her face—on cushions that sat on tatami mats. Not particularly comfortable, especially when Francine told me that I was supposed to kneel—I didn't because I couldn't; my body evidently wasn't aligned that way—but it was worth trying once, with the promise (to myself) that I'd never have to go through such contortions again.

"So let me ask you," Francine said, "How is your mother dealing with this?"

I knew what she meant. "With Corey and me? She's not." And at first I'd forgotten that, as far as Francine knew, my mother was still alive. "By which I mean, I haven't told her yet."

"You haven't told her?!"

I reached my hand toward her mouth to cover it. "Yeah, I know. Great son, aren't I? I just think she wouldn't be able to deal with it. Especially now. Given how possessive she is."

*

A week after my father died, when I was still in my twenties, my mother said, "Morley, I've had my fun. Now it's time for you to have yours."

"Meaning what?" I asked.

We were standing at the kitchen sink. She was washing the dishes and I was drying them. I'd taken over that chore from my father, because when he was still alive I'd leave the kitchen table as soon as dinner was over, and head to my bedroom to read, something I'd just discovered then, or listen to music.

"Meaning," she said, "that if you'd like to date somebody, I don't want you to feel beholden to me. I don't want to stand in your way."

She knew I was asexual, and that I never would date anybody. So I leaned over and kissed her, and she smiled.

"You're not going to, are you?" she asked.

"No," I said, and we both smiled. Was her largesse genuine? I couldn't say. Maybe she'd said that because she knew I wasn't suddenly going to wander out of her life, the way my father had, but it was nice to hear, so I didn't question it.

*

"Have you ever had sushi?" Francine asked.

"Never," I said. I loved sushi. "And I'm not averse to trying it, but right now I'm in the mood for something else."

"Well if you like fish in general, you'll like sushi."

Why? By "fish in general," I was sure she'd meant cooked fish, and sushi didn't taste anything like cooked fish. Nor did its texture resemble that of cooked fish. And the vinegared rice, sliced ginger, wasabi, and soy sauce were not ingredients that one would eat with cooked fish, so I didn't see her point at all.

"All right," I said. "Next time." I was physically uncomfortable enough to not want to go back there, but I remained thrilled that we could speak so easily about getting together again. Because there was no longer the guarantee of our seeing each other every day, our dinners out had risen to the level of something special.

"So," she said, smiling giddily. "I want to talk to you about...oh...a particular matter, but you need to order first."

"Order first," I said. "Okay." And so, obligingly, I did. We did. Appetizers: sashimi for her, shrimp gyoza for me; entrées: the sushi dinner—ten
pieces—for her, duck teriyaki for me. The waitress placed down chopsticks
in paper sleeves when she set down our appetizers. I extracted mine, broke
them apart, and immediately realized that I had no dexterity to pick up my
food with them. Since I'd always eaten sushi alone, I used my fingers to grab
the fish, and a fork to eat whatever couldn't or shouldn't have been handled
manually. But there were no forks on the table. Still, I made what I thought
was a valiant effort, but after taking a single bite of my appetizer, half of the
shrimp slid out of its wrapper, and Francine laughed.

"See? That's just what I mean."

"*What* do you mean?"

Still smiling, she said, "Nothing personal, but you have no table manners."

I sighed loudly.

"And the only reason I'm bringing this up," she said, "is that now that
you're seeing someone, I figured you'd want to make the best impression on
him."

There was something vaguely touching but wildly disturbing about that.
I *wasn't* seeing anyone, and I knew that my table manners were poor, but that
was because I'd simply never cared enough to impress anybody with them.
My parents, God bless them, put on no airs; their manners were no better
than mine, and my father, in particular, loved to slurp soup. In public, when I
was usually alone, I didn't think much about it, and it must have proved how
comfortable I'd become with Francine that I didn't see any need to impress
her, either.

With my chopsticks first, then with my fingers, I picked up the remaining
stuffing from my plate.

Francine turned her face away from me. "What are you doing?" she asked.
She was still smiling, but I could see that it was getting harder.

"I'm trying the place the detritus from my wrapper back inside."

"With your fingers?!" she asked.

Funny, I thought. I expected her to comment on my use of the word "detritus." "Well I don't have a fork," I said.

She widened her eyes. "Ask for one."

"I'd rather not," I said. "I don't like asking for things. I prefer to make do
with what I have. *As you know.*" Finally restuffing the spilled shrimp into my
dumpling, I said to her, "And that's a good way to get through life. It relieves

you of a remarkable lot of frustration. Not asking." Then I bit down, convinced that she'd be afraid to ask me something while I was chewing, in case I'd answer her before I swallowed.

"Okay," she said, suddenly serious. "That's what I don't understand about you. Whether what you say is real or if you just make things up."

Doesn't everybody make things up? How can you go through life and not make things up? But I said nothing. I continued to eat.

"What, are you chewing for the hearing-impaired?" she asked.

Fortunately I was able to cover my mouth with my napkin as I burst out laughing. "Now what?" I asked, before I swallowed.

"You chew with your mouth open."

I did and had for the longest time, but no one had ever told me not to. To myself I'd excused it by reasoning that since my sinuses were often stuffed, I had to breathe through my mouth if I wanted to breathe at all, but then I just started laughing, and she started laughing, and I looked around the restaurant to see if we were attracting any attention, then felt disappointed to realize that the other people there didn't find us nearly as entertaining as we did.

Before the entrées arrived I asked our waitress for a fork and knife, which she brought quietly, but I then realized that, given the dish I'd ordered, she probably would have brought them anyway.

And shortly after I sliced into my duck and tasted it—it was delicious—Francine asked, "Why did you do that?"

"Do what?"

"Switch hands?"

"What?"

"Look," she said, leaning over the table but staring at my plate rather than me. "You skewer your food with your fork, which you hold in your left hand, and that's fine, and cut it with your knife, which you hold in your right hand, and that's fine, too. But then you put down the knife and switch the fork to your right hand."

"I'm right-handed," I said.

"Okay. Then why not just keep the fork in your right hand and cut the food with the knife in your left hand?"

"Because I'm right-handed," I said again, "and don't feel like I have the strength or proficiency to cut food using my left hand." Again I looked around me; everyone seemed absorbed in his or her own affairs.

Francine sighed. "It's just poor table manners," she said.

"Why do you do *that*?" I asked, raising my eyebrows.

"I was expecting that," she said, and waved her right hand at me. "Criticizing me for something I do." She smiled and relaxed her shoulders. "Okay, what is it? What do I do that bothers you?"

"Open your mouth to talk. I'd much prefer it if you kept it closed."

At first I thought it was all terribly amusing, but increasingly I was becoming irritated because it made me wonder if one reason I stayed with—as opposed to by—myself was that I was too embarrassed to present myself in public.

"Is there anything else you'd like to criticize me for?" she asked. "I'm just curious."

"You salt your food too much."

"There's no salt on the table," she said, frowning.

"You're using soy sauce; it's the same thing. And I've seen you elsewhere. Why all the salt? It's not healthy," I said.

"I need a few grains to take you with."

I smiled wanly. "You have an answer for everything, don't you?"

"No," she said, suddenly sober and biting her lower lip. "Not at all. In fact, I have very few answers for anything. Good ones, anyway."

"You never have that problem around me."

"You're different."

"Is that why you like me?" I asked.

She shifted her eyes back and forth. "Because I always have an answer for you or because you're different?" She was sitting up much more rigidly.

"Either."

She looked unusually thoughtful. "Morley," she said, resting her hands in her lap and bending forward. "Why do you think there's only *one* thing that people like about each other?"

"I don't," I said.

"Yes, you *do*. Look," she said, "I think I know you well enough by now to recognize that. You have very elemental ideas about attraction. That's not how it works at all. And it's not even that one thing is more attractive than any other. Not always. Morley, answer me something. Have you ever been attracted to anyone?"

She knew the answer was no, so I said, "Of course I have."

"That's what I thought," she said, clearly answering my "no," rather than what I told her. "But if you ever do—"

"There's Corey," I said. Or had she forgotten about him already?

"Well yes, and now there's another question I want to ask you. I'm sorry if I seem to be jumping around, but—"

"Ask," I said.

"Do you think prostitutes debase themselves? By being prostitutes?"

My, how quickly the focus of our conversation changed. But I knew she couldn't accept the fact that I was dating a prostitute. Which was one reason why I told her I was. To keep her at a distance. Not understanding other people is the best antidote to closeness.

And suddenly I was concerned that other people would be listening to us, and I knew I would have been less concerned, even proud, if any part of my story were true, but nobody looked interested. I rolled my eyes. "Oh, please," I said. "People debase themselves all the time, and not just sexually. But sexually, too, and a lot. Look at it this way: in a relationship between a prostitute and a client, whose debases himself more? The prostitute, whom the client desires for his physical attractiveness and sexual prowess, or the client, whom the prostitute values for his money and ability to validate him?"

She shook her head. "I don't know," she said. "What do you think?"

I was touched by her question, maybe more than I should have been, but didn't have an answer. So I said, "I don't know, either. Both, I guess."

She laughed. "Well that's one way of assuring equality."

I signaled the waitress, then asked her for an iced tea, which she said they had.

"Look, that's something you're not going to find in every relationship."

"But equality varies," Francine said. "Sometimes one person feels more in charge, and sometimes the other one does. I don't think one always feels in control, or wants to."

I did.

If I regretted having mentioned, indeed invented Corey, and if I had only been nicer to myself, I could have simply changed the subject *again*, but I found the conversation so fascinating that I felt I had to tell Francine more, if only to see what her reaction would be. So shortly before we were done with our entrées, I said, "You know, there's a bit of a problem with Corey."

"Your problem or his?" she asked, and I could see her regretting that there was nothing for her to lean against.

"Good question. His. But now mine. But not really."

"See?!" she said. "I knew this was going to happen." And she pushed her open right palm toward me and nodded.

We ordered dessert and I switched back to hot tea.

"I say 'not really' for a reason, and by the way, can we not come here anymore? Sitting on a cushion is not my idea of paradise. Anyway, he's being kicked out of his apartment."

"Why?!"

"Why do you think?" I asked. "He can't afford to pay his rent."

"Does he work? I mean a *real* job, not being a prostitute."

How sad that she thought prostitution wasn't real.

"Oh, yes," I said. "He's a graphic designer. Prostitution is just a sideline. And remember, I'm not paying him anymore."

"For his sexual services," she said.

I had to laugh. "Right."

"So now you're going to tell me that you're paying his rent."

The waitress brought our desserts: mango mochi for Francine and apple tempura for me.

Then I said, "Not exactly," and let my face fall. "Look, if I were paying his rent, he wouldn't be getting thrown out of his apartment, would he?"

"You would have decided to pay it after you found out." She clicked her tongue. "Where does he live?"

"In Arledge."

"I've never heard of it," she said, then concentrated on breaking her mochi with her spoon.

"It's on the way to Bellerson, about a forty-minute drive from Lake Quaintance. To the south."

She nodded while chewing, then swallowed. "Oh, okay. I know where you mean."

"But here's why it's not my problem. He can afford half of his rent, so I'm paying only the other half."

"Why doesn't he have the money?" she asked.

"I don't know."

"You didn't ask him?"

"I didn't think it was any of my business," I said. The restaurant was getting a little more crowded, but the crowd was quiet.

She shook her head. "Morley, what am I going to do with you?"

"I don't know," I said. "What are your options?"

"It's not *my* options that matter, it's yours. If you're going to pay half this man's rent, I would think he owes you an explanation for why he needs it."

"It was my decision," I said. "He didn't ask."

"Even so," she said.

*

When I was twenty-four, and had just finished graduate school, I was the last person among me and my friends to get a job. I'd been made three offers, but I turned all of them down because one school paid scantily, one was in a district with a questionable—*poor*—academic reputation, and one was a little farther from where I lived than I wanted to work. And since I was still living with my parents, I could afford to be choosy. Six months later, though, I started my job in Lake Quaintance, and moved there. I'd saved enough, through other jobs during my six years of college, and summer jobs, to put a small down payment on a small house.

My best friend, Angelo, who taught graphic design, and was never, as far as I knew, a prostitute, lived in an apartment in Arledge, but after a year, for reasons that I would never understand and never ask him about, he told me that he couldn't afford to keep it anymore, and was moving back with his parents. I was fine with the silence, but then, I always would be. And young people just starting their careers felt too embarrassed to discuss their financial shortcomings with anyone but an advisor, anyway. I liked Angelo. We didn't spend a lot of time together, which might have been why I liked him, but I felt as though I should have helped him pay his rent. Could I have afforded to? Probably, as I spent very little money on myself, but the better question might have been *Why?* Likely it was for the same reason that I left large tips: if I could afford it, it would allow me to feel at least a little superior to him. Obviously, I had no idea what living with a relative stranger would be like, but I also knew that I probably wouldn't have enjoyed it, so I let that, rather than my innate frugality, be my reason for not offering.

Clearly, though, the thought persisted with me all those years, which was why I made up my little myth about Corey.

*

"Are we ready?" I asked.

"Just a minute," Francine said. "I want to savor my tea."

No, she didn't. She wanted to talk more. So "Let me know when you're done," I said, as an indication that I didn't want to discuss the situation any further.

Corey SPEAKS

Not two weeks later Francine called me again. I knew she would, because she had to. She couldn't have been satisfied with the way we'd left our conversation about Corey, but I was sure it was because she wanted to give me her opinions rather than because she thought she could help. Two different things; often confused.

"I'm not calling to apologize," she said, "so don't be disappointed."

"I'm not disappointed," I said. It was a Tuesday night.

"I'm just concerned."

But *that* disappointed me. Concern was fine, but telling somebody that you were concerned had an element of self-importance about it, and the suggestion that something was now expected in return.

"Morley," she said. "I think you can do—"

"Stop," I said. "Don't say it, because I've heard it already. You think I can do better."

"No," she said, "I think you can do different."

Did she expect me to compliment her on her cleverness or broad-mindedness?

"Because, look," she said. "You're a very good-looking man."

Funny; I didn't think so. In my mid-forties, I was past the age when anybody but a blind person could find me good-looking. And I don't say that disrespectfully. I knew a blind girl in high school who felt people's faces to gauge how they might have looked, and when she felt mine she told me that I was very good-looking. But I didn't know if she'd been able to see once and lost her vision later or if she'd been blind since birth and had no idea what human faces looked like. I never asked her because, I told myself, it wasn't my place to, but really I was afraid that she didn't know what "very good-looking" meant. But so what? What was the point of it? I appreciated physical beauty, but on some level, because I didn't tie it to sexual gratification, it didn't matter all that much. And I was fine with that. Respect made me feel better than compliments on my appearance. And maybe because I never put that emphasis on attractiveness in other people, I never found myself attractive. Some would find that sad or even maddening, but to me it always seemed natural.

"Thank you," I said. "Corey thinks so, too. But that's not why you called. So tell me the truth. Is my paying half his rent the only thing that bothers you about him, or is there more?"

I could feel her sighing, even if I didn't hear it. "It's not *him*," she said, sounding a little sad, "it's the situation. And you know what? I don't know anything else about him. You haven't told me that much."

Then, I thought, I would really scare her. "You want to talk to him? You can ask him yourself what's going on between us. I'm sure he'll tell you more than I have."

"He's there?!" Her voice was so loud that I imagined a pair of lips coming through the telephone receiver, like I used to see on Saturday morning cartoons.

"Sitting here, right next to me," I said. Let her think that I'd announced something embarrassing or insulting in response to a remark she'd made.

"Oh, God," she said, muttering. "Yeah, sure. Put him on."

One small talent I had, from the time I was a child of five or six, was an ability to speak, convincingly, in dialects. And if I was more apt to impress people who were less familiar with a particular mode of speech than people who were raised to speak it, at least none of the voices that I put on sounded anything like me. Not bad for someone who never traveled. But I was always a good listener.

Professionally this was a real boon in my *Irish Literature* and, especially, *Understanding Faulkner* classes, where my students would seem delighted by the way I could adopt the personae of various characters and turn pages of potentially dreary prose (in my students' opinion, not mine) into something human and relevant.

So, of course, I decided that Corey, like Faulkner, had come from Mississippi, and I didn't even worry that it would make Francine suspicious. Let her think it was part of the attraction.

I covered the transmitter and said, "It's my friend Francine."

"Hey Francine," Corey said in a sweet, lulling drawl. "How're you doing?" I was afraid he was going to say that he'd heard a lot about her, because I'd already told her that I'd never discussed her with my other friends, but Corey didn't mention it.

"I'm all right," she said, forcing some brightness into her voice. "How are you? And what are you guys up to tonight?"

"Oh, sitting back. Relaxing. You know. 'Shooting the shit,' as they say," and he laughed much more loudly than I expected him to, but at least his laugh didn't sound anything like mine.

"You have a great laugh," she said.

Thanks, Francine.

"Do you get together often?" she asked.

"Ah," he said softly, "not really. Because we live so far away"—he pronounced it "fur"—"so usually on the weekends, but not always. But we try to see each other at least once a week."

I never explained to Francine how I spent my weekends, so let her think that I reserved them for Corey.

"Well that's nice," she said, but her voice was so colorless that I couldn't tell if she was jealous, knew it was me talking, or something else was bothering her. It certainly didn't carry conviction. But maybe she'd just soured on relationships by that point. "So where are you from?" she asked more lightly. "You certainly don't sound like you're from around here."

And again he laughed too loudly. "Hardly. I'm from Missippi,"—I was remembering Walter Bailey—"Biloxi to be exact."

"Oh. Big city," she said.

He shook his head, but she couldn't have known. "Not really," he said. "There are no big cities in Missippi. Like Vermont. There are no big cities there, either. I've always wanted to go there but I haven't yet."

And Francine paused, possibly afraid that he was going to ask me to fund his next vacation. Very likely, I thought, since I was already paying half of his rent. "Well look, it was really great to finally talk to you," she said mechanically. "Do you mind if I talk to Morley again?"

Corey covered up the phone and said, very dispassionately, "She wants to talk to you."

I laughed. "Coming," I said, holding the transmitter as far away as I could. Then, holding it next to my mouth, I said, "So. What do you think?"

Another long pause. "I don't know what to think," she said. "I mean, he seems nice enough, and has a wonderful accent, but—"

But what? Did she not believe he was real?

"I don't know. Something about him....All right," she said. "This is what I'm thinking. I thought that after talking to him, maybe I would understand you better—"

"'You' meaning 'us,' or 'you' meaning 'me'?" I asked.

"Either," she said. "Both. But I don't. I just find him very hard to read."

"Francine," I said. "You spoke with the man for less than a minute. Okay, two if you count the pauses."

And that had to have been because she was just checking to see if he was real. Or not real. To confirm her suspicions, although I didn't know what her suspicions were. Because obviously she wasn't interested in getting to know him.

"I know, but some people reveal themselves quickly," she said.

I exhaled deeply. "He's been through a lot," I said, and left it at that.

"So are you seeing him this weekend?"

Actually, I wanted to tell her, I wasn't, because I had plans then, though I had plans for every weekend. So I said, "Probably."

"But you know something?" she asked. "Since you're already paying half his rent, why don't you two just live together? At least sometimes." And this, I knew, was something she was never going to let me forget. But did she think I would always be paying half of his rent? That he would never become financially stable again? Nothing in a relationship with someone else lasts forever, and she, of all people, should have known that. As a friend of mine once said, when you get more than one person together at a time, you're asking for trouble.

So I said, "Oh my God," but in such a way as to let her think I meant, Why hadn't *I* thought of that? "In the first place, he lives nowhere near where I work, and in the second place, what about my mother?"

"Of course," she said gently. "How is she doing? Does she know Corey is over?"

"She knows."

"And she's all right with it?"

"She has no choice," I said. "But really, she's so *not* all right with so many other things, this hardly matters."

"Of course," she said again. "All right. Look, I'm going to go. I don't want to keep you any longer than I already have."

"Sounds good," I said. "I'll talk to you soon." We said goodbye, and I hung up. Neither she nor I wanted the conversation to continue, and my reason was that the thought of Corey being real, and my spending extended amounts of time with him was suffocating. I had to get back to myself. The image of being trapped in a room with two parallel walls moving toward each other was distressingly familiar, but one could argue that it mirrored life, just that the walls moved more slowly than we could realize. But that was how I felt when I spent, or contemplated spending excessive amounts of time with others. The more people who were in the room, the sooner someone would be crushed. One good argument for solitude. But solitude afforded me expansion. On the weekends I usually divided my time equally between reading and listening to music, and both broadened my life by taking me outside of myself and letting me mull over memories and idealize them. A scene that, at the time, seemed usual or ordinary would become exalted and dignified when revisited, but only when I was reading or listening to music. Still, those good feelings would remain with me until the next time I could be by myself and do what I enjoyed. I was lucky enough to always know what made me happy.

The ROLE of a LIFETIME

Then four months went by before I spoke to Francine again, and this time I called her. Specifically to say that my mother was finally feeling well—I hesitated to use the word "again"—and that she was on the mend. She hadn't been to the hospital since the last time Francine and I had spoken, so I thought it would be nice for me to finally invite Francine over and introduce her. Of course, I no longer had a mother to introduce her to, but I did have Helen.

Helen was my neighbor; a seventy-eight–year-old woman who lived right next door, and I'd come to know her through my mother. Helen moved into her house when it was new, six years before I moved into mine. At that time she was living with her eldest daughter, Mindy, but two years after I moved in, Mindy was killed in an automobile accident, and Helen's next-oldest daughter, Katherine—Helen had four daughters—bought the house so Helen wouldn't have to move.

One weekend when my mother was visiting me, Helen introduced herself. She'd been sitting on her front porch, and my mother and I walked outside. Thinking that my mother had moved in with me, or had always lived there, Helen walked up to her, told her what a beautiful neighborhood ours was—it was nice—and what a wonderful town Lake Quaintance was, and began telling my mother all about herself. I could see my mother becoming first disinterested and then annoyed, because, while she could be gregarious, she tended to shy away from new people, and finally excused herself by saying, "Helen, it was wonderful to meet you, and I'd really like to talk more, but I have to go."

Then it was two months before they saw each other again, and I hadn't run into Helen in the meantime, but when they met, Helen started talking more, and my mother, by then knowing better what to expect, seemed much more cordial and voluble, and from that time on, Helen would always count my mother among her closest friends, even if they saw each other maybe half a dozen times a year (I visited my mother more than she visited me).

After Mindy died, I was at Helen's house every night for the first week, after which I was sure I'd made a nuisance of myself, and my mother and I even went to the funeral, but in the days that followed I felt some responsibility to stand in for the woman I loved.

With time, Helen and I saw less of each other, but whenever we would meet she would wrangle me into a conversation, which I actually enjoyed because I knew that once it was over, I would feel relieved. This time, after I invited Francine over, I rang Helen's bell, and she invited me in. She would be perfect for the role of a crochety woman. She was short, slightly hunch-backed, had faded skin, stark white hair, incredibly intense dark brown eyes, and looked careworn. Her voice was harsh and raspy. But she was sweet and had an especial fondness for practical jokes, especially those that weren't explained to the victim.

"So what do you want me to do?" she asked. She laughed, and I could see how much she was relishing it.

"Okay, I have this friend named Francine," I said. She's about my age. We used to work together, for about a year, but then she drifted, and now she's back in my life."

Helen smiled impishly. "You want me to scare her away?" She knew what sort of impression she made on the uninitiated.

"Wait a second," I said. "Don't steal my good ideas." And we both laughed. We were sitting at her kitchen table, drinking tea. "Here's the thing. I want you to pretend to be my mother."

"Your mother?!" she asked, sounding a little offended and a little disappointed. "Your mother was a marvelous woman."

"Yes, I know," I said. "Of course she was. But Francine has never met her. And I'm just trying to give her a good scare."

Helen perked up, and didn't even ask why. She didn't care. As long as she would be able to dupe someone, she knew she was going to have fun.

"So I want you to be as obnoxious and outrageous and utterly unpalatable as you can."

She sighed, then smiled. "You know you're asking me to do a lot," she said. And I was, because Helen wasn't usually like that, if she ever was. "But all right. I'll do it for you and I'll do it for your mother. But tell me one thing."

"Yes?"

"What did Francine do to deserve this?" She sipped her tea slowly.

"Do you really want to know?"

Then she spit it out, laughing. "Oh, I'm sorry," she said, suddenly felicitous. "I just figured I'd ask so you could see how well I can act."

And we both laughed.

Put them all together
they spell "MOTHER"

Why was I doing this? Because, over the years that I'd known Francine, I'd painted such an inaccurate, unrepresentative image of my mother that I had to prove to both of us that it was true. Had I simply described my mother the way she was, calm, quiet, unprepossessing, there would have been nothing to show and nothing to prove. But the enormity of that difference, between what was real and what I'd described, made me determined to convince her that I wasn't lying.

So Francine showed up the following Wednesday night, with the understanding that we'd eat out afterward. And this time I'd decided on Eddie Renn's Steakhouse, which was walking distance from our old school, and was someplace I would never have gone by myself, but I had the impression that Francine loved, or at least liked steak, so it could be a treat after what I had planned for her. And, I thought, why should she be the only one to suffer?

Helen showed up at six o'clock—Francine said she'd be by around six-thirty—wearing a baggy beige dress and an orange woolen shawl, designed, she explained, to highlight the whiteness of her hair. She brought her cat Piers, a ginger shorthair, with her. She'd asked me before if that would be all right, and I'd told her that of course it would, but she'd have to bring a bowl of food, a scratching board, and his litter box as well to make the illusion convincing. My only concern was that the name Piers might remind Francine too much of Peter. I'd explained that whole story to Helen, and she suggested that we rename the cat Gilbert, or Gil for short, as that had been the name of Helen's husband. I had no idea what happened to him.

And when the doorbell rang twenty-five minutes later—Francine was early—Helen apologized. "I'm sorry, sweetness," she said. "Nothing that follows is serious." But from that moment on, at least for the next half hour, she would be my mother.

"Come in," I said when I opened the door. Francine must have heard the tension in my voice.

My mother stood so rigidly and close to my right—our shoulders were touching—that I might have been supporting a body in which rigor mortis had already set in. She extended her right arm, bent at the elbow. "I'm Mrs. Peck," she said, without smiling. "You can address me as such."

Which came as a relief, because my mother's name was Jennie, and I didn't want any confusion with first names. Not that hers would be used in such a situation.

"Pleased to meet you," Francine said, and shook her hand.

"Come on in," I said, as Francine stepped into the living room. "Can I get you anything to drink? Water, lemonade—"

My mother frowned. "Morley," she said, "Don't ask people if they want something to drink as soon as they walk in. This isn't a concession stand."

Francine and I stared at each other.

"Be a gentleman," my mother said, "and show your friend the house. Then we can sit down and talk."

So I showed Francine around. Mine was a ranch-style house. There was no foyer, so the front door opened right into the living room. Every floor, except the floors in the kitchen and bathroom, was covered in thin, worn, olive green carpeting. I didn't like it, but it was there when I'd moved in and I never saw a need to change it since I never entertained. The furniture, which consisted of a sofa, loveseat, two end chairs, all in solid beige, surrounded by a variety of small end tables and an old television set, was functional, not elaborate. Mid-century modern, it drew no attention to itself, like a room full of exceptionally quiet people. There was no wall between the living room and the kitchen and dinette, where there was a modest pine table with four chairs, and, to the right, a hall that led to the two bedrooms, whose doors faced each other. Just to the left of the smaller bedroom was the bathroom. I'd set up that smaller bedroom as a den, but that was for show, as I spent virtually all of my time in my own bedroom. Of course I'd closed the door to the den so Francine couldn't see that it wasn't a bedroom at all.

In my bedroom I had a queen-size bed, which Francine might have thought appropriate, a desk, chest and dresser, wall mirror, recliner, three overstuffed bookshelves, and a rack holding my stereo equipment. Truthfully, I never saw any reason to leave, except when I had to go to work or eat.

Notably, there were no photographs of anyone anywhere in the house. One reason was that I wasn't close to my family, so I saw no need to be reminded of them, but I also disliked photographs in general because they seemed artificial, or at least limiting. They captured one particular instance, but people's lives were composed of an infinite variety of instances, and to look at, or be reminded of just one effectively closed the door on all the others.

"Nice," she said, quietly, when we'd concluded our tour, but I couldn't tell if she was unimpressed—her house was certainly more opulent—or simply cowed by my mother.

Back in the living room my mother told, rather than asked us to sit down. She sat in the center of the couch by herself, a throne, given that it was accommodating a single person, and we chose to sit on the two end chairs. The loveseat would have put us too close together, and I'm sure my mother wouldn't have approved, to say nothing of what Francine might have thought. "I want to know about you," my mother said, staring at her.

Francine swallowed loudly. "What would you like to know?" she asked, her voice dry and caked.

"First of all, what do you do?" My mother scowled and crossed her arms.

Francine sat, hunched forward, with her hands in her lap. "Well, as I'm sure Morley's told you—"

"Don't be sure of anything. I'm asking you, not him."

Francine smiled nervously; I thought she was going to vomit. "I'm a high school English teacher, just like your son. That's how we met. We used to work together, at the high school here."

My mother rolled her eyes. "I know that already," she said. Which, had things taken a comedic turn, would have been a cue for laughter, but there was none. "Do you still teach?" my mother asked.

"I do," Francine said. "As I just said." Somebody wasn't listening. "Except now I teach in—"

"I didn't ask *where* you teach. I asked *if* you teach. Still." She shook her head and sighed. "So I guess you do. All right. Are you married?" my mother asked. That, of course, was what she was interested in.

"Excuse me?" Francine asked, but not archly. In fact, a little too placidly, I thought.

"I know you heard me," my mother said, "because I don't whisper. I can't stand it when people whisper. It's rude. I asked if you were married. A simple question. Yes or no." My mother smiled, not because she wanted to relax Francine, that would have been out of character, but because she was simply enjoying herself. A game, yes, but one she took very seriously.

"Um, no," Francine said, looking like she'd just been struck by a blunt object, so, confused, hurt, and annoyed. "Divorced."

My mother pursed her lips. "Well I'm glad you're not married," she said. "Otherwise I couldn't imagine what you'd be doing here. A woman's place is with her husband. Always."

I laughed to myself. And Francine thought *I* was old-fashioned.

"Don't you agree?" my mother asked.

"Hmm? Yes," Francine said timidly.

My mother settled back. "So whose fault was it; yours or his?" Francine opened her mouth, but my mother said, "Your divorce. Why did you do it?" But before Francine could say anything, my mother shook her head again and said, "It doesn't matter. It's over and done with. So are you dating my son? You'd better tell me now, missy"—a brilliant touch, Helen—"because I'm going to find out eventually."

For a moment I thought Helen and I were carrying things too far, and that Francine must have realized it was all an act, but then I thought, Yes, there probably was dialogue just like this being spoken somewhere by some poor sons of bitches.

I thought Francine looked unusually sad when she shook her head and said, "No, I'm not," but, again, that might have just been me.

Then, deus ex machina, Gil wandered into the living room and sat in front of Francine's left foot, putting his right paw on her leg and purring.

"He must like you," I said.

My mother shook her head. "He doesn't like strangers. You know that."

"I have a cat," Francine said.

"Then maybe he smells him on you," my mother said. "But he doesn't like strangers." Then her expression brightened. "My son's a good man, you know."

"Oh, I know that," Francine said, letting her shoulders fall back. "He treats everyone with respect."

I wasn't so sure, but it was nice to hear, and here, I thought, Helen was just apologizing for what she'd been putting Francine through.

"Can I assume you do the same?"

"Hmm?" Francine asked. "What?" Then, "Oh, of course. You know, you become a teacher and you learn to treat your students respectfully, so they'll return the favor."

My mother raised her eyebrows. "It's not a favor," she said. "Respect is never a favor. It's always given because the person doling it out wants something in return."

Maybe so, I thought.

"So, mom," I said. "Is there anything else you'd like to ask Francine?"

She stood up. "What for? I'm not getting any real answers anyway. Just 'um' and 'hmm.'" Then she walked over to me as I stood up—Francine seemed frozen in place—and asked, "What time will you be home?"

"Not late," I said. "We're not going far. Just into town and back."

"Well make sure it's not late," she said. Then she called Gil and walked toward her bedroom without saying goodbye.

"Shall we?" I asked Francine.

Still sitting in the end chair, she looked too exhausted to say anything.

Table for Two

Eddie Renn's Steakhouse occupied three floors of an old red brick building on Drews Avenue, four blocks north of the high school. The ground and second floors were used for hosting social events, and the restaurant itself was in the basement. If it weren't a steakhouse that might have been a problem, because the absence of windows and, therefore, light, even artificial light during the night, would have made it oppressive, but the shadowiness seemed well-suited to the atmosphere they were trying to convey; something terribly masculine and serious. Suits of armor stood against stucco walls with dark wood beams set vertically and diagonally, though the wait staff was attired in simple white shirts and blouses and black pants and bow ties; no allusion to the Tudor period there. And, likely, the Tudor period wasn't known for wall-to-wall carpeting.

We were seated along the far wall, a couple of tables from the corner, where a round table for six was set. The lighting was dim.

"So why did you decide to come here?" Francine asked. "I know you don't like steak."

"I figured I'd give you a treat," I said. "I'm assuming you do."

"I do," she said, but not very enthusiastically, which dampened my feelings of pride for having done something nice for someone at my expense. Note to self: don't do that again.

We both ordered French onion soup, and she ordered the twin tournedos Rossini—I loved the name!—while I ordered the twin lobster tails.

"You have a nice house," she said.

I laughed. "I don't like it either. Remember?! That's what you said to me, or something like it, the first time I came to your house, and I complimented you on it."

She smiled sadly. "No," she said. "I don't remember that at all."

And I was a little disappointed because, obviously, that meeting had meant a lot to me, but I was relieved at the same time because enough had gone on back then that was better left forgotten.

"So have you lived there all your life?"

I rolled my eyes. "Did the house look *that* old?" I asked, mock-irritated. "No. I bought it after my father died, and my mother moved in with me. It was new then." None of that was true. Then, after a few moments I asked, "So what did you think? About her."

Her expression brightened. "You know what?" she asked. "I just realized something."

"Which is?"

"I really like the smell of air." And we both laughed.

"Yes," I said. "My mother can be very suffocating. But you'll have to forgive her. Wednesday is one of her off days. Her others are Thursday, Friday, Saturday, Sunday, Monday, and Tuesday." And again we laughed.

"Well it does explain a lot about you," she said, but it couldn't have, because that wasn't my mother, and the character who Helen was playing wasn't anything like my mother. But I knew what Francine meant. That growing up in such a stifling environment had to make me turn inward. But no, that wasn't the case at all.

"And I didn't realize you had a cat," she said, leaning back, unfolding her napkin, and placing it in her lap. I'd never seen her do that. Usually she kept her napkin on the table just to the left of whatever dishes were set down, but I always placed mine in my lap, and I wondered if she was picking up another of my habits.

"Oh, yes," I said. "His name is Gilbert, but we call him Gil." Then I remembered that Corey's last name was Gilliam, and I wondered if she was getting suspicious about too many little details fitting too neatly together. But she couldn't have gotten suspicious about that, because that was a coincidence—Gil had been Helen's husband's name—over which I had no control. Clearly, I wasn't trusting myself anymore.

"How long have you had him?"

That was a question I wasn't expecting. How long had Helen had Piers? I couldn't remember, but since Francine and I had stopped talking six years earlier, and I hadn't mentioned having a cat before then, I said, "Five years, I think. Yes, five. We got him five years ago." I was talking too much.

When the waiter brought our soup, Francine said, "You seem nervous. Is everything all right?"

"I'm fine," I said, but I was feeling overwhelmed. First I'd invented Corey, then I'd invented my mother, though that was a story I'd been telling Francine for a long time, and I was getting tired of trying to manipulate so many fabrications. It wasn't that I was afraid of her seeing through my masquerade, it was that I was simply losing interest in perpetuating it. I was anxious to tell her who I was already, and anxious to stop feeling that she would reject me for it because she couldn't understand it. And yet, when I tried to get closer to her, I realized that I just didn't want to. I looked around and saw that there were tapestries hanging on the walls. Easy to miss because of the dimness. "So how long has it been now?" I asked. "Since the divorce?"

She breathed loudly and shook her head. "Oh, over a year," she said. "Closer to two."

"And how have you been holding up?"

She smiled self-deprecatingly. "All right, I guess."

"Which means—"

"Not well."

"Tell me about it," I said, and leaned back.

"Do you really want to hear about it?"

"I wouldn't ask if I didn't," I said, but I didn't, because her life was so different from mine that I couldn't offer her any support or advice, and I knew that she needed both. But I could see her life only in terms of my own, and in those terms there was nothing wrong with it.

"I'm lonely," she said, "but it's more than that. I was lonely when I was married to Peter, just in a different way."

"Is this loneliness worse?"

She smiled obliquely. "Not necessarily. Just different."

"Francine," I said, "please forgive me for asking this, but do you like yourself?"

She looked surprised, and tensed. "I think so. I think I like myself all right," she said.

But not enough to enjoy her own company, I thought. Because Peter, if he existed, must have made her feel so poorly about herself that she could no longer keep herself company. And now she didn't have anyone else.

One of the advantages to being asexual, and there were many, was that, as somebody once told me, when you eliminate sex you can love somebody without feeling like you have to. And sometimes, maybe even often, this person said, people use sex to convince themselves that they love each other when they really don't. True, I'd said, but I still saw no need to love anyone. It either happened or it didn't. It wasn't a requirement for happiness and, more importantly, it wasn't a requirement for satisfaction. But who was I to explain any of this to Francine? And who was she to understand it?

"Dating?" I asked.

"Not yet," she said. I could see the waiter bringing our entrées, which would be a natural cue for us to change the subject.

"It takes time," I said, remembering her decision to not adopt another cat immediately after Tomas died. I shook my head gently. "Give it time," I said, then added, as she once said, "It's always nice having what to look forward to."

After we were served, she said, "So about your mother. Do you think she is the way she is because of Corey?"

"Oh!" I said. "I forgot to tell you. Corey has a new job. He's working again, so I'm no longer supporting him halfway."

"Well good!" she said, looking pleased.

"Yeah," I said. "Helping him out was the least I could do, and, you know, I always try to get by with the least I can do."

She laughed. "Don't say that. I'm glad, though. But do you think your mother is jealous?"

Jealous, I thought. Because I was paying attention to someone else. How hopelessly possessive other people could be. "I'm sure she is," I said.

"Well I can understand that," Francine said. "I never told you this, but for the first few years of our marriage, my mother practically stopped talking to me because she thought I was spending all of my time with Peter, and none with her anymore."

"Were you living at home?"

"No!" She rested her left arm against the back of her chair, which implied that she was going to say a lot. "I was living on my own, and dating, but when I finally found someone, Peter, she closed herself off."

"Sad," I said, but maybe her mother didn't like herself any more than Francine did, and that would have explained a lot.

My lobster tails were delicious, and Francine seemed delighted with her tournedos Rossini.

"Really excellent," she said. "Good choice."

"And you know what's funny?" I asked. "My mother always told me never to order seafood anywhere but in a seafood restaurant, and Italian anywhere but in an Italian restaurant, et cetera."

"She must not have liked diners," Francine said.

"She hated them."

*

Seating ourselves one Tuesday night at the Greenwood Inn, my mother said, "You know what I love about diners?"

"This isn't a diner," I said quietly.

She waved her right hand. "Oh, please," she said. "It is. The absence of booths doesn't make it any less of a diner than restaurants that call themselves diners. But this is what I like about them. You can get anything you want here. Steak, seafood, Italian specialties, Greek specialties. Sometimes even Chinese."

"Yeah," I said, "but it's not as good as the authentic—"

She laughed. "Let me tell you something. I don't know if you've noticed this, but I'm not that young anymore. You know how many doctors I have? One."

"That's because you're in good health," I said.

She shook her head. "It doesn't matter. You know how many doctors my friends have? Five or six. Or seven or eight. Seriously. Everyone's a specialist these days. So one goes to one doctor for her heart, another doctor for her kidneys, another doctor for her liver. It gets ridiculous. And you know why? Because one doesn't know what the other is doing. I'd rather go to one doctor who can treat me *whole*."

"And you'd rather go to one restaurant that can serve you whole."

"That can give me whatever I want."

"All right," I said. "I can understand that."

*

"So how's work going?" I asked. The question one always asked, at least of an employed person, when one ran out of things to say.

"I really like it," she said, and she sounded genuinely happy; very unlike the way she'd sounded when she worked in Lake Quaintance.

"So coming here doesn't bother you. It doesn't bring back bad memories."

"Not really," she said. "Bad memories are easy to overcome if you've got something to replace them with."

I understood that. Did she?

"So about my cat," I said, because I again felt the need to reestablish that alternate reality. "He's been doing something strange lately."

"What?" she asked. She put down her knife and fork, which made me feel that I owed her an elaborate explanation.

"He likes to eat newspaper."

She shook her head. "Why am I not surprised that you still read newspapers?" she asked.

I smiled. "Are you done with your criticisms?" I sipped my water.

"Give me a moment," she said. Then, "All cats like to eat newspaper."

"So you're telling me that my cat isn't unique."

"I'm *telling* you that it's not abnormal, so there's nothing to worry about," she said.

But I wasn't worried, not least because I didn't have a cat. "So you're telling me that uniqueness is abnormal and something to be worried about."

"Are you in therapy?! Because you could make some therapist very happy. Really stuff his pockets."

"And of course you're interested more in your capitalist creed than helping the needy. Put more money in the pockets of the already-wealthy, but don't help the person who needs help."

"You're hopeless," she said. "You're beyond help." And we broke into peals of laughter. Then, a few moments later, she asked, "Did you just shit yourself?"

"What?!" I asked. "No. Why?" I wasn't laughing that hard, but I reached my left hand under the seat of my pants to make sure there was nothing wet there, even though I knew I hadn't done anything.

"Because I smell something...bowely. Is that a word?"

I considered her question. "Hmm," I said. "I don't know, but I like it. If it isn't it should be. But seriously, why do you ask?"

"I just told you. Do you not smell it?"

"I'll have you know that I have an extremely fine sense of smell, and if there was that, I'm sure it would have wafted toward me. But no, I don't." Then I said, "It must be one of your ideas you're smelling."

She shook her head and waved her right hand in front of her nose. Maybe coughing would have been too much. "Well I don't know how you can't smell it," she said.

I shook my head, a little bothered that she hadn't responded to my humor.

Then she looked up as an elderly woman, frail, with short pinkish-red hair and in a long dress, cheap, paper-thin, and black and white, walked past us, and Francine nodded. "It was her."

I turned around to see if I could detect any stains on the seat of the dress, but I saw none.

"Some sense of smell you have," she said.

"It's good. Very good. Didn't I tell you that already? That's why I enjoy eating out so much. I enjoy fine food. And to enjoy fine food you have to have a good, even a highly developed sense of smell."

*

"Run, man, run!" I felt my high school chemistry teacher's hands around my upper arms even before I heard him.

"What—?"

"Cyanide, Morley," Mr. Gray said. "Somebody just released cyanide under the hood." I thought I'd seen him nodding while he was talking to me, but I couldn't have. I looked around and realized that everyone else had already left the classroom. "Come on. Run!" he said. Then later, "How could you not have smelled that?"

"My sense of smell must be off," I said.

"Morley," Mr. Gray said, "you could wind up dead that way."

*

We were nearing the end of our entrées when Francine asked me what time it was.

I looked at my watch. "Eight o'clock," I said. "Why? Are you in a hurry?"

She took a sip of her water and shook her head. "I just don't want you to be late."

"Oh, don't worry about that," I said, then wondered if she'd said what she did to embarrass me. But nothing about that situation was real, so I couldn't have felt embarrassed. "She's probably sound asleep by now. In fact, I'm sure she is."

"Already?!"

"You know, it comes over her all of a sudden. She'll be sitting up watching TV, and the next moment she'll be sawing logs, as they say. Eventually she'll wake up and go to bed."

Francine looked concerned, which I found touching. "You don't wake her up?"

"What, do you want me to carry her into bed, too? No," I said, "she can wake up perfectly fine by herself. She might be on the couch or in one of the chairs, but she'll always get up before midnight and get herself into bed."

We ordered dessert, two strawberry parfaits, coffee, and tea, realizing that we weren't in any hurry. Then I thought about how sad my make-believe mother's life was and how sad, in their way, my real parents' lives had been. When I was living at home, after dinner was over and I'd go off to my bedroom to read or listen to music, my parents would sit in the living room, with the television on, and would both be sound asleep within an hour. Then, at about midnight or one o'clock, one would suddenly wake up and yell, "Oh my God! Look at what time it is! We need to get to bed." Which, within ten or twenty minutes, they would. They would always set up the coffee-maker for the next morning, and put out the bowls and spoons and boxes of cereal for breakfast first, and if I was still awake, I would laugh, thinking how silly that was, and how little they must have had to look forward to, if that had become the focus of their lives. But now, definitely older and possibly wiser, I could miss it, if only because I was glad that I hadn't ended up like them.

After we finished, Francine said, "I want to thank you so much for having me over."

I smiled. "Yeah," I said, "we'll have to do it again sometime." And we both laughed.

We'd walked to the restaurant because the weather was still nice, comfortably cool and slightly breezy, and when we got back to my house I asked her if she wanted to come inside. "Don't worry," I said. "I'm sure she's asleep."

But Francine looked down and said, "Thank you just the same, but I'll pass."

"You sure?" I asked.

"I'm sure," she said. Then she got into her car and drove away, each of us waving to the other while she pulled out.

And not a minute later, Helen came running out of her house, looking concerned. "Hey, sweetness," she said. "I just watched your friend pull away. Was I okay?"

And I had to stare at her to remind myself that she was the same woman who'd played the role of an overbearing mother a few hours before. I smiled. "Helen," I said, "you were perfect."

She smiled back, seemingly surprised. "Really?"

"Yes, really," I said. "Why do you even ask?"

She shrugged. "Oh, I don't know. I didn't want it to be too over-the-top."

I laughed. "It was," I said, "but that's what made it work. That was what I needed."

"My God," Helen said. "Morley, what did you tell that poor woman about your mother?"

Instinctively I glanced at my watch, then decided I had time to talk. "Come on inside," I said, "and let me fix you some tea. Then I'll let you know." But I was stalling her. I didn't want to explain anything, and maybe my offer of tea, which I knew she loved, would help her forget. Seated at my kitchen table, each of us with hot cups in our hands, I said, "Terrible, terrible things."

Helen looked worried and concerned. "Why?" she asked.

"You want to know something?" I asked. "I don't know why." I'd originally made my mother into a surrogate for Francine, but Francine wasn't like that anymore, so now I could have simply stopped the charade, but often, too often, such things can't be stopped. Or maybe I was just reluctant and lazy.

"I would have stayed," she said, "but I didn't know if you'd be coming back with her, and if I was supposed to be waiting for you."

I laughed again. "Please," I said. "Surely you didn't expect her to feel that welcome a second time." And then I wondered how I really felt about Francine, and if I wasn't simply trying to push her out of my life altogether. Well, that could be one more thing for me to think about after Helen left.

A PASSING (not so FANCY)

Then eight months passed. I didn't hear from Francine, but that didn't bother me, which must have meant that I was feeling very secure or very disinterested or both. But one Thursday night, when I was thinking about her again, the phone rang, and I was sure it was her, only it wasn't.

"Hello?" I said.

"Morley," a voice said back, slow and considered. "It's your cousin Harry."

I rolled my eyes. Harry wasn't my cousin. He was, or had been my father's cousin, but after my father died he'd tried to seem—*seem*, not *be*—closer to me.

"Hey," I said. "How are you?"

"Oh, I'm all right, I guess," he said. "You?"

"Fine," I told him. "Just fine."

Harry called me a few times every year, usually around the holidays—Passover, Rosh Hashanah, sometimes Thanksgiving—to let me know he was still alive, as he was in his eighties and not very healthy, and I'd seen him only once in the seventeen years since my father died. "Look," he said, "I have some bad news for you."

I hated it when people told me that, especially people I didn't speak with very often. Didn't they realize that if they were going to stay out of my life as a rule, they should come back into it only when they had something good to say? "Who passed away?" I asked. I knew what he was getting at.

He laughed. "Listen to you," he said. "You're right on top of it." Then he stopped laughing. "Cousin Pearl."

I flushed. Pearl had been married to my father's cousin Sidney, who had been Harry's brother, and I couldn't stand her. Even dead, the thought of her offended me.

"Oh God," I said, my statement uninflected.

"Yeah, I know," Harry said, just as vaguely.

I'd met Pearl once, at the Bar Mitzvah of some distant relative I could no longer remember. I was about ten, and standing in the synagogue with my mother and father. They walked me over to Pearl and Sidney, and "Morley," my father said, "I'd like you to meet my cousins—"

And as Pearl was standing in front of Sidney—typically, as it would turn out—I said, "Oh yeah, I know you. You must be Cindy."

"What?!" she practically screamed. Contorting her face, she opened her mouth, but I continued to talk.

"You're Cindy and Earl."

"No!" my mother said, placing her left hand gently over my mouth, not knowing what else to do, and laughing. "Morley, listen. It's Sidney and Pearl, not Cindy and Earl." To be honest, I'd never met them and had heard them mentioned so rarely that I had to have been forgiven for getting their names wrong.

But Pearl wasn't a forgiving person. "Earl?!" she said. "What the hell kind of Jew names a child Earl?!"

"It's nothing," my mother said. "He was just fooling around." But Pearl was already walking away, looking disgusted and shaken.

Sidney at least smiled, stooped down in front of me, extended his right hand to shake mine, and said, "Well Morley, it's very nice to finally meet you." Then he walked over to join his wife, who, stupidly, still seemed shaken and may even have been crying.

I never saw them again, but I never forgave her for that.

"Self-inflicted wound?" I asked. "Did she get so tired of damaging other people's lives that she finally turned on her own?"

Harry laughed, though strenuously. "Lung cancer," he said. "You know, she was a heavy smoker."

I didn't know, but I didn't care. "So when and where's the funeral?" I asked.

Harry sighed, then told me. He didn't sigh because he was upset that she was gone—I was sure of that—but because anything that required a lot of explanation seemed to defeat him. But then he said, "And you can be sure Gerald won't be there."

Gerald was Sidney and Pearl's son, and he'd stopped talking to Pearl when Sidney died, which had to have been ten years earlier.

"So that's why I'm calling you," Harry said.

"Why?"

"Well, look. No one is going to be at the funeral. Or almost no one. You know that. And the rabbi we have lined up is someone who'd never met her.

So he's going to say exactly what I tell him to. But when he mentions that Pearl was a loving mother—"

I groaned.

"I think it might be nice to have someone there who can make believe he was her son."

"Harry, why?"

"Just to make everything look good."

"Look good for whom?! Who do you want to impress? You just said there isn't going to be anybody there."

"Well, in case anyone comes."

"That's ridiculous, Harry," I said. "They'll know I'm not Gerald." Then, Oh my God, I thought. He was looking to impress the funeral director. But a moment later I realized that maybe he'd been looking to impress himself. And find some comfort by embracing the illusion that his fractured family was still close. For all I knew, Harry was dying as well, and wanted and needed this fantasy to latch onto. And, crazy as the thought was, it gave me a marvelous idea: invite Francine to Pearl's funeral, and pass Pearl off as my mother. After all, their last names were the same. And, after all, I'd done something like that before.

"Harry," I asked, "please forgive me, but...will the coffin be closed?"

"Of course," he said. "Our family always has a closed coffin, just as we had for your father. You know that."

"All right, thanks Harry," I said. "I'll be there."

The opportunity was perfect. My mother had died shortly after I'd stopped talking to Francine, and if we'd still been friends I'm sure she would have come to the funeral, for moral support, something at which she could be especially good. But that didn't happen. So, for a while, I ended up missing her and even considered calling her to apologize, but that didn't happen, either. Now that we were friends again, I'd continued to talk to her about, *and introduced her to* my mother, and that was getting me exhausted. So now I could finally put that part of my life to rest and feel the satisfaction of having Francine at my mother's funeral, which I'd missed so many years before. Fortunately, if surprisingly, she'd never asked me my mother's or father's name—Jennie and Sam, respectively—and though she hadn't met my mother, though she *thought* she had, I had to make sure that the coffin would be closed, as Pearl looked nothing like my neighbor Helen, should Francine still remember her.

So another phone call followed.

It was unusual for me to call Francine, and since we'd already gone so long without talking, I wasn't sure that she wanted to hear from me again. Perhaps she'd figured out that Corey, who we hadn't spoken about in as long as I could remember, wasn't real, and that my mother hadn't been real, either, but now I had news, *real* news, for her, and that got me excited.

"Hello?" she said.

"You'll never guess who this is," I said.

"Did I win a million dollars?!"

"Better than that," I said. "You're talking to me!" And we laughed. "Anyway, I've got some news for you."

"Yes?" Expectantly.

"Remember when I told you that I would have to get rid of my mother before I could be happy?"

"Mm-hmm," she said.

"Well...now I'm happy."

"Oh. Where is she?"

"Hard to say. Heaven's a possibility, but I'm not betting on it."

"She's dead?!"

"Yes, of course. Since nine-thirty last night. What did you think I meant when I said I had to get rid of her? That I'd stuffed her into a broom closet somewhere? And which I'd asked you about the last time." I laughed.

"But you didn't have anything to do with her death," she said carefully. "Right?"

"Relax, no," I said. "No, she stayed with me for as long as she did because she had it so good and didn't want to leave."

And that was where I expected Francine to tell me that my mother didn't want to leave because I'd made things too easy for her, so it was my fault that she'd stayed. Though, of course, that wasn't how things had gone at all. And, of course, that wasn't what Francine said.

"When's the funeral?" she asked.

"Tomorrow morning at ten. I would ask if you could come, but it's sudden and—"

"So what?" she asked. "A cold is sudden, too. So is a stomach virus or a broken ankle. I'll be there."

Well that moved me, and I was glad to realize that I could still be moved, however occasionally, by the nice things that people did. Though I knew better than to count on them.

"Um," she said, and laughed. "Where is it?"

"Al Kappel's Funeral Home in Linning."

"Oh, okay," she said, sounding relieved. "That's not too far. I'll meet you there. The name is Peck?"

"Yes, of course," I said. "Pearl Peck."

LAID to REST

As was my wont, I arrived at the funeral home early, just after nine-thirty, but was surprised to see almost no cars in the parking lot. I knew the place well because it was where both my mother and father had been eulogized, and the burial would take place at the Mount Meron Cemetery in Inman's Bay, about half an hour to the west. My parents were buried there, too, so if Francine asked who Jennie and Sam were, I would tell her they were my cousins, and that Sidney had been my father.

Walking inside I was still bothered by the lack of cars. Had I come to the wrong place? Did I misunderstand the date or time? Had Harry simply not known what he was talking about? I knew Pearl was unpopular, but still. And yet, when I opened the door I saw Harry, looking haggard, standing right in front of me. How many years had it been since I'd seen him?

"Morley. Hello," he said. "Long time no see." He put his arms around me but hugged me less tightly than I expected he would. I just hadn't realized how weak he'd become. I hugged him back. "So sad to be meeting under these circumstances," he said.

Harry had always been tall, but by then he'd become stoop-shouldered, and the skin on his face looked like it was sliding off. His hair was short and white, and he seemed not to have shaved in a few days. He was wearing a light brown checked shirt, a pair of creased khakis, and a burnt umber cardigan. I wouldn't have been surprised if I'd smelled moth balls on him. At least he had on dress shoes, not sneakers. I was wearing a sport jacket, but I'd never known how to dress for a funeral, and almost invariably I would be the only one there who was formally attired.

"Harry," I said, "you look—"

"I look like shit," he said, and laughed, showing a crumpled mouth with a few missing teeth. "I know. I've gotten used to it."

I was sure I'd never heard anyone on my father's side use vulgarities. "Used to what?" I asked. "Getting older or using four-letter words?"

He laughed again. "Both," he said. "They come together."

The entrance foyer, which was decorated with burgundy and gold flock wallpaper, was square and small and led to three larger rooms with double doors, all closed, in dark walnut. A brass stand holding an open book in which visitors were invited to sign their names stood in front of each. "Which way do we go?" I asked, remembering a character from my once-beloved Saturday morning cartoons. That was one way I'd become familiar with classical music, and it seemed appropriate to feel nostalgic just then.

"She's in the room to the left," he said. "And don't forget to sign your name."

"Are we going to be the only ones here?" I asked as we walked in.

He looked sad. "No," he said. "Probably a few more people will show up, but not many. Five or six at most."

I wanted to know how he'd even found out about Pearl's death, since Sidney was already gone and Gerald was no longer talking to her. But I decided not to ask because I really didn't care to get involved.

"Come," he said. "Sit down." He pointed to an unusually long couch to our right. There were only long couches, no chairs, ringing the room, so no one could sit by himself or herself. If you wanted to be alone you had to stand, which would attract even more attention. Unless the room became incredibly crowded.

We sat down. "Gerald's not coming, is he?" I asked.

Harry shook his head, and the loose skin under his chin wobbled. "No," he said. "Gerald's not coming."

"So I can pass myself off as Pearl's son."

"Well," he said, sounding suddenly anxious, "to anyone who doesn't know you."

"Harry," I said, "there aren't many cars here. Yet. And we have only... what?" I looked at my watch. "Twenty minutes?"

"She wasn't well-liked," he said. "Or hadn't you noticed?"

"How many again?" I asked. I needed him to reassure me because the act had to go well when Francine arrived. Which reminded me that I needed to tell him about her.

"You're the only person I told," Harry said, and I felt touched, though I knew the feeling wouldn't last.

I was sitting with my hands on my legs, then I lifted them slightly and said, "Look, Harry, I have to tell you something. I have a friend coming. She's meeting me here. Her name is Francine, and she thinks that this is my mother's funeral."

At first Harry laughed, and said, "The illusion must be spreading." But then he looked at me more seriously and asked, "Why does she think it's your mother's funeral?"

But I couldn't explain my relationship with Francine to Harry because, I was sure, he wouldn't like it. I would have to tell him that I lied to her as a matter of course, and, like most people with whom I wasn't close, which is to say, *like most people*, he wouldn't have questioned it, he just would have let it bother him. My family, aside from my parents, didn't love one another unconditionally. They all remained apart; because of profound dislike on my mother's side, and because of deep indifference on my father's.

In front of each of the couches was a large cocktail table—I guess you could have called them that—in pale wood, where there were rows of un-adorned black satin yarmulkes, two boxes of tissues, a stack of small paper-bound prayer books, and, on the table in front of us, a little plastic cradle, in the corner nearest me, holding a stack of business cards. No, I thought. It can't be. But it was. Business cards with the name, address, and telephone number of the funeral home on them. I was only surprised that I didn't see the words, "Ask for Josh," or some such nonsense at the bottom.

Then three people walked in; a lean, clean-shaven, middle-aged man, a svelte woman with ash blonde hair, and a teenaged girl who wore her dark hair in a bun and had a slightly pock-marked face. They stepped tentatively, staring straight ahead of them, and looking like they weren't sure they'd en-tered the right room. Then Harry stood up. "Mel!" he shouted.

The man turned toward us and smiled. "Harry," he said. "How are you?" He shook Harry's hand more vigorously than seemed appropriate for such an occasion, but I imagined that they hadn't seen each other in a long time. "No, I was sure I was in the wrong place when we walked in, because I didn't see anyone else here." He looked over at me, smiled again, and said, "Hello."

I nodded, knowing only that I'd never seen him before.

"Morley," Harry said, "I'd like you to meet my cousin Mel."

"Your very distant cousin Mel," Mel said. "I don't even know how we're related." He laughed.

"And his wife Valerie," Harry said. Then quickly added, "And their daughter...Melissa?"

The girl blushed then laughed while looking down. "That's right," she said. "Melissa."

A few minutes later three older women walked in, dressed in black and wearing veils. Had they been hired by the funeral home to fill out the assemblage? Had they picked up one of the business cards and volunteered their services because they had nothing better to do? And then I saw Francine standing right behind them. She mouthed the words, "This is it?!" And I nodded.

"So how did you find out about this?" Harry asked.

Mel grinned. "We must be select members of the club. Gloria told me."

I had no idea who Gloria was.

Francine sat down next to me, and asked, "Really?!"

I shook my head, looking unusually serious, lest she think I was enjoying myself. "Told you so," I said, and felt like a child.

"Who is everybody?"

"Cousins," I said. "One or two friends. And my Uncle Harry. Let me introduce you. He was my father's brother."

"Is anybody from your mother's side of the family here?" Francine asked.

"No," I said. "But then, they knew her better." I walked over to where Harry was standing. No one seemed to be paying attention to the three women, who seated themselves on the farthest couch and spoke quietly to each other. "Harry," I said. "I'd like you to meet my friend Francine."

"I'd better run," Mel said, slapping the top of Harry's right arm. "I'll talk to you later."

Harry turned to her and bowed solemnly. "A pleasure," he said, extending his right hand.

Francine looked like she didn't know what to say, so she said, "I'm very happy to meet someone from Morley's family, and am so sorry to hear about your loss."

I could see Harry stop himself from smiling. He said, "Thank you," then, "I'll be right back," and he walked over to Mel, Valerie, and Melissa.

"Who are they?" Francine asked.

"Oh, my cousins," I said. "Melvin is the father, Valerie is the mother, and Melissa is the daughter."

"A Melvin and a Melissa in the same house?" she asked. "I bet there are a lot of stiff necks when Valerie yells, 'Mel!'" We both laughed. "And by the way," she said, a little too loudly, then whispered, "I had no idea you were Jewish."

"I had no idea, either," I said. "I surprise myself all the time." But what was I supposed to say? I couldn't have lied about it anymore, and I didn't want to explain why I tended to keep it a secret.

"A man of a thousand mysteries," she said.

"And counting," I said.

Finally a much older couple walked in, and suddenly I remembered who Gloria was. It was Gloria and Ton—Anton—cousins of my father, and I remembered them from my childhood, though I didn't recall seeing either at my father's funeral, but Gloria and Ton traveled a lot. "My God," she said. "Morley?" I nodded. She hugged me tightly, the way Harry hadn't, and Ton, flat-faced, with bristly brown hair, and always the much quieter of the two, though he'd married into the family, first smiled, then nodded, then shook my hand. "How *are* you?" Gloria asked. As long as she didn't say anything about my mother, I figured I'd be fine.

"I'm well," I said half-heartedly. "You?"

She shrugged. "Not awful," she said. Gloria was short and slightly broad in the hips, had a full head of grayish brown hair, and wide, flabby lips, but the way she carried herself, with her small, tight gestures, suggested the elegance of good clockwork. I was more surprised that she recognized me than that I recognized her, because children change so much more profoundly as they age than adults do. "Who are the women in black?" she asked, and nodded toward the couch where the three women sat, still talking to each other.

I smiled. "Nobody knows."

"Just as well," she said. "Nobody wanted to know Pearl anyway." And we both laughed.

"Big turnout," Ton said, but he wasn't being facetious.

Gloria's expression hardened. "Gerald's not here, is he?" she asked.

I shook my head. "Of course not."

"Bastard," Gloria said, and Ton poked her.

I chose not to introduce Francine to them or them to Francine, because I knew that Gloria, if anyone, would start talking about who I was.

Then someone who looked official, which is to say, dressed in a dark brown suit and tie and wearing a yarmulke, walked quickly into the room, stood straight, and announced, "We're ready to start the service, so if you'd all step into the chapel, please—"

And the eleven of us did. For a moment I panicked that someone had changed his or her mind and decided to leave the coffin open, so I made sure I was the first one to step up to it, but it was closed and I was relieved. Then, because there were so few of us there, I, along with everyone else, sat in the first row. Another stroke of fortune. At a funeral, only the immediate family was supposed to sit in the first row in the chapel, and I was certainly not immediate family, but Francine had to believe that I was.

The rabbi was surprisingly young, and I say "surprisingly" because when I was growing up, and I went to synagogue and relatives' weddings, Bar and Bat Mitzvahs, and funerals far more often than I later did, all rabbis seemed old. But then, most everybody seemed old to me once. He had perhaps too eager an expression on his broad, round face, but I couldn't imagine what he must have thought about the scanty turnout, if he thought about it at all.

"Ladies and gentlemen," he said, in a deep, trombone-like voice that didn't seem to match his lithe figure, "this is a sad day for all of us, because today we're marking a passing. The passing of Pearl Peck"—nice name, I thought, at least coming from him—"beloved mother"—I could imagine Harry rolling his eyes—"caring sister"—was that who at least one of the three women dressed in black was? Her sister?—"devoted wife, and good friend."

And he dutifully explained what a beloved, caring, devoted, and good woman Pearl was, "taken too soon from our midst." Harry told me that she was eighty. "Those of us who knew Pearl"—and clearly he wasn't counting himself among them—"would always talk about her sense of fairness, her sense of justice, her love of the community." And by then it was painfully obvious that the rabbi had no idea who he was talking about, and had never met her. And I was irritated by the fact that, unlike other rabbis I'd heard in similar circumstances, he didn't simply say, "I never met Pearl," because by saying what he was saying he was trying to convince us that he knew more than he did, and I found that offensive.

I looked around. Nobody was crying. I would have been surprised, even shocked if anybody had been, though I couldn't remember being at a funeral that was so quiet and so still. And again I wondered what the rabbi thought of it, unless it was more common than I realized.

Fortunately, the rest of his speech, full of bland generalizations in which "observations," where the deceased's name was used to take the place of blanks, were interspersed with readings from the Bible, lasted only about ten minutes, and seemed to go faster as he went along. Then he asked if anyone wanted to come up and say something, and when nobody did, he concluded with a prayer, announced where the burial would be, mentioned that he, of course, would be joining us, excused himself, wished us a safe drive there, and walked away.

"*Where* is she being buried?" Francine asked.

"In Inman's Bay," I said. "The town, not the body of water."

She laughed, then covered her mouth. "Yeah, burials at sea have become so passé."

Francine and I would ride to the cemetery together in my car, and after we got outside I realized how stuffy the chapel had been; surprising, considering how few people were there.

The service at the cemetery, and all eleven of us were there, took even less time than the service at the funeral home did. As was traditional in my family, the coffin had already been lowered into the grave—I wasn't the only one who found it unbearable to watch it descend—and when people were handed the shovel to scoop in dirt from the tall pile that stood next to it, I was the first to oblige, as I had been with my mother. But then, there weren't that many others who could do the same.

Almost everything the rabbi said was in Hebrew, though he repeated, in English, a few of the words he'd spoken at the chapel but, of course, his options were limited. As Harry had explained to me the night he'd called, the rabbi was just saying what Harry told him to.

Francine looked around but didn't walk off. "Your whole family is here?" she asked.

"My father's side," I said. "My mother's side is buried at another cemetery, but that's a lot farther away." It wasn't.

"Do you want to visit anyone else's grave?" she asked.

That touched me, but I said, "No. I come here often enough." I hadn't been there since my mother died and was, of course, surprised to find myself there again. Unlike some people, I never felt significantly closer to the dead at a cemetery, primarily because when I remembered people I remembered them the way they were in life, not the way they were six feet underground. Cemeteries didn't depress me, but they didn't inspire me either, and as long as I was reading or listening to music I could see anyone I chose to whenever I wanted.

When it was over, Harry asked me and Francine, "Do you want to come back to my house?" Then he said more loudly, "I have plenty of food at home, so anybody who wants to come is more than welcome." It looked like Mel, Valerie, and Melissa would, and Gloria and Ton said they would join them.

"So where do you live?" I asked Harry.

"In Cohancy," he said. "Or Cohan's Sea, as it might originally have been named." Odd, I thought. My parents and I had lived in Cohancy when my father died, and I didn't remember hearing from or about him in all our time there, until, that is, he came to my father's funeral. And did older people always think about what was *original* once? Which was just another way of thinking about the way things used to be.

"When did you move to Cohancy?" I asked.

"About a year ago," he said. Well that explained it. "I'm in a retirement community now. Just don't ask how many things other than jobs I'm retired from."

We all laughed awkwardly.

"Well, thanks for the invite, Uncle Harry, but I have things I need to do at home and—"

Harry smiled maybe too broadly. "No, that's fine," he said. "It's not going to be a big turnout anyway."

Even if I'd wanted to go, and I didn't, I couldn't have gone, because Francine would want to come with me, or feel obliged to come with me, and with Mel and his family and Gloria and Ton there, I was sure she would have realized that I wasn't Pearl's son. So I hugged Harry, Francine shook his hand, and I waved goodbye to Mel, Valerie, and Melissa, kissed Gloria, shook hands with Ton, didn't see the three women in black, who may have been the Weird Sisters, for all I knew, and walked back to my car with Francine.

"Someday," she said. "Someday I'll have to ask you to explain your family to me."

"Someday," I repeated.

EXPLANATION, please

That day came three years later, because Francine and I didn't talk to each other again until then, aside from a single phone call she made the next day to tell me, once more, how sorry she was for my loss. "I know you sit now for a week. Is that right?" she asked.

I was impressed. I didn't know where she'd learned about the Jewish tradition of the bereaved sitting shiva—the name meant *seven*—for a week, where friends and relatives came by one's house to pay their respects, but she did. But since I clearly wasn't sitting for anybody—though, of course, I had for my mother—I said, "It's optional for people like me, who are not very religious." Not very religious, true; optional, not so much. So she told me to call her if I needed anything, I told her that I would, and that was the last we heard from each other for more than a thousand days (and nights), long enough, I supposed, for Scheherazade to spin all of her tales. And I wondered whether she'd lied to her sultan as much as I lied to Francine. So, once more, I was both concerned and relieved by the thought that Francine had given up on me, was tired of my incessant lying, and was too busy dating men, or caring for her cat, or devoting herself entirely to teaching, or doing whatever it was she did, to be able to call me. But by then, time itself had waned, so it didn't feel long.

But call she did, one Wednesday night, and, picking up exactly where we'd left off, invited me to dinner the following week.

"Where are we eating?" I asked.

"You like Chinese?" she asked.

"Of course I do," I said. I hated Chinese food.

"Ming's Dynasty."

I laughed. "Funny name," I said. "But clever, I guess. Where is it?"

"In Oberlies," she said.

"Oh. Are we meeting at your house?"

"Why don't we meet at the restaurant?" she asked guardedly. "I'll give you directions."

I was disappointed that we wouldn't be meeting at her house because I felt that she was trying to put some distance between us. Again, I hadn't called her—could have, but hadn't—in three years, but then I was thinking that the reason she didn't want me there was that she was seeing someone, and that bothered me. It must have been pride because there was nothing else it could have been. And hate Chinese food though I did, I remained so impressed that she'd asked about my sitting shiva after Pearl's death that I figured I owed her something, however small.

Ming's Dynasty, evidently a new restaurant, was on Posner Street, the main thoroughfare in Oberlies, and looking up and down the street, I was reminded why so many people thought the town was wealthier than it was: it was neat and extremely picturesque, but with a slight sense of artificiality about it.

Inside we were greeted by a large brass Buddha—I'd never seen one who wasn't smiling; what did he know?—and a middle-aged Asian man in horn rim glasses, which looked terribly old-fashioned—immediately I pegged him as someone who was underpaid—showed us to a table. The walls were dark pink, almost red, with black wainscoting, and were decorated not with images of dragons or Chinese characters but with colorful abstract paintings that, to me anyway, looked decidedly Western. The overhead lights were pot lights; not a single lantern hung anywhere. I decided that rather than try to pass itself off as a "traditional" Chinese restaurant, Ming's Dynasty wanted to appear more fashionable and cutting-edge—not that there was anything *un*fashionable about traditional Chinese eateries—possibly with the hope of attracting a larger clientele, and likely fitting in better with the tenor of the town. But the menu was completely conventional, and that disappointed me because it meant I'd have little chance to avoid the usual list of dishes I didn't much like.

After handing us our menus, our waiter came back with a teapot, teacups, dishes of duck sauce and a surprisingly pale yellow mustard that I was sure would be spicy—it was—and a bowl of crispy fried noodles.

"Let's order first," Francine said, "because there are a lot of things I want to ask you."

So we did. She ordered egg drop soup, spareribs, and shrimp in lobster sauce, and I ordered hot and sour soup, a spring roll, and the fried crispy half duck. One thing that bothered me about Chinese restaurants was the belief that dishes there, but seemingly nowhere else, were meant to be shared. There was so little that I liked from a Chinese menu that I didn't want to give up any of what I ordered to someone else. And chances were that I wouldn't care for what the other person, or other people asked for, or I would have asked for it myself.

We folded our napkins in our laps, poured our tea, dipped our noodles into the duck sauce, and Francine said, "Okay. I asked you here for one reason. I need an explanation."

I smiled. "One explanation?"

"Many explanations," she said. "Or at least as many as you're willing to give. But, to be honest, I'll settle for one, because even that would make me happy."

I shook my head. "It doesn't take much, does it?" I asked. I was enjoying myself immensely because of all the power she'd given me.

"It's your family. I want to try to understand them. Because if I can, I feel, maybe I can understand you."

"Naïve," I said, dipping another noddle into the duck sauce.

"Am I?" she asked.

"Don't you know?" I asked. "Because if you don't, nothing I tell you is going to change anything."

"I don't want you to *change* anything; I just want you to *explain*. All right, can we begin?"

The waiter brought us our soup, and I said, "First course. A good place to start. And by the way, I can't believe you've waited three years for this."

"What can I tell you?" she asked. "I like a big build-up. So first tell me about your mother. And here's what I want to know. When you found out she had cancer, how did that make you feel? Happy? Sad? Guilty? Some of the above? All of the above? None of the above?"

For a moment I had to remember that my mother never had cancer. So I imagined what might have gone on between us if she had, and made believe that I'd actually felt as uncomfortable with her as I'd told Francine I had. The only problem was that, after so many years, Francine was no longer the thorny person, my surrogate mother, she had been, so I had to make everything up.

"Well, okay," I said. Then I took a handful of noodles, put them in my soup, tasted my soup, and said, "You have to understand one thing. At the time she'd been diagnosed with cancer, she didn't let me know."

"She didn't let you know?!"

"Nope," I said. "Not a word."

"Then how did you find out?" Francine put down her spoon.

"Too hot?" I asked.

"Too interested," she said. Which buoyed me.

"Well, come on," I said. "After a while it became painfully obvious. She was losing weight. She lost twenty-five pounds in that first month, and was sleeping all the time. And that was pretty hard to ignore. I mean, looking into her bedroom and always seeing her in bed, I knew something was wrong. 'I'll be up soon,' she would say, but she sounded terrible. Very weak."

"Was she getting any treatment?"

"No. They decided against chemotherapy. 'They' meaning her doctors and her. She knew what it would be like, or *could* be like, everyone was different, *though she didn't understand that*, and I couldn't blame her. Besides, her disease was so advanced by that point that there was nothing much they could do."

Francine started eating her soup again. She shook her head. "That's terribly sad," she said, but the word "terribly" struck me as artificial.

"And you know what's really ironic?" I asked. "Maybe a month before she was diagnosed, she'd said to me, 'Maybe I ought to leave.' Meaning the house. 'Why?' I'd asked her. 'Because you don't want me here,' she'd said, and I'd laughed. 'Do I make it *that* obvious?' I'd asked her. And she'd said, 'Yes. Sometimes you do.' And by 'ironic' I'm pointing to the fact that, again, she had no place else to go, she would soon be leaving for the hospital anyway, and she just didn't have that much time left."

Francine looked at me curiously. "Time," she said, and lowered her gaze. "Have you found forgiveness yet?"

I shook my head. "I don't know," I said. "Which probably means no."

*

"Morley," my mother said. "Sometimes I just don't think I'm going to make it." This was about four months before she died, and I didn't even know how sick she was. I was visiting her for the weekend.

"What brought this on?" I asked. She was lying in bed, and I was sitting in the lounge chair next to her. It was close enough to allow me to hold her hand.

She smiled. "I don't know," she said. "I just haven't been feeling right lately. But I'm going to the doctor on Monday, and we'll see what he says."— *We*'ll, not *I*'ll.

"Have you felt this way before?" I asked.

She sighed. "I have," she said, "but when was the last time I saw you?"

"Last week," I said. "You were at my house."

"Then don't you see?" she asked. "I couldn't have said anything then, because of where we were. Sweetheart, I wanted you to hear it here, not in your house. Because I didn't want you to associate this with where you live. I'd rather you associate it with here. Because after I'm gone, you'll have no reason to come back. You can forget about it."

My music and my reading helped me to never forget my past, and I was glad. So I asked, "When have I ever forgotten anything?"

*

Next came the spareribs and spring roll, less heavy and greasy than an eggroll. Francine dipped her first sparerib into a spoonful of duck sauce mixed with mustard that she'd put on her plate, and asked, "Were you at least supportive of her after she told you she had cancer?" Then she bit into it and chewed slowly, possibly to give me time to answer.

"Oh, she never told me," I said.

Francine stopped chewing. "Never?! I thought it was only at first."

"Oh, no," I said. "I found it out, *officially*, from her doctor, when I went to visit her once in the hospital. But I never mentioned it to her because I knew she didn't want me to, so I guess that was supportive enough."

"I guess," Francine said.

"Though one night I got so mad, I told her something that I knew I shouldn't." I cut into my spring roll and ate a few bites first, to heighten the expectation. 'I wonder if I'm ever going to come to terms with whatever is wrong with me,' my mother said. Again, notice, '*whatever* is wrong with me.' And by then I was just so fed up with it, with her, with the whole situation, that I said, 'Maybe you will and maybe you won't. Sometimes it happens and sometimes it doesn't.' But we both knew she wouldn't, so it couldn't have come as a surprise to her."

"That's still horrible," Francine said.

"Agreed," I said. "Now. I don't suppose 'she taught me well' would be an acceptable explanation, would it?"

"Nothing would be," Francine said.

I picked up another forkful of my spring roll and said, "Well, you asked. So I'm just being honest."

*

At around the same time, my mother asked me, "Morley, are you afraid to die?"

In fact, I never really had been, but I couldn't tell her that, in case she was. I didn't want her to think there was anything wrong with or unnatural about such a fear. So I said, "I'm not sure. Why do you ask?"

"Well," she said, "I've heard that some people come to terms with it, with death, before they pass, and others don't."

"Look," I said, "it depends entirely on how it happens. A protracted death, in some ways, I won't say *many* ways, can be easier, because it gives you the time to make peace with yourself and those around you. But sometimes people die in the middle of—"

"A sentence?" she asked, and we both laughed.

"To be honest," I said, "I'm not worried about you. You'll be fine. It's just that when you find out that something is wrong, you suddenly become so enveloped by it that you can't imagine ever feeling any other way. It's too much to get your head through. But eventually you do. Mom, is anything wrong?"

"No," she said. "I was just wondering."

And I believed her because we both wanted me to. She would ask me that again, whether I was afraid to die, and not long afterward, but I would give her a very different answer the next time.

*

When the entrées came, I said, "Okay, first, I don't want to sound like a louse, but can we please not share?"

Francine shrugged. "That's all right with me. I don't care. What did you order, again?"

"The duck," I said.

"Oh, good. I don't like duck that much anyway."

I didn't know if she was being honest, but it was nice to hear.

"So tell me now about the rest of your family," she said. "Aunts, uncles, cousins. I know you have them."

"Oh, the people at the funeral were distant cousins, and my Uncle Harry wasn't really my Uncle Harry."

Her eyes bugged out. "Who was he?!"

"He was my father's Uncle Harry. But, you know, we were always close, so I just call him Uncle Harry."

"Well that makes sense," Francine said, piling several spoonfuls of rice onto her plate and topping it with the shrimp in lobster sauce. "You don't like shrimp?" she asked. She knew I did.

"No," I said. "So anyway, about my family," and, as I usually did, I decided to use real names, just changing the character of their personalities. "My mother, Pearl, had two sisters, Emma and Elaine. And the funny thing was that her mother, my grandmother, was named Edna, so there were a lot of 'E's in that family."

"You're lying to me," Francine said.

"No, I'm not," I said. "I'm telling the truth. Anyway, who knows, maybe that was why my mother felt left out, because she was different."

"Why did they name her Pearl, and not some other name that began with an 'E.' Do you know?"

I had no idea. And her name was Jennie. "Oh, I know," I said. "My grandfather, whose name was Lem, short for Lemuel, was so tired of everybody's name sounding alike, and seriously, I don't think his hearing was ever very good to begin with, that he decided that my mother would have a unique name. Anyway, Emma, who was the oldest, was married to Bert, and Elaine, who was the middle child, was married to Seymour, but we all called him Sy."

"Any cousins?" Francine asked.

"Each of my aunts and uncles on my mother's side had one child. Emma and Bert had Naomi, and Elaine and Sy had Russel."

"And what about on your father's side of the family?" Francine asked.

"My father's brother, as I'd mentioned once before, though that was a very long time ago, was Olin, and his wife was Doro, short for Dorothy."

"That's right," Francine said, scooping a large shrimp onto her fork, "I remember that. Did they have any children?"

"None," I said. They had four.

"So how did they all get along?" she asked. "Your family."

I shrugged, stared at and skewered another piece of duck, and said, "Just fine. Pretty well, at least. You know, the funny thing was that the two sides of my family were, *are* remarkably alike. Nothing really to report on. Ours was always a boring family. As I suppose most families are."

*

Every Sunday when I was growing up, from about the age of three until maybe the age of eleven, either my Aunt Emma and Uncle Bert would invite Elaine,

Sy, Russel, my parents, and I to their house, or my Aunt Elaine and Uncle Sy would invite Emma, Bert, Naomi, my parents, and I to their house. We almost never entertained, both because our house was considerably smaller than theirs and because, simply put, neither of my parents wanted to be bothered. We all lived less than half an hour from each other, and we would get to the house of whoever was hosting that week by two o'clock and leave by six. It was decided that dinner wouldn't be served, because of the expense and the hassle, and because neither of my mother's sisters was a very good cook. Each family would thus go its own way afterward.

The most obvious problem with this weekly setup was that I never got to see Emma and Bert without Elaine and Sy, and never got to see Elaine and Sy without Emma and Bert, and seriously, you would have thought that *somebody* could have gotten sick at least once, but no one ever did. The larger problem, though, was that Bert and Sy hated each other. Not disliked; hated. Nobody knew why, but because it had always been that way, no one ever questioned it; they simply accepted it as something that could never be changed. The three sisters got along famously, but the two brothers-in-law attacked each other viciously. My father, wisely, always ignored them, walking into a bedroom when the yelling got to be too much, and sitting down by himself to watch television or do the crossword puzzle in that day's newspaper.

"You want to try a good Italian restaurant?" Bert asked once. A tall, thin man with red hair and a bulbous face, he was by far the more excitable of the two. "Try La Stella in Cohancy. Di-vine."

"I know La Stella in Cohancy," Sy said. "Their food tastes like shit." Sy, also tall and thin, but with black hair and a pendulous face, always seemed soft-spoken at first, but within moments would fly into a rage, and his rages seemed worse than Bert's because no one knew when they were going to come. If Sy didn't explode right away, my family would hold out hope that he wasn't going to, but he always did. Tranquility wasn't his forte.

"Have you ever tasted shit?!" Bert asked.

"Yeah," Sy said. "I've had your wife's cooking."

And then the two of them would simply sit and hurl invectives at each other, the veins bulging from Bert's neck and Sy's forehead. Neither was funny, clever, creative, or original, and neither was very intelligent. They were both high school dropouts; Bert was a white goods salesman and Sy had been a baker. So once the yelling began, Russel, Naomi, and I would walk into the kitchen to play cards, usually poker or gin—Russel always carried a deck with him—though I just watched when I was younger, and the women would walk into whichever bedroom my father wasn't occupying, sit by themselves, talk, and laugh.

My Uncle Olin and Aunt Doro were the exact opposite, and maybe to a fault, which is to say, they never said anything. Or almost never. We spent Thanksgiving and Passover with them every year, when other members of the family would join us, so that would liven up the proceedings a bit, but on the very rare occasions when my parents and I would visit them without anyone else there—when I was very young my four cousins were away at college, and when I got older they all moved across the country, so I never got close to them—the afternoon would always go like this: we would say hello. Everyone would shake hands. There was no hugging or kissing. Then we would be seated in the living room, where there was classical music playing in the background, usually from the radio, but sometimes from my uncle's LP collection, but that actually annoyed me, because it was too quiet for me to concentrate on, and too loud for anyone to talk over. And that must have been the reason it was always on. To discourage chatter.

My aunt, to her credit, was a great cook, and she would put out wonderfully inventive hors d'oeuvres, such as sun-dried tomato basil rollups; brie, fig, and prosciutto on toast points; and prunes soaked in red wine and wrapped in bacon, to name some of my favorites. Then ten minutes would pass without anyone saying anything—one simply didn't speak while one was eating—and when we'd finished the dishes of hors d'oeuvres, my aunt would rush into the kitchen and bring out more. Occasionally someone would ask of someone else, "So how are you?" and, after a moment, the answer would come back, "Fine," followed, very occasionally, by "Good." Dinner, needless to say, was eaten in silence.

*

"So you're not going to tell me," Francine said.

"About what?" I asked. We were just finishing our entrées and were about to order dessert—the usual: vanilla, chocolate, strawberry, or pistachio ice cream; pineapple chunks; orange sections; or candied kumquats—so I asked, "What more do you want to know?"

"Everything," she said. "Because that still doesn't explain who you are."

I sat back. "Look," I said, sounding more serious than I meant to. "Nobody's life is so simple that it can be explained by what kind of family he or she was raised in. There are too many variables. But ultimately, you know, it doesn't matter. If you want to know who I am, hang out with me, observe me, and draw your own conclusions. Don't look to copy from someone else's paper by trying to figure out why I am the way I am by learning about my past. I just am."

She shook her head. "I can't buy that," she said.

"Well good," I said, "because it's not for sale."

"All right," she said, "tell me this. Have you ever had any major run-ins with any of your relatives? I mean, other than your mother?" She daubed the corners of her mouth with her napkin.

"Oh, of course," I said. "But doesn't my relationship with my mother explain enough?"

"No," she said, "it doesn't."

And Good, I thought; it shouldn't. Especially since she had no idea what it was like.

We ordered our dessert, candied kumquats for her and pistachio ice cream for me, and she said, "And it doesn't, because it all seems too easy."

"All right," I said. "Maybe this will tell you something. My relationship with my cousin Russel was always troubled. He was Elaine and Sy's son. Russel was ten years older than me, and when he was twenty-two, so when I was twelve, he married this woman, Rebecca, who I couldn't stand. And, notice, I'm speaking in the past tense. That's because Russel died about ten years ago, and I couldn't have been happier." I loved Russel and Rebecca, both of whom were still very much alive, and I was made the godfather of their eldest son, Jason.

"Oh, nice," Francine said, as the waiter brought our desserts.

"Anyway, after his marriage, I think, he became intolerable. To me at least. His whole life became a show; all he was concerned with was impressing everybody. He grew up in, as they say, very straitened circumstances, but he made a lot of money, and not only did he want everyone to know it, he couldn't stand 'poor people,' like me, anymore, which is to say, people who weren't as well-off as he was."

"I've known people like that," Francine said, breaking into a sigh.

"So the last time I saw him, and this is already going back maybe twelve years, we got into a fight. He said, 'Poor people are poor because they want to be. They look for handouts. They're lazy.' And I interrupted him to quote one of my mother's favorite lines, 'Russel,' I said, 'I hope you live long enough to bury your own children.' He had three."

"You didn't," she said.

I smiled. "I got it from my mother," I said.

"You did." She put her spoon down loudly and shook her head. "I...I don't know what to say anymore. I—"

"Then don't say anything," I said. "You know what, Francine? You're a phony."

She puckered her mouth and stared straight ahead. "Excuse me?!"

"You tell me that you want to know the truth. That you want to know more about me. So I tell you the truth, and then you decide you don't like it. Well too bad, that's the way it is. I'm sorry if my truth isn't convenient enough for you." Listen to what I was telling her! Playing the poor woman like the proverbial goddamned violin.

She nodded. "No," she said, "you're right there. I do. But...I don't know. I guess maybe I don't like finding out so much about you."

"Look," I said, "there are ugly parts to all of us. You, of all people, should know that." And that was the wrong thing for me to say, because I didn't want her to think about what went on between us after she'd told me that she'd tried to commit suicide.

"Is there more?"

I laughed. "Oh, yeah. But please try to put this in perspective. Russel was the only person in my family I ever hated so much."

"Russel and your mother," she said, wiping her mouth and pushing her empty dessert plate aside.

"My mother I'm not so sure about," I said, "because that was different. She was my mother, and we lived together, so maybe it was a little easier, because...well. Okay, think of it this way. After Russel got married I would see him maybe once a year, if that much. And in the time between visits, my anger and hatred would grow because there was nothing to deflect or lessen it. With my mother, on the other hand, there was always the possibility that she would say or do something, and sometimes she did, to calm me down. So a few years ago, when my mother and I were visiting the family cemetery, *her* family, not the family at the cemetery where she's buried, I pissed on Russel's grave."

"You what?!" she asked much too loudly, then smiled, presumably from embarrassment.

I laughed. "You heard me. And I think everyone else here heard *you*. No, but as I was saying, I knew I was going to do it, and I didn't make a big deal of it. I had to go to the bathroom anyway, and I was wearing black pants, so it wasn't going to show. 'What are you doing?' my mother asked me. 'Nothing,'

I said. 'I'll be there in a minute. So I stood over his grave, making believe I was reading the headstone, and peed."

*

My mother outlived my father by a lucky thirteen years. Every year, on the Sunday closest to the anniversary of his passing, I would drive her out to the cemetery in Inman's Bay, to pay our respects, and leave a small stone on the grave marker, a sign of respect in the Jewish religion. My mother and I were always heartened to see how many stones would accumulate on my father's marker.

"Do you think there'll be that many stones for me?" she asked me once.

"Maybe more," I said.

We stood there and stared. We didn't pray and didn't say anything to the departed or to each other, but she, at least, felt better for having come.

"What are you looking so antsy about?" she asked, though not unkindly.

I'd started jiggling my right leg. I laughed. "I have to go to the bathroom," I said.

"Well don't do it here!" she said, and we both laughed.

"Obviously," I said. "I'll stop at the men's room by the gate house on the way out."

And walking back to the car, my mother said, "Oh my God. Morley. Look at that." She was pointing down to a headstone that said:

BABY BENJAMIN

January 13, 1895 – January 19, 1895

FOREVER IN OUR HEARTS

"He lived for six days," I said.

"Morley, there's nothing worse than burying a child. Remember that. And don't ever wish it on anyone."

*

"So now that you've heard all about my family," I said, "is there anything more you'd like to know?"

Francine laughed. "There's actually a whole lot less I'd like to know," she said.

"Then let's make it a deal," I said. "The next time we meet, I'll take it all back."

"Can't wait," she said.

We paid our bill, left a tip, and walked out.

Teachers' convention

The State Teachers' Convention was held for two days each November. The location would always change, and that year it was being held in East Moser, a pretty, coastal town, but at least a three-hour drive from Lake Quaintance. At that time I'd been a teacher for twenty-two years, but teachers in our state were not required to attend the convention, so I'd never gone. Neither, as I was soon to find out, had Francine.

"Morley," Leo said to me one early fall morning, when he met me in the hallway in front of his office. "You doing anything on the ninth and tenth of next month?"

I shrugged. "Next month? November? I don't know, I...oh, wait a minute. School is closed because of the teachers' convention and—"

Leo smiled and held up the index finger of his right hand. "And I want you to go."

"Why?" I asked.

"Because it'll be fun."

"Leo—"

"All right," he said, stepping back. "It won't. I know that, but you don't, because you've never been to one. So that's why I want you to go there now."

"To find out how little fun it's going to be?"

"Exactly!" Leo said, and laughed. "No. Because everybody else from this department has already gone at least once, so I'm giving you this golden opportunity—"

"Doesn't gold tarnish?"

"Silver tarnishes," Leo said, then laughed again. "So I'm giving you this *silver* opportunity to broaden your horizons, expand your mind, and...come on," he said, "this is the point where you're supposed to walk away."

I shook my head. "Where do I sign up?" I asked.

"Come into my office and I'll show you."

That night I called Francine. "Well, guess what," I said.

"What?" she asked.

"I'm going to the teachers' convention next month."

And "Oh my God!" she said. "So am I! You want to go together?"

"Well, yeah, sure," I said, and the lack of excitement in my voice genuinely surprised me. Try to keep the enthusiasm down, I expected to hear, but I didn't.

"Are you checked into Cavender's?" I asked.

A pause. "No," she said. "Gail couldn't get me a room there."

"Who's Gail?"

"My boss," she said.

"Do you like working for a woman more than you liked working for a man?"

"Hmm," she said. "Let's talk about that when we see each other."

"So where did she book you?"

"The Van Ness House," Francine said. "It was either that or the Heldrich, but this looked nicer." She pronounced it Held*rich*, when I imagined it should have been pronounced Held*rick*.

"Can you give me ten minutes?" I asked. "I'll call you right back."

"Okay," she said, and we hung up.

I did some investigating online, and saw that Cavender's was the largest and newest, meaning *most modern* hotel in East Moser, but the Van Ness House, though much older, looked like it had more character, and I decided then that I must have been old—I was all of forty-six—because I couldn't buy into the argument, if ever I could, that *newer* meant *better*. So I cancelled my reservation at Cavender's, booked myself a room at the Van Ness House— they were about the same distance from the Convention Center, where our workshops would be held, and about the same price—and called Francine back to let her know.

If our drive down together was quiet, I didn't mind, because quiet almost never bothered me, and I knew that we would have a lot to talk about when we got there. She might just have been waiting for the right moment. Also, we'd left shortly after six that morning, as our first workshop started at eleven, and I thought Francine might have been tired. As for me, I didn't say anything because she didn't, which meant that either I respected her silence or didn't want to realize that she didn't feel much like talking to me.

The Van Ness House was a twenty-four–story concrete structure that must have been at least a hundred years old. The lobby was shallow but wide and paneled in dark walnut. Two ostentatiously sweeping staircases that ran for two stories stood at either end, and half a dozen Tiffany fixtures hung from the ceiling, which was three floors high. The carpeting, overlaid with embroidered rugs, looked clean but worn, and the curtains on the front windows seemed thinner than they probably should have. I understood then why everyone tried to book their reservations at Cavender's. Besides, I would later find out, Cavender's guest rooms had terraces whereas the Van Ness House guest rooms did not, but that was all right, as we were there on business, not for vacation. And, in fact, that thought, that we weren't on vacation together, relaxed me.

Stepping up to the front desk, we were greeted by a clerk who couldn't have been more than twenty-five, and when he smiled at us I knew he thought we were a couple. Whatever makes you happy, I said to myself.

"Name, please?" he asked.

"Peck," I said, because I was used to speaking before Francine. "Morley Peck."

"Room for two?" he asked, still smiling.

I smiled back. "Sorry," I said. "Room for one."

His smile, no longer comfortable, faded quickly. "Oh, I'm terribly sorry, sir," he said.

And Francine, laughing, said, "Don't worry. People mistake us for a couple all the time."

Well wasn't *that* news to me? And again I wondered what, exactly, she thought about when she thought about us.

Our rooms weren't adjacent but at least were on the same floor, the twenty-second, and we both had nice views of the beach. A few minutes after we settled in, Francine knocked on my door, and when I opened it, she said, "I hope I didn't embarrass you."

I shook my head. "Not at all," I said, "but you know what this reminds me of?" And then I figured that I had to mention Corey, so long absent from our conversations, to reestablish myself as a man who couldn't be had, at least by her. "Corey. The first night we checked into a hotel."

She had an equivocal look on her face. "Oh, I bet it does," she said.

"The only difference was that, when we checked in, the guy behind the front desk, and it wasn't a hotel that looked anything like this, didn't ask if we were a couple."

"I would guess not," she said.

But I could see that I'd upset her, so I said, "To be honest, I just checked in by myself. Corey was standing by the elevator."

After Francine and I had spoken the night I'd called her about the convention, we changed some of the workshops we'd signed up for, so we could attend everything together. The Convention Center was only a few blocks from the hotel, and the weather was nice, sunny and cool, but it was strange being in a coastal resort out of season, because I always expected to see crowd-ed beaches, not empty ones.

Once inside the Convention Center we waited on line for about twenty minutes to sign in, register, and be handed portfolios filled with brochures that I knew we would never read, and notepads, and then be given nametags that we were asked to wear around our necks, though some of the men wrapped them around their belts, which I found vaguely offensive; too ma-cho. We were told, at the beginning of each workshop, that we'd have to sign our names on another form, so it could be verified that we'd actually sat in on that workshop, and the man in charge of the first workshop, *Race in Litera-ture*, said, jokingly, "There'll be no cutting class today."

His name was T.J. Nathan, and he was an older man, probably nearing sixty. His graying hair was neatly combed, and he had an endearing if odd smile. His two front teeth were so much wider and larger than the rest, that it looked as though someone had punched him in the mouth but his teeth swelled rather than his lips. The session lasted for two hours, was attended by close to a hundred people, and was, in turn, encouraging and irritating. En-couraging because I liked the idea behind his argument, that racial stereotyp-ing often crept into, but had no place in "even great literature," but irritating because he couldn't seem to tell the difference between writers who were prej-udiced themselves, so couldn't create fully developed characters who weren't like them, and writers who simply recorded what went on around them. Mr. Nathan began, predictably enough, by apologizing for Twain and *Huckleber-ry Finn*, but, much to his credit, praised Faulkner, particularly later in his career, for his inclusiveness. "One can see, in Faulkner's writing, how much more accepting he became of people who were different from him, as he got older. For instance, in *The Mansion*," he said, which I taught, he wrote sym-pathetically about blacks, which often appear in his fiction, and even Jews."

I had to stop myself from laughing. Right, I thought. *Even.* But I didn't agree with what he'd said about Faulkner's sympathies broadening as he got older, so when the lecture was over and the floor was opened for discussion, I spoke up.

"Does anybody have anything they'd like to say?" Mr. Nathan asked. "We're running a little late, so if nobody does, that's okay."

And as he turned his head, I said, "I do." It wasn't my fault that he'd spo-ken beyond his allotted time.

"Well, okay," he said, sounding flustered.

"I don't agree with you," I said.

He looked confused. "That's okay," he said, and tried to smile. "You're allowed."

"Thank you for the privilege." I knew I sounded angry but I wasn't. I was just anxious because I wanted to tell him something but knew I didn't have much time to say it. "You said that Faulkner became more accepting of others, by which I assume you meant 'outsiders,' as he got older. But that's not true. Faulkner was always marvelously accepting in his writing. Look at Benjy in *The Sound and the Fury*. He was an idiot. And Temple Drake in *Sanctuary* was a victim of rape."

"What I *said* was that in his late works he wrote understandingly, more understandingly, of outsiders. Benjy and Temple were not outsiders. They might have been victims but they still belonged to the group of white Anglo-Saxon Protestants with whom he lived and, let's presume, most often associated. I'm sorry," he said, "I'm out of time."

An interesting point, I thought, and one I would have loved to discuss with him further, but we both had other things to do. I watched him step down from his lectern and walk out, and Francine and I walked across the hallway to our next session.

"What was all that about?" she asked.

"Nothing," I said. "Somebody who was unprepared lecturing somebody who knew. That's all."

"I'm sorry," Francine said, "which role did you play?"

Next came *Understanding Childhood Trauma*. Poor Francine—I had to laugh—must have thought I'd signed up for it because of what I'd been through with my mother, but I'd signed up for it because I admired the open-mindedness behind it: appreciating that some students weren't as receptive as others because of past encounters with "authority figures." And because I'd never seen my role as a teacher as an authority figure, I was glad to see other people being "taught" the same thing, though that workshop had a lot fewer attendees, or just more empty chairs, than the one before it. Typical, I thought.

Ruth Meister was the speaker, and she was young and petite but had a fiery demeanor that must have surprised everyone; it certainly surprised me. "Students," she said, "are not our inferiors. That's the first thing we need to understand. It's not that they know less than we do, it's that they know different things than we do. Too often, though, we tend to look down upon them. And that's especially true in the case of students who have suffered early losses or early devastations. So that's what I'd like to talk about today." I looked around the room but, much to my surprise, saw no one walking out. But after a short while the lecture, and it *felt* like a lecture, started to bore me, because she kept repeating the same few key points. Maybe my agreeing with her put me at a disadvantage, as I didn't need to be convinced, but by the time the session was over I was sure she'd made many enemies. I knew a lot of teachers who treated their students as inferiors, and for all I knew, that was why they taught; to show other people how much more they knew and, as a result, how much better they were. And I was sure that my, or, rather, *our* views on teaching were shared by only a handful of others.

Again, as soon as the lecture ended, and this time the speaker left herself plenty of opportunity to answer any questions, Ms. Meister, said, "I'd like to open up the floor to discussion," and then simply stood there for the next twenty seconds while people said nothing or got up and walked away. So I walked over to her. "Thank you," I said.

She smiled, and asked, "For what?"

"For bringing up a number of valid points." Which, I knew, meant, For agreeing with me. Francine drew closer. "Childhood trauma leaves lasting marks and—"

And at that point, Ms. Meister picked her head up, looked away, called out "Yes?" And then, a moment later, during which I didn't hear anything, she said, "I'm sorry, but I have to go. But you're welcome," she said, as she walked off.

Francine laughed. "Well that'll show you."

"What is it with this bullshit?"

"Come on," she said, "they open themselves up to questions to be nice. They don't want to be asked anything because they're reading from a script and wouldn't know how to react to anything they haven't been prepared for."

"You sure you've never been to one of these conferences before?" I asked.

"I've been around," she said.

Our last workshop of the day, much less interesting to me, was *Introducing Computers Into the Classroom*. Computers, at that point, had been introduced years before, and I couldn't imagine anything being said about them that hadn't been said already. While almost all of the other teachers in the English department at Lake Quaintance High School didn't even hand out books anymore, preferring that their students did all of their reading online, Brendan and I—no surprise there—were the holdouts. But in my case it was because I loved the very look, feel, and even smell of books, and had since I was a child. When I was growing up, one of my favorite things to do was visit bookstores—both of my parents were avid readers—where I would be seduced by the neatness, tidiness, and elegance of bound volumes. And while I thought hardcover books were all right, I loved paperbacks, particularly for the precision with which the front and back covers and inside pages were aligned. The covers had to be unbent, of course, and none of the pages could be wrinkled. I would thumb through paperback after paperback, and as soon as I found one I liked, based, again, only on appearance, never content, because I didn't read in those days, I would ask my parents to buy it for me. Invariably the reply would come back, "Isn't that a little too advanced for you?" But I insisted, and I was a spoiled child anyway, predictably enough, as I was an only child and adopted, so I would add it to my shelf of unread tomes.

"You still pass out hardcovers, don't you?" Francine asked me when the workshop ended.

"Hardcovers and paperbacks," I said.

"Mm," she said.

I didn't ask her if she distributed only online reading materials, as I was sure she did, and I didn't feel like explaining to her why I did what I did. Besides, the books that I passed out invariably suffered from a lot of wear, though I would never pass out a book with underlining in it, because I encouraged my students to make their own marks, decide what was most important to, or most difficult for them, or rip out pages and turn them into origami if they wanted to, so my nostalgia didn't have quite the hold on me that it once had, but it still had enough.

For dinner that night we had two choices: dine with most of the rest of the convention attendees in a large dining hall at the Convention Center, which was free of charge, or have dinner on our own, for which we'd have to pay. We decided to have dinner on our own, and the main restaurant in our hotel, Vagabond's, which billed itself as an Irish pub, seemed like a good choice; convenient and interesting.

"You don't like the crowd, do you?" Francine asked, while we were waiting for the elevator to take us down to the lobby. I looked around to make sure no one was near us.

"They're not bad," I said. "But the funny thing is, you can tell who all the teachers are. They just have a particular look about them."

She smiled, as if just realizing something. "Yes, don't they, though," she said.

If asked, I don't think I could have described exactly what made us, as teachers, stand out. Perhaps it was arrogance, perhaps it was a thinly disguised goofiness, perhaps it was simple humanity, but even without seeing a nametag on somebody, and many people had taken them off long before the end of the day, we could tell who was and who wasn't a teacher.

The only windows in the restaurant looked out into the lobby; none faced outside, but I found it fascinating to watch other people, so we asked for, and were seated at a table by a window. And since the restaurant itself was so dim while the lobby was so bright, that gave us the opportunity to see each other better, as well as whatever food would be placed in front of us.

I virtually never drank, which meant that one glass of hard liquor could leave me incredibly loquacious, but never hungover, so I ordered a glass of bourbon from a young man who came only to take our drink orders, and Francine, playing my role, asked for an iced tea, which I would also ask for later.

"So I have some news for you," she said. "Big news."

"Uh-oh," I said, but I was smiling. "What is it? And please don't say, 'Let's order, first.'"

"I can't," she said. "We don't have any menus."

And just then a white-haired waitress with a surprisingly young face came up to us, handed us our menus, and, as though she'd been listening in on our conversation, said, "Take your time."

I glanced at the menu, decided to go with the Irish brown bread crackers with artichoke and spinach dip, and the fish and chips, and Francine ordered a bowl of potato soup and the smoked salmon with cabbage. "So what's your big news?" I asked.

"I think we're going to have an opening," she said. "At my school."

"Think," I said. "You don't know."

She shook her head and smiled. "No," she said, "but one of our teachers in the English department is leaving next year, well, after the spring semester, and there's already talk about hiring someone to replace her, so I thought you'd be perfect."

I smiled very awkwardly, and said, "Thank you. No, I seriously appreciate the consideration, but—"

"But what?" she asked, looking disappointed already.

"I'm not quite sure I'm ready to leave yet," I said, and I thought, And am pretty sure I don't want to work with you again. To be honest, I'd come to value our friendship much more highly since we'd stopped working together, though that may have been as much because of her divorce from Peter as because of her separation from me. And yet, it made me realize that, should things ever not work out where I was, though as far as I knew, they were working out fine, she might be a good contact to find me another job, so one more reason why I should remain friends with her. And then, I recognized, there was another reason that I didn't want to follow her to Janesboro. She'd already been there for eight years, but who was to say that, as soon as I got there, she wouldn't leave to go somewhere else? Again. I almost certainly wasn't the reason why she'd left Lake Quaintance, but from time to time I liked to tantalize myself with that idea. So I said, "Let's see. It's not for a while yet, anyway, right?"

"Well they want to start interviewing soon," she said.

"So it's definite that this other teacher is leaving," I said.

"Pretty definite," she said, "but not positively. Still, they want to be prepared, and you have to admire them for that."

I sipped my bourbon then folded my hands in my lap. She was trying to sell her school to me. So I said, "In a way, yes. You certainly don't want to be left without someone if you can help it, but what about all the people who are going to take time off from their regular jobs to interview for a position that might not materialize?" I didn't like that.

I thought I'd made a good argument, but she just said, "I see what you're saying," and tightened her lips until her soup came.

To me "I see what you're saying" meant "You just don't want to change," and for the first time in a long time I remembered the kind of tension that used to exist between us whenever we talked. And that, too, convinced me that I was better off staying where I was. "So tell me about the people you work with," I said. "You've never mentioned them." And I looked out on the lobby rather than at her.

She held up the index finger of her left hand, while she took another spoonful of soup, then put the spoon down, smiled, and said, "Sorry. Oh, okay. So the first person I should tell you about is Gail. She's my boss, and you'd asked me whether I liked working for a woman more than I liked working for a man."

I remembered that.

"And my answer is, yes and no."

"Well that covers all the bases," I said.

She laughed. "And what I mean by that is, I enjoy working for Gail more than I enjoyed working for Leo. So yes, in that sense, but *no*, in the sense that I enjoy working for Gail because she's *Gail*, not because she's *a woman*."

Very progressive, I thought. My ideas must have been rubbing off on her.

I scooped a cracker through my dip, ate it, and asked, "So what did you have against Leo?"

"Nothing," she said, and shook her head, "but I could see that I didn't, and probably couldn't have had the type of relationship with him that you had."

I rolled my eyes. "Why?" I asked. "Because we're both men? Don't forget, I'm gay." I hated saying that.

"But still," she said.

I felt disappointed, so I turned my head to look outside again, then around the restaurant, which was filling up quickly, and getting noisy. So she really did believe that people congregated only with their own kind. Sad, I thought, but then thought that maybe she was right.

"And Leo was sort of goofy," she said.

"Very goofy," I said.

"Gail, on the other hand, is a strict businesswoman," she said. She took another few spoonsful of soup. "Not that she's not fun; she is. She's a lot of fun, in fact. But she just seems a little more focused than Leo ever did."

I could understand that. Our entrées came, and after the waitress asked us if we wanted anything else and I told her no, I asked Francine, "So who else do you work with?"

She smiled sadly and said, "That's it. The other teachers in our department don't really hang out much together."

"So it's just like it was at Lake Quaintance," I said.

"Yes," she said. "Just like at Lake Quaintance."

The fish was surprisingly good; crispy and flaky on the outside, tender and moist on the inside, and flavorful and clean, not fishy. "You like your salmon?" I asked.

"It's delicious," she said, but I could see that I'd lost her, at least for then. Then she suddenly brightened and said, with an almost malicious smile, "So on the subject of Corey—"

"Yes?" I asked.

"I noticed that he wasn't at your mother's funeral. Why was that?" She was leaning forward, and I half-expected her to say, "Come on. I want to *hear* from him again." Because she must have thought that she'd caught on to me. That I would then confess either that Corey wasn't real or that my mother wasn't real. But I said, "You know the answer to that yourself, so why even ask?"

"Because I want to hear what *you* have to say."

I could have explained that he was sick, but I'd played that card with my mother so many times that I didn't feel like turning it over again. "The family," I said. "They wouldn't have understood."

"What family?!" she asked. "No one was there."

"There were eleven of us there," I said, proud that I could remember the exact number. "Including you. But they wouldn't have understood," I said again, and took another forkful of fish.

"Don't they know that you're gay?"

I cringed. "Of course they do. Everybody does. And they're all fine with it as long as I keep it at a distance. As long as it's some abstract concept that they don't have to think about and don't have to deal with, they're fine with it." And there I was remembering something that had been said at a lecture I'd attended at my one gay social organization. "But if I showed them that I actually have someone else in my life who's a man, they would run away. You know? That would make it too real."

I had no idea what she thought of that; whether she "bought" it, as she liked to say, but at least it quieted her down, and the rest of the meal found us discussing only the workshops we'd be attending the following day.

Maybe someday I would let her know that I was asexual, but that seemed even more daunting than pretending to be gay, but, again, as long as I was only pretending, there was no threat attached. No perceived danger of anyone rejecting or even attacking me for being someone I wasn't.

There were four workshops scheduled the next day. Again, we had a choice of eating (breakfast) with everyone else at the Convention Center or eating by ourselves in the hotel, but at a different restaurant than the one at which we'd eaten dinner. This was a breakfast nook called Josie's, and the eggs Benedict that Francine had and the peach pancakes that I had were very good.

Our first workshop of the day was titled *Evaluating the Quality of Students' Reports*. "You realize," I said to Francine as we were walking into the assembly room, "we haven't partaken of any of the social events they have lined up." And there were a lot.

She shook her head. "Oh, please," she said, not smiling. "Did you want to?"

"No," I said.

"Me, either," she said.

She was no more socially outgoing than I was, but it was for different reasons, fear rather than desire, so it didn't draw us together.

The first workshop was conducted by a young, tall woman with exceptionally long grayish-blonde hair almost the exact color of Francine's. Her name was Kristen James. For some reason I always looked askance at people whose last names could double as first names, and I wondered how many of them had cruel parents who would, or would try, depending on the laws in their state, to give their offspring a first name that was the same as their last name: James James, or even, a little less damagingly, Robert Roberts.

But the workshop was fascinating even if I had one problem with it, and that problem became more bothersome as the workshop went on. Grading a student's reports, I believed, wasn't, and couldn't be the same as going through a list of true-or-false or multiple-choice questions where one answer was clearly right. Yet, Ms. James argued, it should and could be if you applied a strict set of criteria. The more criteria the report satisfied, the higher the grade would be. And yet, that all seemed like nonsense. So at the end, when the discussion section opened, and, as Francine must have known, nobody raised his or her hand, I said, "I'd like to argue a point with you, if I may."

Ms. James looked at me defensively. Had I sounded combative? "Certainly," she said.

"Okay," I said. "I understand what you're getting at. That by going through a list of criteria, it's easier and, possibly, more accurate to grade papers, because you're removing, or trying to remove the subjectivity. But this isn't math. You have to make allowances for people whose arguments don't necessarily convince you or coincide with yours."

She smiled. "Tell me more," she said.

"Okay," I said. "If a student of mine argues something passionately in a report, even if it deviates from the topic at hand, I will likely give him or her a higher grade than I would a student who stuck to the topic more conscientiously but argued it with less enthusiasm."

"I like that," she said, and smiled. "And do you know why I like that?"

"I don't," I said, then realized I was in trouble.

"Because you're arguing exactly the same point that I'm arguing."

I couldn't stand the laughter.

"Look," she said, "you're applying a strict set of criteria just as I am. It's just that yours are different than mine. And, I should let you know, I like the criterion of arguing something passionately. I'll have to use that."

"Do you feel humbled?" Francine asked me, and laughed, as we walked out.

I shook my head. "I don't even know how," I said, "because I've never had any reason to. What's your next stupid question?" I wasn't sure how seriously I meant that, but she said nothing.

Our next workshop was *Inclusive Learning*, and was purported to help teachers deal with students who were out of the mainstream; specifically gay, lesbian, bisexual, and transgender students, but also students of minority representation, and since more than ninety percent of the students in Lake Quaintance were white, I thought it would be a good choice for me, as I rarely thought about students who belonged to minorities. The lecture was led by a squat Korean man named Aaron Kim, who smiled a lot and seemed unusually delighted with his own asides. Unfortunately, most of those asides were spoken so quietly, and often not into his microphone, that I, at least, had no idea what made them so funny.

But the lecture was stimulating and good, and he focused on the fact that many minority students allegedly did poorly because, he said, "They're mentally so preoccupied with being 'different,' that they can't devote as much attention to their work as their mainstream counterparts, and in high school, fitting in counts for just as much as it did during the McCarthy era." There was a lot of laughter over that, but I made sure not to look at Francine because I was certain she didn't agree with it, and I didn't want to be reminded of that.

"You didn't say anything," she said, when we walked out. I was sure she was being funny, or maybe she was alluding to Mr. Kim's political remark, but I was becoming incredibly annoyed, and No, I thought, I don't want to work with this woman again.

Lunch consisted of salads arranged, and sandwiches stacked on platters covering several long tables around a room only a few feet away from the one we'd just left, and then there would be only two workshops to go, then we'd drive back, and I wasn't looking forward to the silence that had kept us company on the way down. During that drive I didn't mind it because I knew that we'd be talking soon afterward, and any fears I might have had about Francine feeling uncomfortable with me would be laid to rest. But now there would be no such intimacy to follow, and for a moment I wondered again about working with her because, if I did, I wouldn't have to worry about such protracted quiet. But, ultimately, I decided I was better off simply appreciating it.

The next-to-last workshop was *Teaching Students How to Write*, and I signed up for that because it promised to focus as much on teaching fiction writing as nonfiction writing. The speaker, a surprisingly sloppily dressed man named Tim Ocean, spent the first thirty minutes discussing the writing of students' reports and essays, and I wasn't sure he even knew the difference between them. Okay, I thought, fair enough. But that was followed by another thirty minutes of his discussing the writing of students' reports and essays. I looked around me, but no one seemed restless or even, for that matter, especially interested, and that might have been why Mr. Ocean spent the next forty-five minutes discussing, of all things, the writing of students' reports and essays. Finally, with fifteen minutes left, he said, "I'm sorry, I wanted to address the writing of fiction by students today, but I guess time got away from us." Not from us, I thought. From him.

The last workshop was titled *Emotional Learning*, and it was my favorite of the seven, so a nice way to conclude. The speaker, an older, overly made-up woman named Hannah Rilsen, said that the underlying point of her argument was that literature, *like music*, appeals to us emotionally long before we can absorb it or understand it intellectually. The difference between literature and music, and what put literature at a disadvantage, was that while people returned to favorite recordings repeatedly, almost nobody ever read a book, especially a long and involved one, a second time.

"Let's remember," she said, "Thomas Mann felt that everyone who read *The Magic Mountain* should read it twice. And there's a lot of sense to that, not just because you pick up more the second time around than you did the first, but because you read in a completely different way. The first time you read a book, or a story, half of your mind is occupied with the question, 'What happens next?' And, closer to the end, 'How does it all turn out?' But the second time you read it, you know the answers to that already, so you can concentrate on so many other things."

Wonderful. Then she said, "Let's look at it another way. Some books and short stories are allegories, and they really need to be read twice. Once on the surface and once to understand what they represent or what they're really saying." For an example, she picked out Mann's short story *Mario and the Magician*. She detailed its outline, explained a few ways of interpreting it, especially the most common way, as a critique of fascism, then showed us why, the first time you read it, it was hard to accept on its own terms and as a political satire. "Read it first only as a story about a German family vacationing in Italy and going to be entertained by a magician and hypnotist. Then read it as a political allegory. Because if you try to do the two at once, you miss out on both."

And before the discussion was over, she said, "Think of it this way. Say you're in a movie theater to see a film. You watch it, and you love it, and you think, when it's over, Well, yes, I captured all that I needed to. But now think about how many times you blinked during the showing of that film and, as a result, how many specific seconds of it you missed."

I was so thrilled to hear someone else espouse the ideas that I'd often espoused that I resolved, from that point on, to teach my students, if not to read every assigned book twice, then to reread any "incomprehensible" passages over until they made sense, or at least comforted them, and then reread that entire chapter, or whatever had been assigned, again, to put the once incomprehensible passage in its proper context. I would face more than a hundred and fifty students every day, and I knew that if I could convince one of them that I was right, then I would be happy, because convincing other people of something often meant convincing only one particular person of something, and that one person didn't have to be me.

IAN remembers YOU

It was two and a half years before the job in the English department at Francine's school opened. She called me one night, fairly bursting with enthusiasm, and said, "It's *open*!" And I knew exactly what she was talking about. We hadn't gone without speaking to or seeing each other in all that time; in fact, we had probably spoken and gotten together with each other more than we previously had, but we never revisited the topic of my working with her again until that night.

"So now it's official," I said.

"Yes," she said. "Now it's official."

"If you don't mind my asking, what took so long?" I was modulating my voice carefully; I didn't want to seem overly enthused or unenthused by her news, because my feelings about staying in Lake Quaintance and avoiding her professionally had changed. Pano and Brendan had both left and been replaced, leaving Alice, Leo, and me as the only stalwarts, and even Francine's position, that had once been taken over by Ian Baines, had finally been filled. But she didn't need to know that. And if I was certainly glad to see Brendan go—I was less sure how I felt about Pano—it wasn't so much that I didn't like the people who replaced them as that I found them colorless. If they'd been offensive, at least they might have been interesting.

"Oh, the woman who was going to leave decided to extend her contract for two more years, but when it was up she finally thought it best to pack her things," Francine said.

"Do I see a dinner coming up?" I asked.

"Absolutely," she said. "And I've got the perfect place for us. Adele's International in Pelton."

"Adele's International *What*?" I asked.

"Oh, that's it," she said. "It's just called Adele's International. And the idea is that they serve food from all over the world, so there's no concentration on any one type of cuisine."

"Sounds intriguing," I said, and we made a date to meet there the following Wednesday night. I thought it sounded horrible. You spread yourself too thin and you don't do anything right. And Pelton was an hour north of me and hardly closer to her, so I'd have little time to prepare after I got home. Alas, I thought, I'm getting tired of this.

Pelton, which I remembered Francine telling me was the town where she grew up—how much of what I told her did she remember?—reminded me a lot of Willemoes, the town where my mother had lived. Both were in the northern part of the state, and they shared a number of features: small; hilly if not quite mountainous; heavily wooded, which meant surrounded by a lot of state forest land; and, depending on your point of view, bucolic or provincial. I didn't have to live in either so I could find them both enchanting. In Pelton, all of the shops, restaurants, and conveniences were located along Cadensia Avenue, and though there may have been something quaint about the town rolling in its sidewalks at nine o'clock, you were out of luck if you wanted to buy a container of milk, find a place to eat, or fill your tank with gas after that. Even Adele's International closed its doors at nine, and since we didn't get there until seven, we knew we'd have to eat more quickly than usual, probably not order coffee, tea, or dessert, and not linger over any morsel of food or observation that one or the other of us made.

What surprised me about the place was how small it was, fitting all of twelve tables. Yes, understandably a small restaurant in a small town with very little traffic, but the appellation "International" implied something big. That said, I felt comfortable when we sat down. The walls were forest green, appropriately, embossed with gold maps, also appropriate. And the floors were covered in low-pile beige carpeting, probably not the best choice, because it was going to show wear, unless they simply didn't get many customers. The night we were there, only two other tables were occupied. But the menu, which ran to half a dozen pages, was huge. Thirty-five countries were listed, and beneath each, native appetizers, entrées, and desserts were explained.

"I like this place," I said. "Why have we never come here before?"

Francine didn't smile. "Who wants to drag all the way up to Pelton?"

I leaned toward her. "Obviously you do," I said. "You come here often?"

She unfolded her napkin and laid it in her lap. "I try not to," she said. "This is the town where I grew up, and...well, I'm just as happy to put it behind me."

When we'd gone to Eddie Renn's Steakhouse in Lake Quaintance, she'd told me that bad memories were easy to overcome if you had something to replace them with. I wondered what had happened in the meantime. "You don't look happy," I said.

She shook her head and said, "I'm not. So why don't we talk about the position that just opened up at my school?"

"Would you rather talk about what's bothering you?" I asked. I saw the waitress walking toward us.

"I'd rather talk about the position that just opened up at my school," Francine said and forced a laugh. That, at least, was the Francine I knew.

We'd decided in advance to skip dessert, but when I ordered, I decided to skip the appetizer course, too, and Francine did as well. I wasn't feeling as comfortable as I had a few minutes earlier, but that was because I really didn't want to work with her again. Clearly her earlier bonhomie had all been an act—I was good at recognizing those—and this was what I'd be dealing with if we went back to working together. For all I knew, she was thinking the same thing but was telling me about the job because she felt obligated to.

Her country of choice was Spain, and she ordered the ham and Béchamel croquettes, which were served with baguette slices topped with ratatouille, and my country of choice was Denmark, and I ordered the broiled cod filet, which was served with caramelized white potatoes and pickled herring on rye toast points.

"I have to tell you," the waitress said, "this is going to take time, because everything here is made to order." She was short, young, had curly dark brown hair, and tried to appear perky but seemed edgy.

"I would hope so," I said to Francine when the waitress left. "Who wants to eat food that's been popped into a microwave?"

But she still wasn't smiling. "So tell me how things are in Lake Quaintance," she said. "Same old same old? And what are you celebrating now, fifty years there?"

I laughed, to see if I could lighten the mood. "Twenty-four. Next year will be my silver anniversary."

"Oh," she said, laying her arms against her chest. "Do they give you anything for that?"

"Probably a pink slip," I said. "After twenty-five years they're bound to be tired of me."

She took a sip of water. "Tell me," she said. "Is Leo still alive?"

Alive? I thought. Why didn't she ask if he was still *there*? "I don't know," I said, "I'll ask him the next time I see him."

She looked surprised. "But he's still there, isn't he?"

I leaned back and looked around. The people at the other two tables, who hadn't been served yet, were sitting as still as mannequins. "Of course," I said.

"So is everybody else. Same group as when you left. Even the students are the same." But still no reaction.

Fifteen silent minutes later, she asked, "My God, what are they doing? Killing the cow?"

"No," I said, "they're choking the chicken." I laughed heartily, but she didn't even break into a grin. Note to self: avoid masturbatory jokes around women.

But then the food was served, and Francine's mood changed completely. I noticed that the other tables were being served at the same time we were, though all of the people there had been seated before we'd even walked in. "So let me tell you all about the job," she said. "It's for an English teacher, but they'd like someone with at least ten years of experience."

I didn't need a knife to break my cod because it was so flaky. "Why?" I asked.

"They've had trouble with the other people in that position, none of whom had very long résumés," she said. "And, I'm sorry to say, none of whom lasted very long either. Except the woman who just left, but they were happy to see her go."

I ate a piece of cod, took a bite of the pickled herring and a sip of water—neither of us ordered drinks—and asked, "What's the turnover rate like at your school? Is it high?"

She pursed her lips. "About average, I'd say."

I pointed my right index and middle fingers at her. "Which means it's high," I said. "The turnover rate at our school"—and I deliberately said "our," rather than "my"—"is very low."

"I know," she said, looking sad again, and then cutting into her first croquette. "But oh," she said, again suddenly enlivened, "we just interviewed somebody I think you know. He remembers you."

I was hoping she wasn't going to mention Brendan or Pano, because I'd already told her that they were still with me. But she said "*you* know," not "*we* know," so it couldn't have been either of them.

"Ian Baines," she said, and smiled.

And a faint wave of nausea came over me. "Ian Baines," I said, almost mumbling it. "Well yes, I certainly do remember him." Ian was the man who'd taken over Francine's position the semester after she'd left. And with whom I virtually never spoke, though I still didn't like him. "Did you interview him?" I asked.

"Me? No," she said. "Gail did. I didn't even see him or read his résumé, but Gail liked him, so if you're going to apply, you'd better do it quickly."

And that worried me tremendously, because I didn't want her to know that I'd lied to her about Ian. Of course I'd lied to her about so many things, but this lie would have been especially caustic, because it dealt with her, not just with me. For a moment I relaxed. Maybe she was just telling me to apply quickly because she really wanted me to work with her again. And maybe Gail hadn't liked him at all.

I put my fork down, then picked it up because I didn't want her to think I was mulling over something. "How do you know that I know him?" I asked.

She swallowed what was in her mouth, wiped her fingers on her napkin, and said, "Oh. Gail told me."

"Told you what?" I didn't like the tension in my voice.

"That he knew you. He evidently told her that he'd worked with you."

But *why*? I asked myself. I couldn't figure that out. The only thing that came to my mind was that he'd listed his year as an English teacher at Lake Quaintance High School on his résumé—some people didn't list short-term jobs—and Gail said something to him because she already had somebody else from there, Francine, working for her. But where did I fit in? If Francine had told Gail about me, and I bet she had, Gail still wouldn't have mentioned me, another (possible) candidate, to Ian, and I couldn't believe that Ian would have mentioned me to Gail. "I still don't understand it," I said, shaking my head.

"Are you all right?" she asked, looking concerned.

I laughed but didn't smile. "No," I said, "I'm not."

"Did something go on between you?" she asked, scooping some ratatouille onto her fork. "Something must have. Because you look a little peaked." Now there was an old-fashioned expression to gladden my heart.

And then I did something remarkably ugly. "Yes," I said gravely. "Something did happen between us. He came on to me." All these years later I still can't understand, and certainly could never justify why I said that, except to make sure that she didn't hire him and find out that he was the man who'd replaced her.

Her periwinkle blue eyes shot together. "What?!" she said, though it was almost a shriek.

"Look, it was a long time ago," I said, trying to calm her down.

"When?!" Still anxious.

"A long time ago," I said again. "Before you even started teaching there." What was she getting so upset about? I was just trying to protect her feelings.

"When?!"

"I don't want and don't need to talk about it," I said, trying to sound as angry, or maybe as victimized as I could. And now things were falling into place. That was my rationale for never mentioning Ian; because of what he'd done. Although, of course, he'd never done it. And if she did end up reading his résumé, or even if she'd seen it already, she could just assume that he'd changed the date of his hire at Lake Quaintance High School to distance himself from that nastiness.

She calmed herself down. "What the fuck went on?" she asked. I assumed her use of the word "fuck" was deliberately punning.

"Okay," I said, finally laying down my fork, leaning back, and twisting each of my wrists, in turn, with the other hand. "Nothing much," I said, and smiled. "In fact, nothing at all."

She looked confused.

"He just said something to me that he shouldn't have, and that was the end of it." Now, having explained things to her, I decided to take them back. Or tried to.

"Could you tell me what he said?" she asked, leaning forward.

"I'd rather not," I said, waving my right hand.

She leaned back. "Okay," she said. "I can understand that. But what happened? Afterward, I mean. Did you report him?"

I looked at her. "I didn't report him because he didn't do anything. He just said something at which I took offense, and believe me," I said, and laughed, "that happens all the time."

"No," she said, shaking her head. "It doesn't."

"Well, I mean...he never touched me or anything."

"The perfect gentleman," she said.

"He was. In that respect, at least." Brother Devil, as Leo had called him. "Look, all he did was take me aside one afternoon and suggest we do something that I didn't like. So I let it go."

"But why?" she asked. She still hadn't started eating again.

"Because I wanted, *needed* to be in control," I said.

"You could have gotten control—," she said, and stopped. "You could have gotten control," she said more quietly, "by getting him fired."

"It wasn't worth it," I said, then thought, Why not make myself as offensive now as I'd just made him? "And besides, I was impressed."

She looked sad because she knew how I was going to answer her next question. "Impressed with what?"

"His attraction to me." I was hoping that would end the conversation, but if it didn't, I was prepared to tell her that Ian had left after a year, and that he'd said what he'd said just before he'd taken off. But why did I bring up any of that? I don't know. When you lie to somebody else for so long, you end up wondering how honest you've been with yourself, and maybe, *honestly*, I wanted that job at her school so badly that I had to eliminate, or try to eliminate Ian's chances of getting it. "Look," I said, "I don't want to change your mind. If you think he's the best-qualified man for the job, you should hire him. As I said, all of this happened a long time ago, and he never touched me."

She shook her head. "That doesn't matter," she said, then looked at me apologetically, as though to tell me it did.

"Well look at it this way," I said, and smiled bleakly. "You and Gail have nothing to worry about."

"But we *do*. It's not an all-women department and, God," she said, "it's not an all-girl's school." She took a few more bites of her croquette. "Okay," she said. "Can I be honest with you?"

"Why start now?" I asked, and laughed too loudly. Because the question implied that she hadn't been.

"I don't think Gail liked him," she said.

"Then why did you tell me that she did?" And I knew how she was going to answer my question, but I asked it anyway, to bring her dishonesty a little more into the open and maybe counteract some of mine.

"Because I want you there," she said. "Working with me again."

I hadn't had anything to drink that night, but in retrospect I would always wonder if I had, because I could think of no other reason to explain what I'd said next. "Who do I call about the job?"

"Vera Starcey," she said.

Unless I was just so touched by her appreciation, but I doubted it. I finished the last morsels of food in my plate and asked, "Vera Starcey?"

Francine laughed, and said, "Yes, and when you meet her you'll see that she looks just the way you imagined."

I didn't know what Francine thought I was imagining—a woman in her late fifties or early sixties, fading orange hair in tight curls, sharp creases around her eyes, half-glasses, and a pointy nose—but at lunchtime the next day I called the number that Francine had given me just before we'd left the restaurant, and set up an interview for the following Monday morning at nine-thirty. Then I told Leo that I needed to take Monday off because something personal had come up, and he told me that was fine.

Why did I set up the interview? I had a few thoughts on that. Maybe I was trying to punish myself for my assassination attempt on Ian's character. As a result of which I'd have to give up the job I loved and head into something less secure and certain. Or maybe I wanted to prove to myself, Francine, and her colleagues, that I was a better teacher than Ian was. Or maybe I really did want to work with Francine again, and that desire resulted from more than feeling flattered by her wanting to work with me. I didn't know because I could no longer tell the difference between black and white.

And yet, when my alarm rang at seven o'clock on the day of my interview, when I'd set aside enough time to eat a quick breakfast—tea and toast—take a shower, get dressed, and be out of the house by eight, I simply reset it for nine, at which time I would call Vera, thank her again for having granted me the interview, and let her know that I couldn't make it that day because I'd been involved in an automobile accident. Nothing serious, nobody hurt, no real damage done, but enough to interrupt my plans. I would tell her then that I'd call her back to reschedule it, but I knew I never would. And I never did.

Learning HOW to THROW

Four years later, during which time Francine and I almost never spoke to or saw each other and she never mentioned the open position at her school again, though she couldn't have been surprised that I'd bowed out, she called me on a Monday night, once more as though no time had passed and nothing had happened, to ask if I wanted to try something new.

"What's new?" I asked. "And please don't say, 'Nothing much. What's new with you?'"

She laughed. "I'm signing up for a pottery class," she said, "and was wondering if you'd like to join me."

I had to think that over. I was actually good at art, very good, when I was a child. I painted, drew, and even worked with clay, though never on a potter's wheel, instead sculpting heads freestyle, and I enjoyed it all so much, and won enough awards at school and in various competitions in which my teachers entered me, that I considered taking up art as a profession, until I realized that, in those days anyway, it was hard to find a job with an art degree, and the jobs that were available didn't pay well. So the pottery class that Francine suggested sounded intriguing, except that it likely meant meeting weekly and for an extended amount of time—it did—and I wasn't sure I would enjoy that, and not just because of her.

"Where is it being held?" I asked.

"In Oberlies," she said, "so it's very convenient."

I laughed. "Yeah," I said, "for you. What's the schedule like?"

"It's three hours every Monday night, from seven to ten, for nine weeks," she said. "It's supposed to be very relaxing."

Standing among a group of strangers for three hours a week could not, in any way, be relaxing, especially if Francine was among them, and I would have to commit myself, because it made no sense to take one class and then leave. Unless I decided I didn't like it, or something else came up to occupy my time. And the term "relaxing" never appealed to me; I always looked to be stimulated, not relaxed. But maybe I was still feeling guilty for not having investigated the job opportunity she'd passed my way four years earlier, or maybe I was interested in seeing her in a different context, so I told her all right, I would go to the first class with her, but if I decided I didn't like it, and I'd already decided that I wouldn't, I wouldn't come back, but she shouldn't take it personally.

So the following Monday night I met her at the Arts Center of Oberlies, on Hanover Street, a busy and wide thoroughfare, to see what the class was all about.

The Arts Center was a surprisingly large building, having three floors and lots of floor-to-ceiling windows that faced north, to afford painters the best reflected light, which gave them the most control over their colors, because north light doesn't shine from different angles during the day. Or so I'd been told. The room we were in, however, while large enough to hold twenty pottery wheels and five kilns, had no windows, which was just as well, but by the time fifteen men and women—the class was divided almost equally between them, and they ranged in age from their early twenties to, I thought, their early seventies—had gathered, in anticipation of our instructor's arrival, I was already longing for other stimuli, such as anything I could see through a window. At first I was surprised that Francine didn't introduce herself to anybody, but then I remembered that she was, ultimately, as solitary a creature as I was, just not one who was happy about it. In fact, I'd expected her to walk around saying, "Hi, I'm Francine, and this is my friend Morley, but he doesn't talk." Then I could take offense at her and have a perfect reason to not come back, but that didn't happen.

"My name is Peggy Greenwich," a voice called out from behind us, and the voice pronounced it *Green-witch*, rather than *Gren-itch*, and belonged to a tall, young woman, who we all turned around to see, with pinched features, a bedraggled expression, and effusive blonde hair that fell halfway down her back. "And I'd like to welcome you to tonight's class." She didn't move. "Just a few things before we get started," she said. "This course lasts for nine weeks, and we'll be engaged on four two-week projects. Tonight is going to be an introductory class only, so you'll know what to expect when you come back next week, by which time you'll no longer be beginners." She laughed, then, putting on a voice that someone else might have used to imitate a pirate, said, "Arrr, I don't want to see any beginners here next week," and she cawed. Maybe she'd always wanted to be a kindergarten teacher. This, I thought, is not going to be fun.

I also noticed, unsurprisingly, that nobody was dressed as formally as I was. I didn't have on a sport jacket, but I was wearing a red-striped button-down shirt and charcoal gray flannel pants and black wingtips, while almost everyone else there was dressed in casual shirts or T-shirts and jeans, sneakers, or sandals, though one man was wearing worn corduroys and a pair of moccasins.

Peggy walked over to me and said quietly, "If you'd like, there's a smock in the closet," and then she said more loudly, "There are smocks in the closet for anyone who wants one. Protect your clothes; protect yourself." That impressed me; her not making me stand out, and three of the men and two women actually did put them on, as did I.

Walking to the front of the room, she pointed to her pottery wheel, the bags of clay that were lined up alongside it, a small basin of water and a small sponge next to it, and a scraper, and proceeded to explain what everything was used for.

"Come, stand around me," she said. "Stand around my workspace. I don't mind attracting a crowd. At least that's what my husband always says." She sat down.

"And it's 'Mrs.,' not 'Ms.,'" Francine had said on her interview. Why did so many people think that other people were interested in them sexually? Or was I just misinterpreting what she'd said?

"So let me show you the basic steps of pottery. And please don't worry. These are electric wheels, not what we call kick wheels, so if you want to work out your legs, you'll have to go somewhere else."

Nobody laughed. Then I wondered if she'd meant to be funny.

"The first thing you're going to want to know," she said, "is how to throw clay, but first let me explain what 'throwing' clay is."

And I thought, The *next* thing I want to know is how much longer I'll have to be here. Nothing personal, I assure you.

"Throwing clay is the act of shaping clay on the potter's wheel."

I'm bored and I don't know why. Working with clay was fun when I did it by myself as a child. Maybe she lacks charisma—she does—maybe I hate sharing my time with other people—I do—or maybe, because I'm a teacher, I don't like being taught. Don't doctors make the worst patients?

"So first we're going to cut a square, or, basically, a cube of clay and shape it into a ball." She opened a box, pulled up the rectangle of clay, which was covered in plastic, pushed down the plastic, then took a wire to cut a wedge, which she then placed on the wheel. She cut the wedge into four squares, took one square, and patted it between her hands into a ball. "This is maybe two ounces of clay, just so you know," she said, "and I'm going to let you do this yourself after my demonstration is over."

Nice of her.

"Now we're going to start the wheel spinning."

Are those really "ooh"s and "ah"s I hear? People's lives must be more bereft of pleasure than I realized.

"Make sure your wheel is wet, but not drenched, because you'll need the clay to adhere to it and not slide around. And dipping my hands into the water," which she did, "I'm going to wet the clay, too," which she did, "and then draw it up between my hands. Notice, you'll want to keep one hand in front of you and the other about one hundred and eighty degrees around the clay, and push your hands together."

Open, shut them, open, shut them, give a little clap.

"Now you can see how that little ball of clay is starting to rise."

I swear it looks like a penis. Corey! Of course. Gee, Francine, I'm so sorry, but I can't come back next week because I need to see Corey.

"Now if you take your dominant hand and press the clay down, voila! You'll notice that it's starting to spread and widen."

I won't even say it.

"And in a few moments I'm going to press down the center and start to create a bowl. Chicken soup, anyone?"

What's wrong with him? Hmm. Something awful. Cancer? No, it couldn't be, because my mother had cancer, and I don't want Francine to think I'm repeating myself. AIDS? No, too passé. Most people didn't die from AIDS anymore, and it was emotionally charged, too. I don't need her telling me that that's what you get for being gay. Would she?

"So now, by pressing down in the center with one hand, and holding onto the outside of the clay with the other, you can see that I'm forming my bowl. But if I push the clay inward," and she did, "it will start to rise up, and I can make a vase. So you're going to push and pull."

I have a push-pull amplifier at home. I don't know what that means, but I know I have it. And why am I not there now, listening to music? The Sibelius First would be nice.

"Now we're going to widen the rim, as you can see me doing, and, taking my thumb and index finger, narrow it, and now look at what I have."

Hepatitis! I saw a commercial about some drug for it just the other night. That would be original.

"And here's something important," she said.

I'm listening. And, by the way, it's about time.

"I want you to fail." She laughed.

That's poor of you. No teacher should ever say that, even as a joke.

"The pieces you're going to work on tonight are not pieces you're going to keep or come back to next week. They're just going to be pieces to get you used to the feel of clay between your hands. How many of you have never worked with clay before?"

I looked around the room and was surprised to see that ten of the fifteen people raised their hands, and then I felt guilty that I didn't, too, and worried then that more would be expected of me because clay wasn't a foreign medium.

Her demonstration lasted more than half an hour, and when I got to my wheel and began cutting my cubes, forming a ball, wetting the clay, and manipulating it between my hands, I suddenly realized that I liked the feeling of it, but then Peggy walked over, asked me how I was doing, I told her that I was doing well, and I lost all interest in it.

"Remember, people," Peggy called out from her wheel at the front of the room. "Whatever you make is not going to be kept for posterity, so don't worry."

And again, that disturbed me. When I create something I want to create something lasting, or at least meaningful, and, at least, meaningful to me. Or not "at least." *Importantly*, I want it to be meaningful to me. But she was encouraging us to not take the assignment seriously, and though she could write it off as simply getting us familiar with the feel of the clay and the feel of the potter's wheel, to me she was canceling any sense of pride I wanted to take in what I was doing.

"What are you going to make?" Francine asked, looking at me. She was standing at the wheel next to mine.

"You'll see," I said. "What about you?"

"I don't know," she said, and already sounded spent. "Maybe a vase first, or a bowl. I'll see."

If I wasn't going to make something to be proud of, I thought, I'd at least make something clever. That would have a touch of me about it.

To be honest, spinning the potter's wheel became quickly monotonous, and anything I could end up making would, of course, be circular, but I never liked circles. I always preferred angles to curves. And while that was something that could be provided by a canvas, or a piece of charcoal paper, or even working with clay freehand, it wasn't going to be provided by what I had to work with.

But in the end, I made an aspirin tablet. What could be simpler? I put my ball of clay on the wheel, pressed it down so it elongated, kept it high in the center and lower around the sides, then turned it upside down and did the same thing so both the top and the bottom looked alike. Then, just to be fancy, I took my wire, held it vertically while my tablet was spinning, and flattened the sides. Yes, I'd worked with clay before.

Peggy walked over, stopped short, looked concerned, smiled, looked concerned again, and finally said, "I don't know what to say. This is marvelous."

"It's no big deal," I said, but I knew it was, but it was because it was *different*, not because it was *good*. It was a ridiculously easy piece to make, and the vase that Francine was still working on looked a lot more elaborate and inventive.

"I'd love to show this to the class," Peggy said, "but I can tell you don't want me to." She smiled and shook her head. "So carry on." She walked quietly toward another bench.

That surprised me. I'd been smiling, too, I didn't look apprehensive, but she saw right through it. "I didn't think I was that easy to read," I said.

"You're not," Francine said, walking toward me. "At least I don't think so. But maybe I just can't read people very well."

"You like it?" I asked.

"I do," she said.

"Or maybe you just can't read *me*," I said.

"Maybe. Morley?" she asked.

"Yes?"

"You don't want to be liked, do you?"

And for a moment I froze, because I didn't know what to say, but then I realized that I'd never felt so proud, both of her and me, or had a greater desire to walk away from her than I did then, and walking away would have answered her question perfectly.

After another hour, my phone rang or, rather, vibrated. Actually, it didn't, but I wanted it to, so I walked out to answer it and came back five minutes later with a concerned look on my face.

"Is everything okay?" Francine asked.

"I'll tell you later," I said, but then, thinking that I was being too manipulative, said, "No, but it's nothing new."

"I knew something was bothering you," she said.

In fact, nothing had been bothering me except the class, which I was back to finding boring, but she never seemed attuned to that, my boredom, possibly because she was responsible for so much of it.

Forty-five minutes later the class finally ended. The few people who were wearing smocks took them off, and after one man hung his back in the closet, Peggy said, "Don't bother. Just leave them on the chair. They'll have to be cleaned anyway." And while I was sure she'd said that to be helpful, it sounded vaguely accusatory, as though she were blaming him for getting his smock dirty.

When we walked outside, Francine asked, "So what is it?"

And I said, "It's Corey."

She clicked her tongue and asked, "What does he want from you now?"

"What the fuck do you mean by 'now'?" I asked. "We haven't spoken about him for six years."

"Yeah," she said, "but he's always after something. First it was your money—"

I sighed. "That, remember, was my idea."

"Yeah," she said, "but he bought into it." She shook her head. "I don't know. I'm sorry, but I've always felt that he takes advantage of you." She was like the parent who can't stand to see her child grow up, so still thinks of him as a three-year-old even though he's entering middle age. I was glad she didn't have any kids.

We got to our cars. "Where now?" I asked.

"I'll drive," she said. "I know a little place that serves tea."

Lerner's Teas was only about a dozen blocks from the Arts Center, but it could have been in a different town. Located in a residential neighborhood similar to, but nicer than Francine's—*nicer* in the sense of more affluent—it was small and dark, and I wondered if they were still open. I saw a large white sign with black lettering in the window that, at first, I took for a message that they were closed for repairs, but it said:

NO COFFEE SERVED HERE

"Well that'll show 'em," I said, and we walked inside.

It was crowded, terribly noisy, and smelled of nothing in particular, which surprised me. Unless the aromas of teas weren't as potent as the aromas of coffees. The atmosphere was inky.

"Okay, so the idea of this place," Francine said, "is that they serve just tea, but a lot of teas from all over the world. And bakery items, too, of course."

"Like Adele's International," I said.

"Exactly," she said.

What was it about small towns? Did they host these eateries that offered foods and beverages from everywhere because they were trying to prove how open and inclusive they were? Maybe so, but coffee wasn't allowed here, so that clearly was discriminatory. Which, who knew, might have pleased the townsfolk.

We were seated at a small table in a corner and were handed two menus, which, like the menus at Adele's International, were absurdly large. I'd never heard of half the teas they mentioned, and didn't feel like taking the time to investigate, at least not just then. Boredom is exhausting. So I ordered a cup of something familiar, which I loved, jasmine tea, and a Napoleon, and Francine ordered a cup of peach cobbler guayusa and *not* a peach cobbler, but a lemon bar.

"So what did you think?" she asked. "Of the class." A hard question to answer, not because I didn't know what I wanted to say—I hated it—if I chose to be honest, but because I didn't know why she asked it. Presumably she wanted me to confirm her feelings, but I couldn't tell whether she'd enjoyed it or not. Of course, I hadn't paid that much attention to her.

"I don't know," I said.

Her shoulders slumped. "Oh," she said.

I widened my eyes. "Why? What did *you* think of it?"

"I thought it was all right," she said, but she didn't sound all that enthusiastic. The waiter brought us our tea and pastries.

"That was fast," I said. "So was this your first pottery class?"

She nodded. "My first time working with clay."

"Mine, too," I said, but that was too obviously a lie, and I needed to change the subject. "So Lerner's tees, T-E-E-S. Is that what one wears over learner's bras?"

She frowned. "They're called *training* bras, not *learner's* bras," she said. "But how could you be expected to know that?"

"Just because I'm gay," I said, "doesn't mean that I don't know anything about women."

"No," she said, "there must be some other reason." And we both laughed. "So seriously," she said, "what does Corey need from you this time?"

"Oh, we're back to that," I said. But that was perfect because I needed to tell her why I wouldn't be taking any more pottery classes with her. "*Wants*, not *needs*. He wants me to visit him."

"Why?" She looked around the room.

So I looked around, too, saw our waiter, who appeared to be in his mid-thirties, smile at me, so I smiled back, and said, "Because he doesn't have that much time left."

She looked flustered. "What?!"

"Francine," I said, "my friend is dying from hepatitis."

I had to end it. Corey's life, I mean. Because it was keeping Francine and I too close. I'd invented him only for her benefit, or at least her knowledge, and getting rid of him would just put that much more space between us; she and I.

"Do people really die from hepatitis?" she asked, but she sounded more surprised than suspicious.

"No, Francine" I said, "he's going to be the first, and make history. He always wanted to go out with a bang." I sipped my tea, which I rather enjoyed. "Of course they do. Not as often as people used to, because there are more and better medications around, but yes, some people still do succumb."

"Did he drink a lot?" she asked.

"Not as much as he should have," I said, and laughed. "It's led to liver failure and, you know, at first his doctors thought they could control it, but not now. Not anymore."

"How horrible," she said, and shook her head, though then she took a sizeable bite of her lemon bar, which implied that she was putting on an act for my benefit. "God, first it was your mother, now Corey," she said. "I feel sorry for you."

"My mother died nine years ago," I said. But my mother had died five years before that, and Corey never did, so she had nothing to feel sorry about. But still, while I didn't enjoy people feeling sorry for me, I tremendously enjoyed realizing how much better my life was than I made it out to be.

A smile. "You know what I'm thinking about?" she asked.

"Is it legal?"

"Stop trying to be funny," she said. "And you'll notice that I said, 'trying to be,' because, really, you're not. So you know what I'm thinking about?"

I took a bite of my Napoleon, which I thought might have been stale. "How am I supposed to answer you now after an introduction like that?" I asked. But then I smiled and asked, "No, what?"

"A scene from *I Love Lucy*. Did you ever watch that? Of course you did. We're of that generation. Anyway, you might remember this. Lucy was taking a course in sculpting, but, of course, she couldn't put together anything that looked even remotely like a sculpture. And Ricky was bringing a friend of his over to show off Lucy's talents. Which, of course, she didn't have. So Lucy, quick-thinking woman that she was, powdered her face and hair white and stuck her head through a hole she'd cut into a table, with a cloth covering it, to pose her head as a sculpture. And when Ricky brought his friend home, they were floored. Wow, they thought. This woman's got talent. But when the friend tried to lift what he *thought* was the sculpture off the table, Lucy started screaming." She laughed.

"Surreal," I said. "It must have been a hoot." Another sip of tea.

"You never watched it."

"I watched it," I said. "It was silly. But I guess it served a purpose." One more sip.

She looked down. "Yeah," she said. "Some."

"Actually, my grandmother, my mother's mother, liked to watch it, and would force me to watch it with her when I was over at her house on a Saturday night." I looked around the room. It was ten-forty on a Monday night, but the place was crowded. Good for them.

"Force you?"

"Well, not really *force* me, but when my parents went out, as they sometimes would on Saturdays, I'd spend the night at my grandmother's house. She was my babysitter. And, of course, we'd watch *I Love Lucy* together. You know, she was lonely, since my grandfather died—I never knew him—and television kept her company."

"And you," she said.

"And me."

*

"Grandma, you want to watch *I Love Lucy*?"

No answer.

"Grandma, *I Love Lucy* is on. You want to watch it?"

Still no answer. So I turned on the television set, switched it to the right channel, sank back on the couch, and laughed.

"I love *I Love Lucy*," I said.

And still she didn't say anything.

"And I love watching it with you."

I felt her smile, but there was only silence. And there would always be only silence, because my maternal grandmother was dead. Gone for seven years when I was born, and my paternal grandmother had died three years before that. But I always imagined what things would have been like if they'd still been alive.

Excursion into parts UNKNOWN

Corey died early the following year, but Francine never brought him up again. He and I had been together for almost ten years, which, back then, would have been considered "long" in the gay community, but I had no idea how long Francine and Peter—or was it "Peter"?—had been together. I didn't mind the fact that Francine never asked me about Corey, rationalizing that she felt either guilty for not having thrown more emotional support behind me when he was languishing, or jealous that I had him in my life at all. And although I had no sexual desire for Francine, and honestly much preferred the time we didn't spend together to the time we did, her jealousy, if that's what it was, could still be flattering.

I called her the night it happened, one night sooner than I'd called her after my mother's death, but, given my respective feelings toward them, as far as Francine was concerned, that made sense.

"I bet I know why you're calling," she said, when she answered the phone.

"Francine," I said gravely. "Corey is gone."

A silence, then, "When did it happen?"

"Just a few hours ago," I said. It was ten o'clock. "I was at the hospital with him when he died. It happened at about seven."

"Which hospital was he in?"

"Weller Regional. Just outside of—"

She breathed out loudly. "I know where it is. So when and where's the funeral?"

Then it was my turn to sigh. "Fortunately, it's not until Friday. And today is only Monday. But it's out of the way for a lot of people, so they have to give time for everyone to get there."

"Get where?"

"Biloxi. Actually it's a few towns over, in Lyman."

"You're going all the way to Mississippi?!"

"What choice do I have? He wanted to be buried with his family, and his family is there."

"Did they ever come to visit him?"

"No," I said. Then, "At least not that I know of. He never mentioned them."

"Well, I'm glad you're going," she said. "And do me a favor. Call me along the way and when you get there, so I know you're all right."

I was expecting that. Eventually, most people act out of guilt. Which was why I'd booked a trip to Mississippi starting the next day. When I called Francine, I knew she would be able to find out where I was calling from, so I had to make sure I was on my way to, and in Mississippi, not sitting in my bedroom. Of course she would probably never try to track my calls, simply because it was easier to be lied to than to be suspicious—fewer headaches— but I didn't want to take any chances and, besides, it would give me a chance to visit Faulkner's house, Rowan Oak, and the town, Oxford, that he made so famous as Jefferson in his fiction. My vacation, which I'd told Leo about three months before, would last two weeks: two whole days to Biloxi by train, one day to relax, a bus ride up to Oxford the day after, a two-night stay there, then another bus ride down to Biloxi, one more night spent there, and finally a two-day train ride home. I would spend the remainder of my time enjoying myself or, if Francine asked, trying to get over Corey's death.

Why was I taking the train? Two reasons. I hated flying, finding it boring and monotonous. To me airplanes were the equivalent of modern architecture, streamlined and faceless. The more important reason was that I felt the need to lower myself into Mississippi gradually, seeing how the atmosphere changed en route, rather than simply ending up, a few hours after taking off, in a land I was sure was going to feel foreign in the worst sense of the term.

So the next morning, Tuesday, I took a taxi to West Ellis, where I boarded a train for a seven-hour ride to Berriman, which was three states away. In Berriman I would transfer to a train to Chicago. That ride would take nineteen hours. Then, after sitting in Union Station for ten hours, unless there was someplace else I wanted to go, I would take a fifteen-hour ride to Jackson, where I would have to wait for only two hours, before transferring to a train to Biloxi, which would get me there three hours later. And I would enjoy the comfort, if that's what it was, of my own room, officially a roomette, on the trains between Berriman and Chicago and Chicago and Jackson. A room, I should add, with two beds, both available only to me.

But when I stepped onto the train in Berriman, I was surprised and disappointed. Surprised because there were so few people on board—we were, after all, headed toward Chicago, the rail hub of the nation—and disappointed because the train looked just like the commuter trains I would take to make less-than-two-hour trips somewhere. Perhaps the seats were a little wider, and there were curtains on the windows, which I hadn't remembered from earlier trips, but any image of romance, which I'd associated with taking the train to Biloxi, quickly disappeared. I walked down a couple of cars to see where I would be staying and to set down my luggage, which consisted of one toiletries bag, one large valise, and two garment bags. The halls were extremely narrow, and I rubbed my shoulders against the two facing walls. If Chicago was the city of big shoulders, nobody from there would have fit.

I had three choices when I booked my trip: reserving only a seat, which didn't appeal to me, because I would spend a fair amount of time sleeping; reserving a bedroom, which was a lot more expensive; and reserving a roomette, though, upon seeing it, I decided that it was designed for people of my generation who were getting sentimental for telephone booths. Inside there were two chairs, one on each side, in navy blue leather, or faux-leather, which would be converted into a bed later (I wouldn't need the second bed), a folding sink, which was something I'd never seen, and a wide window, also with curtains. And that made me think of another reason why I didn't like flying: once you were off the ground there was nothing much to see. All right, I thought. This could end up seducing me.

I'd gotten onto the train in Berriman late that afternoon, and as it was still winter, the sun would be setting soon. So, after a time, I headed toward the dining car. It was only six o'clock, and I wasn't especially hungry, but I'd heard someone say that it closed at nine, and there was already a line of fifteen or twenty people waiting to get in. Each of the tables in that car sat four, and I felt a little awkward, asking for a table for myself. Still, I looked at the families and small groups of friends sitting together and enjoying themselves, and was glad I was alone.

A redheaded woman with a swollen left eye, who was standing in front of me, turned around to ask if I'd given my name. I told her I hadn't. She told me that I needed to, so I walked up to where a short, young woman with frizzy dark blonde hair stood with a pad and pencil and, without picking her head up, asked me what my name was and how many people were in my party. Surprisingly, when I told her it was just one, she said it shouldn't be more than a couple of minutes, as a man two tables in front of her was about to get up, and suddenly I realized that I wasn't looking at families or friends but collections of strangers who were talking to each other. I hoped nobody at my table would ask me any questions, but if they did, I thought, I would say that I couldn't talk because I was in mourning.

After dinner I thrilled to seeing cities and towns collecting themselves as we pulled into our various stops. At each one seemingly more people got on than got off, and at one stop I had to laugh when I realized that, even with the train officially docked at the station, half of it extended far enough back that the traffic on the town's main street had to be stopped for it.

At ten that night I called Francine. "No idea where I am," I said. "Seems like the middle of nowhere, but I'm enjoying it."

"Don't they announce the stops on the train?" she asked. "They must."

"Oh, they do," I said. "I'm just not paying attention to them because I know I don't have to get off yet." And since it doesn't involve me, how interested can I be?, I thought, but I didn't tell her that.

"What time do you get to Chicago?" she asked.

"Ten to ten tomorrow morning," I said, "so about twelve hours from now, if we stay on time, but word has it that we won't."

"Are you going to make your connection?"

"I'll be in Chicago for ten hours," I said, "so yeah, I think so."

My chairs had been converted into a bed by the car attendant, and the bed looked surprisingly comfortable and welcoming. I was looking forward to laying down, reading for maybe an hour, then looking outside and noticing the differences in the towns and cities I would pass. That was something I'd always enjoyed. I loved the night, too, and had from the time I was a child; preferring night to day and, because of that, winter to summer. Darkness was cozy. The things that I savored were quiet things that were better done at home and in private than outside or in public. The night respected that. It didn't tempt me the way the day did.

So I snuggled beneath the covers, read until nearly twelve thirty—I brought two books with me, as was my reading habit at home; a novel and a nonfiction book, in this case a biography of Ravel—and then, after getting dressed again, I walked into the sightseer car, where two rows of seats sat facing the windows and, alone, I watched the scenery swell and dwindle. If my trip had ended there I would always have remembered it as a great vacation. So much for my not enjoying travel. In fact, I thought, it wasn't travel I disliked, it was most destinations that I found disappointing.

The next day, after a remarkably sound sleep and decent breakfast on the train, we pulled into Chicago's Union Station at nearly one-thirty, more than three and a half hours later than we were scheduled to. But that cut my free time down to six and a half hours—the train to Jackson would leave at eight o' five—during which I could wander around the station, eat at the two-floor buffet that was open to travelers who'd booked a roomette or bedroom on the train, and read. The novel I had with me was *A Fable*, and it was my second time reading it. I didn't usually read novels more than once, but this deserved a second reading, as I wasn't sure how I'd felt about it the first time and, as there would be so many distractions at a busy train station, it made sense to bring something I could read less carefully than I would something I'd never read before.

I called Francine.

"Where are you now?" she asked.

"Stranded in Chicago," I said, and laughed. "Not really stranded, it's just that I've got six and a half hours to kill and don't know what I'm going to do." I knew what I was going to do and was doing it.

"You should walk around the city a little bit," she said.

"I would," I said, "but I'd be so afraid of missing my train to Jackson that I'd be too anxious to enjoy myself."

She laughed. "Yeah," she said, "that sounds like you."

I was anxious, but in the good sense, to get on the train to Jackson, because I wanted to see if and how the scenery changed and how the people who boarded the train changed as we got closer to Mississippi. Unfortunately, in that respect, I was booked into a roomette, not a simple seat, so my exposure to others was limited. Thus, I decided to spend as long as seemed allowable whenever I sat in the dining car, visit the snack bar far more frequently than I otherwise would, and sit in the sightseer car whenever the opportunity presented itself, to do just that: sightsee.

Not until we were two hours outside of Jackson, which meant shortly before we'd crossed the border between Tennessee and Mississippi, did I notice a change in the people around me, and even that was slight. There were more blacks than I'd seen since I'd left West Ellis, which wasn't saying much, but the people on the train didn't look heavier—Mississippi had one of the highest obesity rates in the nation—or poorer—Mississippi also had one of the highest poverty levels in the nation, and Damn it, I thought. We're all tourists.

"What are you doing now?" Francine asked when she called. I was starting to feel hounded.

"I'm writing my eulogy," I said.

"*Your* eulogy?" she asked.

"Oh, please," I said, "the eulogy I'm giving at Corey's funeral."

"You don't think anyone else is going to give one?"

"I have no idea what anyone else is going to do," I said, "but I let his aunt know. She's been my contact."

It was my first night in Biloxi. Why had I ever picked that city, of all places? I hadn't realized that it was a gambling mecca, so finding a decent-looking hotel without a casino wasn't easy, but the Holiday Inn into which I booked myself didn't have one. Imagine if it had, I thought.

The next day, I decided, I would spend in bed. I ordered up breakfast through room service, but by noon was anxious to get dressed and read. I would call Francine that night to let her know that the funeral had been rough and that I wouldn't be able to talk to her for the next few days. I would be in Oxford but I would tell her that I simply needed time to myself. When I got back to Biloxi I would call her again.

At nine o'clock the following morning I checked out of my hotel and boarded a bus for Oxford. The depot was only six blocks away. And as soon as I got on the bus, where I would sit for the next five and a half hours, I knew I was among a completely different crowd of people. The first thing that worried me was that if I could tell so easily that they weren't like me, they must have been able to tell, even more easily, that I wasn't like them. *More easily* because I would be the only one, or one of only a few, who stood out. I couldn't say how they were different. Or maybe I didn't want to, because it would have been disrespectful, and I didn't like thinking of myself that way. I liked most things about myself; my intelligence, my fairness, my open-mindedness, the way I dressed, the way I carried myself, the money I earned, and those were things that, unfairly, I was sure, I didn't see in them.

I situated myself four rows back from the driver, in a seat next to the window, and stared straight ahead of me, turning my head very rarely, so as not to attract attention. Or was I attracting attention by doing that? The crowd was quiet, which I didn't expect. I thought the bus would be filled with people all of whom knew each other, or acted as though they knew each other, but everyone was still, and I quickly disabused myself of the idea that it was because there was a stranger in their midst. But I didn't stop thinking that sometimes it was necessary to try to fit in, and I hated myself for feeling that way.

Oxford was more beautiful than I'd expected. The flat lowlands in the southern part of the state gave way to rolling hills that helped me relax; a letting-down of the shoulders. The town square, what I would have called a village green back home, was dominated by the courthouse, and the first thing that struck me about it was its whiteness. Had that been deliberate? Were justice and justness white? That seemed too easy; clearly I was reading more into it than I should have. Besides, it was the whiteness of a large head, suddenly blanched and terrified. And, for all I knew, maybe that was deliberate. But even the brick and concrete facades of the stores that surrounded it, while more colorful, seemed a little faded. It must have been the heat.

So I began to imagine running into the characters I loved. Look, over there. Isn't that Jason Compson? And surely that must be Gavin Stevens, or "Lawyer," as Ratliff liked to call him, looking just the way Faulkner had described him. And then I figured out what was wrong with my being there. For an artist to connect with an observer, the artist has to evoke something familiar in the observer's mind. So when I look at a street that a writer knew, and presumably knew well, because works of fiction aren't usually created after a single visit, I'll never be able to place myself *there* because I've never walked down that street; I don't have that writer's memory. But I've walked down other streets, streets that have their own attraction to, and meaning for me. And sitting at home, alone in my bedroom, I can walk down any one of those streets and appreciate what the artist is trying to conjure. That's how the artist and I connect. But here there was no connection. The town's reality left no room for my imagination, and the people around me were strangers.

I thought about the Thanksgivings I'd spent at my Aunt Doro and Uncle Olin's house. I always enjoyed them, and much more than I enjoyed any other times I spent there, and that was because of what went on, a happy gathering of family, not where it was. Too many people make that mistake. They have a good memory of something that occurred someplace, and think that if they can just get back to that place, they'll be happy again. But they never are. The place feels sterile, because the memories were memories of what happened, not of where it happened.

I gave myself half an hour to walk along the streets that surrounded the square, looking in the windows of the couple of coffee shops, clothiers, and book stores I passed—it was, after all, a college town—and then I stopped in front of what looked like a multifamily dwelling, whose front door was open, revealing a long carpeted hallway with two closed doors near the end of it.

"Can I help you?!" a woman's voice rang out, and I almost jumped.

"No," I said, perhaps to myself, and ran away, trying to convince myself that she wasn't talking to me, but thinking, just the same, that I didn't belong there.

I walked to Faulkner's house then, more out of a sense of obligation—my God, I'd traveled all the way to Mississippi for that—than excitement, but that turned out to be more fulfilling than I'd expected. In the first place, the house, as seen from the outside and from a distance, at least, was gorgeous; a grand Southern mansion built in the Greek Revival style. I approached it by walking down an avenue of cedars, and I remembered that, when I was growing up, my parents had a cedar closet in their bedroom, and I'd always loved its smell. So there was the artist reaching out to me, and an instance of incident, not place connecting us. If I were to revisit my childhood home, I thought, I was sure it wouldn't have brought back the memories that this had.

And looking at the mansion, I said to myself, Yes. There *is* justice in the world. Such a great writer deserved to live in such a great house. But during the tour it was explained that the house, which was about a hundred years old at the time Faulkner had bought it in nineteen thirty, was in disrepair then, and he went into debt first by buying the house and then by renovating it, though he did many of the renovations himself. And inside, everything looked worn, old, and dated and, I thought, must have looked that way even when Faulkner was alive. Aside from plumbing and electricity, the tour guide said, Faulkner allowed for nothing "modern" with the exception of a small radio in his daughter's bedroom, which I saw. Surprising, I thought, for a writer who was, in so many ways, pretty modern himself.

Perhaps the most fascinating part of the visit was the study on the first floor, where Faulkner had written parts of his outline for *A Fable* on the walls. *A Fable*! But who writes on walls? I thought. And that got me to wonder if he didn't respect or didn't appreciate his house. Similarly, there was a telephone set on a small table in a corner just outside the kitchen, where people's phone numbers had been written on the walls. "I guess it was easier than pulling out a notepad," the tour guide said, and I smiled.

And half an hour later I was done. I decided not to visit Faulkner's grave; I'd seen enough. Was I disappointed? Maybe. Which meant yes, at least a little. But the visit enriched me; it taught me a lot of things about Faulkner and about myself, and I never minded disappointment if I could learn from it.

On the night before I left for home, Francine called, and we spoke briefly. "So how did it all go?" she asked. Of course she was referring to Corey's funeral and its aftermath.

"All right," I said. I was tired. "But you know what they say, no place like home, and all that happy horseshit." I clicked my tongue. "I'm glad to be coming back."

"I'm glad you are, too," she said. "And I'm glad you went there. You needed to, and you did what you had to."

But no, I didn't. I did what I'd *wanted* to. And that explained the difference between us. To her, friendship was an obligation; to me, it was a choice, just not one I made often. And her statement, maybe better than anything else, explained why.

Everything's coming up ACES

Almost two years passed before we spoke to each other again. "Okay," Francine said, when she called me one Thursday night. "Crazy question. Do you like potatoes?"

I shook my head slowly. That was her way of reconnecting; making it seem like we'd been talking only moments before, rather than years ago, and if, at one time, I'd found that genuinely charming, I no longer did. I wished we'd either remain friends with our longest hiatuses lasting only a few months, or simply go our separate ways. At least that was what I'd told myself. Because after that, I scraped together a modicum of appreciation for hearing from her again, and said, "Do I like *potatoes*?! Yeah, I guess. I mean, who doesn't?" In fact, I didn't. Or at least hadn't when I was growing up. I'd liked every other vegetable I'd ever tasted, and I'd tasted many, just not potatoes. Not boiled, broiled, baked, mashed, or fried, and I couldn't think of many other ways to prepare them. But, with time, I'd come to like them more. Enough. "Why do you ask?"

"Because a new restaurant just opened up," she said, "called One Potato, Two Potato."

And for a moment I thought that if a new restaurant hadn't opened up, I wouldn't have heard from her, and I wasn't sure how I felt about that. "Where?" I asked.

"In Oberlies," she said. Of course. When had she become so wildly unadventurous? "But here's the deal. Everything they serve is made with potatoes. *Based* on potatoes. So potatoes determine the character of each dish; they're not served on the side."

"Is it vegetarian?" I asked.

"No," she said quickly, "not at all. A lot of their dishes are made with meat, it's just that they all contain potatoes."

Then "Okay," I said. "Let's try it." To be honest, it sounded pretty intriguing, and I was curious to see what a chef could do, knowing that he or she had to involve potatoes in everything that he or she made. So we decided to meet there the following Wednesday night. I knew better than to ask if she wanted to meet at her house.

The restaurant was, technically speaking, in the middle of town, but two blocks off Posner Street, where it sat like an afterthought. The inside walls were brown tile, an appropriate touch but, hilariously, they were covered with framed photographs, some in color but most in black and white, of potatoes, and each bore a message—"Best of luck!," "Love this place!," "Bite me!"—and a signature.

We were seated by a host wearing a dark brown turtleneck shirt and dark brown pants that didn't quite match but were close enough, and then a young redheaded waiter, similarly attired, came by, asked us if we wanted drinks, and handed us our menus. I, of course, ordered an iced tea but Francine said she'd be fine with just water. And that was something that made me feel old. I still remembered when water was served immediately upon an individual or party being seated in any restaurant. Our table was small and square—it obviously couldn't hold a lot of dishes, so I hoped that nobody on the staff would let them accumulate as dinner wore on—and had two cane back chairs. We were, as we always seemed to be, sitting next to a window.

"Well, I have to tell you," I said, "I *love* the décor." And I did. Invariably I would enjoy myself with Francine more than I'd expect to, but it seemingly never made me want to see her again any time soon. I didn't know why.

"Isn't it clever?" she asked. "But wait till you see what's on the menu. You'll notice something interesting, I think."

I opened the menu and looked through it, but wasn't sure what she was referring to. It was divided into three sections. The first was titled *Just Potatoes,* and listed appetizers and entrées that were made, pretty much, only of potatoes, such as potato soup and potato pancakes, but also a variety of potato fritters, or rösti, as they were called. The second was titled *With Potatoes,* and featured more standardized fare, such as chicken pot pie, shepherd's pie, and moussaka, that was made with potatoes; and the third was titled *Tasted But Not Seen,* the idea being that potatoes, as explained on the menu, were used primarily as a thickening agent, not as part of the dish per se, so there was beef Stroganoff and Swedish meatballs, the potatoes presumably used to thicken the sauces that accompanied them.

I sat back and said, "Well talk about a niche market." I smiled, but didn't mean to.

"Did you see what was interesting?" she asked, and, after a moment, looked disappointed, either because I hadn't commented on it or because I evidently hadn't found it interesting.

"No," I said. "What was it?"

"The way they have their menu divided," she said. She raised her eyebrows; a little punctuation.

And I felt peculiar. That was it? Of course I'd seen it; how could I not? And I started to think that Francine was falling back into the self she'd been when I'd first met her, less sharp and agile than she'd seemed for the longest time in the years since.

She ordered a potato salad, which was an actual salad of sliced raw potatoes with other vegetables and a champagne vinaigrette, not the mayonnaise-based glop that one found elsewhere, and the potato pie, and I ordered the potato soup and the potato rösti garnished with broccoli and grated cheddar cheese, a nice variation on sauce.

"So how are things?" I asked, leaning forward, not because I wanted to, or because I really cared, but because if I didn't it would have been too obvious how my interest had waned.

She shrugged. "All right, I guess."

"That's not very convincing," I said, and sipped my iced tea, which the waiter had just brought.

"You know what?" she asked. "I'm getting tired."

I'd expected that. "Of what?" I asked.

"You name it," she said, "I'm getting tired of it." She pushed herself back in her seat and crossed her arms, something I'd never seen her do.

"Are you dating anybody?" I asked.

She glowered. "No," she said, sounding almost angry. "And that really bothers me, because I know I'm missing out."

I rubbed my wrists with my opposite hands, and smiled, "Yeah," I said, "but look at it this way. You, and not just you, but all of us, are always missing out on something. You decide to go out for Italian one night, you miss out on eating Chinese. You decide to go out for Chinese one night, you miss out on eating deli. You decide to wear blue one day, you miss out on wearing brown. You decide to get married, you miss out on being single. All decisions are restrictive."

That seemed to refresh her. "Yes, exactly," she said, pushing her hands along the tabletop toward me, "but don't you see? It's not my decision not to date."

I shook my head. "Well unless someone is telling you not to or, I don't know, have they passed a law against it? You know me; I'm not up with the times. But unless they did, it's very much your decision. Why do you decide not to?"

"I don't know," she said, and looked down. "Can we talk about something else, please?"

"Sure," I said. "Let's."

The appetizers came, with the waiter repeating the names of the dishes loudly when he put them on the table. Not that potato salad or potato soup could have been mistaken for anything else, but maybe he just wanted to make sure he'd gotten the order right.

"So what's happening in your life?" she asked.

I shrugged. "In the world of Morley?" I asked. "Not very much. Well, actually, one thing that I've noticed is that some days I don't get mail." It wasn't, I realized, that I was a good listener, it was simply that I didn't enjoy talking about myself. Yet one more reason to lie.

She smiled. "Maybe there's just no mail for you those days." She tasted her salad, said it was delicious, and told me that I should try it. I did, and agreed.

"Impossible," I said. But, of course I was just making that up. "With all the junk mail around, I find it impossible that anybody's mailbox can be empty for a day."

"Then you should talk to him about it," she said, waving her fork, which held a bite of salad on it.

"Talk to whom?"

"Your mailman."

"My mail carrier is a woman," I said. "So I guess that makes her my *fe*-mailman."

She laughed. "That makes her sound like a drag queen," she said, and we both laughed. A temporary felicity.

"Is that it?" she asked.

"That and other things," I said.

The entrées were brought out before we'd finished our appetizers. I hate being rushed during a meal, and the waiter asked if we'd like the kitchen to keep our entrées warm for us, so we said yes. "I guess slightly warmed-over food is better than cold food," I said.

"So tell me," she said. "Who's still there? At Lake Quaintance, I mean." I opened my mouth, but she said, "It's been seventeen years. Change does happen, Morley. Maybe not in your life, but it does."

If she'd been smiling I wouldn't have been bothered, but she wasn't, and I could feel her old disapproval of my stasis, or my suspicion of her disapproval sneaking in again. "Pretty much everyone who was there when you were there," I said.

But that wasn't the case at all. Francine (and, later, Ian) had been replaced by Ellie O'Connor, a slender biracial woman, and the first in our school, whose staff was otherwise blindingly white; Pano had been replaced by Stanley Brill, who made me think of a nineteen seventies TV game show host— was it the way he dressed? The way he smiled? The way he wore his hair?—and Brendan had been replaced by Mark Elidis, who, much to my consternation, insisted on being called Eli. If at first I'd found them a drab bunch, I'd since come to admire Ellie—whom no one would ever mistake for Eli, though when one spoke about them, one had to add "her" or "him" after the person's name—for her fairness and, from what I could tell, the respect she showed her students. "They teach me more than I teach them," she told me. Which, I thought, was the way it should be. About Stanley and Mark—I refused to call him Eli—I was less sure. Stanley still seemed insipid, but Mark, I'd realized, was looking to take over Leo's position, and had been since he'd started. And Leo, I knew, had no desire to give it up. But maybe, by then, he should have. After all, the people he was hiring were obviously at the bottom of the barrel. But, as the old saying went, just when you think you've reached the bottom of the barrel, you realize you've only scratched the surface. Perhaps there were simply fewer good teachers around then than there had been once.

"Tell you what," Francine said, suddenly livening up. "Let's give it ten years."

"All right," I said. "Let's." And then our entrées were served. "Meaning what?" I asked.

"Meaning that if neither of us is seeing someone at that time, we'll move in together." She smiled wistfully. "All right?"

I smiled too, but not, I was sure, for the same reason. "Well, if I'm not still seeing Kim," I said carefully, "let's." I sobered my expression.

Her face fell. "Who's Kim?" she asked, and tasted her food, after which she raised her eyebrows, meaning, I supposed, that she liked it.

"Good?" I asked.

"Mm-*hmm*," she said.

"So yes, Kim," I said. Who was Kim? Kim was the name I would use in the days when I still thought I might have been gay, to talk about whoever I would be "dating"—and that was "dating" in quotation marks, because I'd never dated and never had the desire to date—as it was gender-neutral. Now, of course, I didn't need to use such names, but it was the first one that came to my mind. "Um, Kim Samuels. He's the guy I've been going out with since Corey died." Samuel had been my father's name.

"Going out with," she said slowly. She lowered her gaze but looked around the room, presumably at the floor.

"Yes, going out with," I said, and took a bite of my potato rösti, which I thought was delicious. "Great place," I said, to change the subject.

"Since Corey died," she said. And her look of disappointment reminded me of the way she'd looked that day she'd asked me out to dinner eighteen years earlier—I still remembered!—and I'd told her that I couldn't go because I had other plans for that night.

But I couldn't tell whether she was disappointed because I was seeing someone or because, as I'd made it seem, I was seeing someone so soon after Corey's death. So I thought I'd play that up. "Yes," I said, "we met about a month after Corey died."

"Well wasn't that nice of you?" she asked, picking her head up. "I mean, waiting till the body cooled down. What, was this new guy second on your list?"

I clicked my tongue. Well you know what they say, I thought. We homosexuals are oversexed. Did people still believe that? "No," I said. "He was legitimate. I met him on a real dating site."

She shook her head. "I don't believe you," she said.

I took a bite of my rösti and a sip of my iced tea. "What don't you believe?" I asked. I looked away and made believe I was concentrating on something going on at another table.

"Any of it," she said. She put her utensils down, which I took to mean that she wanted to talk, or at least wanted me to listen to her. By then she must have known that I didn't always.

"Oh, Kim is very real," I said. "I can send you a picture, if you'd like." How hard could that have been? I'd find something online. But I knew she wouldn't care if I did, and I didn't want to, because I was tired of my charades.

"Do that," she said. "How old is he?"

"Older than Corey was," I said. "He just turned thirty." And I ate more of my rösti.

"Well isn't that grown-up of you? Somebody who's only, what, thirty years younger than you?"

I smiled. "Twenty-five," I said. "But you do know how to age me." That, at least, was true.

She sighed. "Morley," she said. "Why do you lie to me?"

"What makes you think I lie?" I asked.

She waved her hand. She still hadn't picked up her utensils. "Oh, please," she said. "You lie to me all the time. I'm not stupid. I know it. And you have for as long as I've known you."

Okay, I thought, but had it really taken her eighteen years to figure that out, or had she deliberately not said anything? I wasn't scared or bothered by what she was saying, because she didn't mean enough to me to scare or bother me anymore.

"But please tell me. Be truthful with me just this once. Why do you do it?"

I leaned back. "Why do I lie?" I asked. "Because lying is the quickest and easiest way to expand your mind. It lets you see familiar things in a different context, and all to the good, right? Because if you like the way they look, you can bask in that fantasy for a while, and if you don't, meaning that if the pretend reality isn't as good as the real one is, you end up appreciating the real one that much more."

She shook her head. "Total bullshit," she said.

And it was. But so was everything else I'd ever told her. So "I don't know why I lie," I said, but, of course, that, too, was a lie. There were more reasons for lying than there were lies. Each lie can be rationalized in at least five or six different ways, and different rationales provide different degrees of comfort. What matters, ultimately, isn't whether what I say is the truth or a lie, but how comfortingly I can rationalize it. Which leaves the truth at a disadvantage, because it requires less rationalization. So it offers less comfort.

She started eating again, and for several minutes we sat quietly. Then she said, "So how are things going with Kim?"

"Um...not as well as they might be," I said. I shoveled the rösti into my mouth as quickly as I could, not because I didn't want to talk—I didn't—but because I wanted her to realize that she was annoying me.

"Meaning what?" she asked.

"Meaning," I said, "that I think he's pulling away." I ate more and sipped my drink. Now I couldn't tell if she really cared, was pretending to care, or was just humoring me.

She stared at me. "That's probably your fault," she said. Maybe she cared only enough to try to hurt me. Angry woman.

"Excuse me?" I asked. Mock-indignation.

"Morley," she said, "you're the one who's pulling away. And seriously, I don't know if you realize this, but you are. You've got to be. You build a wall between you and everyone around you, and then you complain that people aren't as close to you as you'd like them to be."

When had I ever complained? I must have lied to her more often than I realized. "Not true," I said. And it wasn't.

"Not true how?" she asked. She picked up a large forkful of her potato pie but only nibbled at it.

"I was very close to Corey—"

She shook her head.

"And used to be very close to Kim, but now I'm not. We're not. I mean, don't get me wrong. We still see each other, but—"

Suddenly she smiled impishly. "Do you still have sex?"

I rolled my eyes. "Oh, yes," I said, and swallowed, though there was nothing in my mouth. "We still have sex."

That seemed to pacify her. "Well good," she said. "At least you're still having sex. That's important."

"It is important," I said, and nodded so she wouldn't think I was mocking her, though I was. "In that regard, anyway, nothing has changed." Well that, at least, was true.

"I'm glad," she said, and let her shoulders drop.

Like most people, and some asexuals, I masturbate, and when I pleasure myself I think about what makes me happy and what satisfies me, what I find attractive and what I find fulfilling, the same as they do. It's just that I never think about people. I think about music. Brahms makes me hard. But how could I have explained that?

For dessert we both ordered the house specialty, which was, predictably enough, potato ice cream. "We would offer potato pudding," our waiter said, "but the chef realized that potatoes don't make a good pudding, so we offer ice cream instead." He smiled apologetically.

"Sounds divine," I said.

Neither of us liked it.

"Is it just me," Francine said, "or—"

"Oh my God, no; it's not you," I said, and laughed. "This is inedible. I can't imagine what the pudding must have tasted like."

"Well, you'd better finish your ice cream anyway," she said, "or you'll disappoint the waiter."

I wondered what she'd meant by that. Did she think I was attracted to him? He was young, probably in his early to middle twenties, and not bad looking, presumably even good looking, but what did that matter to me? She still had no idea who I was, and never would.

"All right, look," she said, when the waiter cleared away our dishes and brought Francine coffee and me tea, "it's obvious that I like you more than you like me."

And after a pause I asked, "Are we back to this again?" Though, to be honest, I never remembered hearing it.

She sighed.

I nodded. "I guess," I said, then looked up. "Are you okay with that?" But I said it jokingly because I was sure that she was joking too.

Then her face collapsed and she started shaking her head. "No," she said. "That's not right. You're supposed to say, 'That's not true. I like you just as much, if not more.'"

"Sorry," I said, but I didn't mean it, and she knew that.

"So yes," she said, agitated, "I'm okay with it because I have to be. What other choice do I have?"

I smirked. "Well," I said, "we can stop talking to each other. *Again*."

She laughed, then I laughed. "Yeah," she said, "wasn't *that* fun?"

But by then, or perhaps suddenly, I knew better than to answer her.

PART THREE

ONE last dance

How does one think about the passing of time? When one does virtually the same thing every day, one can't look back five years and say, "Of course. I was doing *that* then." Because one was also doing that five days ago. Or perhaps it was yesterday. But that was one of the advantages, and there were many, to living a carefully circumscribed life. Because there was so little variety, I was always looking for the subtleties that separated one day from the next; subtleties that most other people overlooked or took for granted. I also ended up regretting very little, in contrast to the people who let their lives pass differently—both differently from mine and with each day different from every other—as long as I enjoyed whatever sustained me, and I enjoyed it all very much. Listening to music, reading, and teaching were still my principal interests, and if people shook their heads when they looked at me, and thought, Poor soul, well, let them. I always loved being different, and being happy, I'd come to realize, was the easiest way to set myself apart.

And then, one Monday night, Francine called. At that time we'd gone without seeing or talking to each other for more years than I cared to remember, and I say that not because I was old—I'd just turned sixty—but because I'd become so used to not hearing from or seeing her that her call struck me as an imposition. But, of course, I would never let her know that.

"Morley?" she asked.

"Francine," I said.

"How are you?"

"Fine," I said. "Just fine. You? And, my God, what, are we just meeting again? Because I'm sure this is the conversation we had when I interviewed you."

She laughed, but her laughter was strained. Not forced but darkened.

"Is everything all right?" I asked.

She laughed again. "All these years and you still ask the same stupid questions," she said, then added quickly, "I'm sorry, you know I didn't mean that."

I paused to let her think I was hanging up, but I said, "It doesn't matter. Really it doesn't."

"Well I'm back on the dating scene," she said.

"Yeah," I said, "it was lonely without you. The scene, I mean. So what's his name?"

"Freddy," she said. "Freddy Assenza. Nice Italian man. He's older than me."

"Wow," I said. "I didn't realize there were people older than you."

"You're older than me," she said.

"Yes," I said, "but at my age memory plays tricks, and I forgot." We both laughed. "I'm glad to hear it, though."

"Well—," she said.

"Well what?" I asked. "Aren't you?"

"I don't know," she said gloomily. "I keep thinking I should be, because I keep telling myself that this is what I really want, but now I'm not so sure."

I rolled my eyes. How some people never change. "Tell you what," I said. "Why don't we meet for dinner sometime soon, and you can tell me all about him."

"There's not really that much to say."

"That's fine, then," I said. "We'll get together next week and we can talk about whatever you want, or *not* talk about whatever you want."

"You still know how to comfort me, don't you?" she asked. But I couldn't tell whether she was being sincere or sarcastic. "Next week I'm free on Tuesday and Thursday."

"Great," I said. "I'll see you on Wednesday."

"Deal."

I didn't really want to see her and discuss her new boyfriend, but I said I would because part of me still thought I could help; part of me was still accepting her as a challenge. And she wasn't happy with him because she needed to look elsewhere for that.

For once I decided to choose a place to eat, and I decided on the *New* Harmony Diner. That was "*New*" in italics, to distinguish it, a plaque on the wall in the entryway said, from the old Harmony Diner, which used to stand there but had been torn down and replaced. And also, I thought, so people didn't think it was in the town of New Harmony. There was no town of New Harmony in our state. In fact, the diner was in Arledge, a substantial drive for both of us, but, again, I needed and wanted time to think on my way there.

I remembered the diner because Angelo and I used to eat there sometimes, though back then, and that was thirty-four years earlier, it was still just the Harmony Diner. And that night I preferred thinking about the past to thinking about the present, or, more specifically, thinking about Angelo to thinking about Francine.

The *New* Harmony Diner looked, of course, nothing like the diner it replaced. That had been a diner in the old sense of the term, built to resemble the railway cars on which it had been modeled. This, like Roscoe's Diner, offered a large dining room, faux-crystal chandeliers, marbled walls, a fountain, and Greek statuary but, in that respect, it seemed a pale imitation, a knock-off. Maybe it was because Arledge wasn't as affluent as Saloway, or because whoever owned it and whoever designed it just didn't care, but likely it was something else that I wasn't even thinking of.

I sat in a booth facing the front door for fifteen minutes before Francine walked in. We must have fallen out of the habit of coordinating our schedules. The hostess set two menus down on the table, but I chose not to open mine because I didn't want to decide on what to eat before Francine got there, then have her feel rushed to make a decision. I saw her run toward me—she was wearing a raincoat, though the sky was clear and had been all day—looking distraught, while I sat back sedately and said, "Don't worry about it. Calm down." Then, "Is everything all right?" and, damn it, I knew it was going to happen, and it did. I started to feel better about myself and better about seeing her, and glad when I saw her smile and heard her explain that "Yes, I left school later than I expected to, I didn't bother to go home, and, by the way, I'm not teaching in Janesboro anymore." She breathed in deeply, smiled, and said, "Jesus, is it just me or does time seem to go faster as you get older?"

"It doesn't go faster," I said, "it just takes longer to do everything."

"So how are you?" she asked. She stood, took off her coat and placed it next to her, first on the portion of her seat that extended into the aisle, then on the portion that extended to the partition, then breathed out loudly.

"Since when?" I asked.

"Since always," she said, but her smile had faded. "Oh, you mean when did I change jobs," she said. "A few years back. Four to be exact."

I laughed and said, "I'm fine; thank you for asking. Clearly we've got a lot to talk about."

Gently she bit her lower lip. "Don't we, though?"

Our waitress, Melody, a middle-aged woman with a bouffant hairdo, told us she'd be pleased to take our order. But Francine had just gotten there and I hadn't looked at my menu yet—clearly Melody hadn't been pleased to notice that—so she told us she'd come back in a few minutes, which, I knew, meant she wouldn't be back for a while.

"Have you been here before?" Francine asked.

I nodded. "Before it was new."

She sighed. "So you still wear sport jackets, I see."

I shrugged and smiled. "What can I tell you? I like them."

"But now tell me this. Do you own any suits?"

"No," I said. "I'm at that age where all of my friends who are going to get married have already gotten married, and you don't need a suit for a funeral."

"Are you okay?" she asked, looking genuinely concerned.

"Never been better," I said, which was true enough, but I didn't want to be there.

"Good," she said, "because I'm not."

The radio was on, as it was in most diners, pumping music through the PA system, but it seemed louder than it should have, and I found that annoying. Or maybe it was just the situation that I found annoying.

"Okay," I said, "let's do this. We'll look at our menus, decide what we want, order, and then we'll spend as long as you want talking."

Chicken consommé with rice and pot roast with extra gravy for her, and split pea soup—"With croutons?" "Of course"—and filet of flounder stuffed with crabmeat for me. With cocktail sauce. Both of our entrées came with mashed potatoes, and she asked for carrots and peas on the side while I asked for broccoli.

"Where should I begin?" She glanced at me.

I leaned back. "Tell me about Freddy," I said, "because that was the first thing you'd mentioned when you called."

"Wait a minute," she said, and opened her pocketbook. "It's not working out." She was looking inside and shaking her head. "And *now*...just a minute, please, I'm going to show you why." She took out her cell phone, swiped it a few times, and said, "Look."

And there was a picture of, as she'd told me, an older man, with a round face, high forehead, graying hair neatly combed back, a pencil-thin mustache, and a very shy smile. To be honest, I thought he was handsome.

"I'm looking," I said.

"So?" she asked. "Isn't it obvious?"

I shook my head then looked at her blankly. "No, it's not," I said. "What am I missing?"

"Morley, the man is ugly."

"Do you have any other pictures of him?" I asked. "Because, I'm sorry to tell you—"

Melody brought our soup.

"I don't see it at all. In fact, I find him pretty attractive," I said.

Francine looked disappointed. "Maybe *you* should be dating him then, not me. Morley, look at his face. How can you not see how ugly he is?"

"Look," I said seriously, "unless this is a joke, and I can tell by looking at you that it's not, I don't see what you have against him. Is it because he's older? What is he? In his sixties?"

"Yes, but that's just it," she said, smiling limply. "He looks his age."

I took a spoonful of soup. It was all right but notably thin. "So what?" I asked. "So do you and so do I. And there's nothing wrong with that. You know what I hate? When people ask me how old I am, and I tell them that I'm sixty-two—"

"You're not sixty-two."

"Close enough. I tell them that I'm sixty-two, and they say, 'Really? You don't look it.' Now yes, I know, there are three stages to life: youth, middle age, and 'Really? You don't look it.' But it's insulting, especially when they tell me that they mean it as a compliment, because what they're saying is, I look *good* by *not* looking my age. What bullshit."

She sat back and raised her eyebrows. "You're being honest with me now, aren't you?"

I was. So I said, "Of course not. I hate growing old, too." But I didn't. And I certainly didn't mind turning sixty, which, since I'd hit my late fifties, I refused to think of as *old*. When people asked me how it felt, I would tell them it felt fine. I'd been born old, and now I was finally catching up. "So tell me about your school."

"All right," she said, pulling up the sleeves on her blouse. She tasted her soup but shook her head, meaning she didn't like it. "I left Janesboro four years ago and now I'm teaching in Gerta."

"Gerta?! Do they even have their own school district? What's the population there, a hundred and three?"

"A hundred and one," she said. "Two people died."

"They must have eaten here," I said, and she laughed. "Do you like it? The school, I mean, not the soup."

She sighed. "I guess. I mean, the staff is okay—"

And all I could think was how perfect it would be if the next thing they played on the radio was *I've Heard That Song Before*.

"But Morley, it bores me. I'm bored."

Boredom, somebody once told me, was the shell around depression. You crack through the boredom and you realize you're depressed. I'd never understood or appreciated what Francine must have been going through for most of her life. I knew that. I thought back to my attempts to *save* her, when we'd first met, thinking that she just needed companionship, or a laugh, or somebody to make her feel better about herself, the way she'd often made me feel better about myself. And though that might have helped, I realized soon enough how naïve I was. And yet, I persisted, because, in some crazy way, that realization comforted and released me. When I try to help somebody, but see that I'm not, I end up feeling that I've failed the other person—failed to make him or her happy—and failed myself—failed to do what was expected of me. And yet that never stopped me, because continuously trying was more about exonerating myself than satisfying someone else.

So all I could say was, "Why don't you come back? To Lake Quaintance, I mean. Would you ever consider it?" I was staring right at her.

"Morley, I can't," she said, and pushed her raincoat farther into the corner. "I'm too old."

"Too old for what?! I don't know if you realize this, but it's the students who have to be young, not us."

At least she laughed. "True that," she said, "but you know, there's something sad about teaching. You develop a relationship with your students, class after class, and then, at the end of the semester or the end of the year, they move on, and usually you never see them again. Then a new group comes in and you start all over. But while the students remain young, you get older."

"Are you giving up?" I asked.

"On teaching? No," she said.

"Hmm. That's not what I meant," I said. But I didn't think she understood me.

Melody brought out the entrées and sides, but to me they looked about as good as the soup had tasted. My flounder was noticeably undercooked, and the gravy on Francine's pot roast looked serous and pale; no pan drippings there, unless the beef had been braised for thirty seconds in tap water.

"How are things there, anyway?" she asked.

I knew she wouldn't come back, so I could tell her whatever I wanted to. I spread my legs in front of me and stretched my arms. "Different," I said. "Very different. Leo retired. That's the big change, and they still haven't found anyone to replace him."

"Really?!" she asked.

"Yeah," I said. "I was surprised, too. But, maybe I shouldn't have been. We're all getting older."

*

About a month before, I'd noticed that Leo hadn't come to school for three days. At first I thought he was on vacation and had either forgotten to tell me—he was, after all, nearing seventy—or I'd forgotten that he'd told me, but then, dismissing that, I walked into Ron's office, Ron being Leo's boss, and asked him if he knew what was going on.

Ron shook his head. "I don't," he said. "He hasn't called me, either."

"Did you call him?" I asked. I was agitated, and didn't like sounding that way.

Ron pressed his lips together, shook his head very slightly, then said, "I didn't. But," he pointed to his desk, which was littered with papers and books, "I've got a lot going on. Why don't you call him and let me know."

"Thanks," I said tepidly. "I'll do that."

I could have asked one of the other members of our department—Alice, by that time, had been replaced by Maddie Katz, a lesbian who I rather liked—but I didn't feel close enough to any of them and didn't want to find out that Leo had told them something he hadn't told me.

So that night I called his house. His wife answered. "Hello?"

"Hello...Maline?" I asked.

"Yes," she said.

"Maline, hi. This is Morley. Morley Peck. I don't know if you remember me, but I was at your house for a holiday party a while back"—twenty-three years ago—"and I work with your husband—"

"I know who you are," she said, but she sounded angry and suspicious, almost as though she were blaming me for something.

"Okay, good," I said. "Um, can I speak to Leo, please?"

"No, you can't," she said, then added, "he's not here."

"All right," I said, feeling extremely nervous. "Could you have him give me a call, please, when he comes back?"

"He's not coming back, Morley," she said. "He's dead."

I nearly dropped the phone, and felt a cramp in the bottom of my stomach. "What?! When?"

"A few days ago," she said. "Saturday morning. Heart attack, while he was in bed. And the funeral was Monday, so please don't ask."

"Maline," I said, "I'm so sorry." I was. "I don't know what to say." I didn't.

"Good," she said. "Then why don't you not say anything except good-bye?" Then I heard her crying. "That's all I was able to say."

And I understood, or *thought* I understood, though I probably didn't, just how she felt. That night, Ron and the entire staff of the English department—Ellie, Mark, Stanley, Maddie, and I—visited her, and I came back for two nights afterward.

The following week Mark was put in Leo's position, and was made my new boss. Just as, I'd long assumed, he'd always wanted to be.

*

"Well I can't say I blame him," Francine said.

"Who? Blame whom?"

"Leo," she said. "He was getting near retirement."

"Francine," I said, "he was well past it." By two years.

"Morley," she said, looking at me intently. "How long have we known each other?"

I shrugged. "Hmm," I said. "Let me think." But I didn't need to. "Twenty-three years."

"That's a long time," she said.

I took a bite of the fish. Tasteless. "Well you have to put it in perspective. In the history of the world, no. In the history of our lives, yes."

She puckered her lips. "Morley," she said. "This is a dangerous question, I know."

"All questions are dangerous. The good ones, anyway," I said.

"Are you afraid to die?"

I took another bite of the fish. Had she been reading my mind? Still tasteless. And when I dipped it in the cocktail sauce, not fresh, I was left with tasteless food that suddenly had the flavor of cocktail sauce. "Good question," I said. "I mean, sure I am. Aren't you?"

Francine put her fork down. "I am, but I don't want to be," she said. "But who am I kidding? Sometimes I'm not."

The woman who'd attempted suicide two and a half times. Death, or at least the thought of death, couldn't have been unfamiliar to her.

*

The second time my mother asked me if I was afraid to die came four weeks after the first. We were in her apartment, sitting in the living room. She had been on the couch and I'd been sitting on the loveseat, and she said, "Why don't you come over here? I want to ask you a question."

That was just like her. She would never simply ask me something; she had to announce it first. So I moved to where she was sitting and said, "Sure. What would you like to know?"

She stared at me so steadily that I thought she was going to tell me something terrible about her health—I always feared it, but could never quite accept it—but she said, "Sweetheart, okay. I'll ask you again. Are you afraid to die?"

"Mom, why?" I asked.

"Because I asked you that before, but I wasn't satisfied with your answer. You said you didn't know, but I could tell you were holding something back. So please tell me. Are you or aren't you?"

I sighed and stretched, digging my feet into the carpet in front of me, and reaching my arms forward, but not toward her. It wasn't a question that required a lot of thought—the answer was no—but I wanted to make it seem as though it did because I didn't want to come across as glib. "Mom, if I were afraid to die," I said, "I would have to regret something, and I don't really have any regrets in my life."

"No?" she asked, but she didn't smile. Was she surprised?

I shook my head. "Not really. I've always known what I've wanted and what I've liked, so it's been easy to make myself happy." And then I wondered if she'd been able to make herself happy, too, but I continued. "You want to know something? I've been one of the lucky ones. I've accomplished pretty much everything I've wanted to in this life and now, if I had to, I really believe that I could leave it with no regrets. And I say that without any bitterness or depression that I'm aware of. It's like I'm all packed for a long trip and know there's nothing else I need to bring with me."

She smiled, didn't say anything for a moment, then leaned over and kissed me. "That's all I wanted to know," she said.

It was also what she'd wanted to hear, but that wasn't why I'd told her that. I'd told her that because it was the truth, and I almost never lied to my mother.

*

Neither Francine nor I was enjoying the meal. We alternately picked at it, put our forks down, tried it again, then put our forks down again.

"This place is terrible," she said.

"It's not what it used to be," I said.

"Is anything?" she asked.

I shook my head. "I don't know," I said.

Stupidly, perhaps, we ordered dessert, but it was just Jell-O for her and chocolate pudding for me. How bad could that be? And I could tell that she wanted to talk more.

And, sure enough, she asked, "Can I say something?"

"Please do," I said.

"Since I turned sixty I've started thinking about 'last times,'" she said. "Now you can't possibly know what I mean by that, and no, it's not biblical." She laughed. "So I'll explain it. When I go to the grocery store, for instance, I wonder if that will be the *last time* I'll go there. When I go to the beauty parlor, I wonder if that will be the last time I'll go there. When I go to the gym, I wonder if that will be the last time I'll go there. And so on. Now that might sound crazy to you—"

"It might," I said.

"Does it?"

"It might," I said again.

"But anyway, that's the way I feel. That's the way I've been feeling. Wondering if everything I do is going to be the last time I do it."

I leaned back. "Look, Francine," I said as seriously as I could, "it *is* the last time you're going to do it. Until the next time."

"I don't get you," she said.

"Of course you do," I said. "Francine, there's always going to be a next time, until there isn't anymore. But you'll never know it, so I don't see why you worry about it."

"Well that isn't very consoling," she said.

Melody brought our desserts and, as expected, the Jell-O and the chocolate pudding were completely without flaw. Only hard water, I thought, might have ruined them.

"What do you want me to say?" I asked. "I understand what you're telling me, really I do, but it seems like you're worrying for nothing. Because when the end does come, you're not going to know it...if you're lucky."

"If I'm lucky," she said.

*

Brahms' Fourth Symphony—still, I thought, his supreme masterpiece—was one of the first pieces of classical music I ever heard. I'd discovered it one Sunday afternoon when I was in high school. My Aunt Emma and Uncle Bert and Aunt Elaine and Uncle Sy were over. We were living in a small garden apartment then, and while my parents were entertaining them—again, something they rarely did—in the living room, I retired to my bedroom, which was across the hall, and shut my door so I could listen to music relatively undisturbed, and so that I wouldn't disturb them.

That was in the day when there were many classical radio stations on the air, at least where we lived, and live concerts were broadcast frequently. I'd never heard the Brahms Fourth but I'd read a lot about it. My high school library was well-stocked with nonfiction books, and I loved nonfiction to the virtual exclusion of fiction, so I'd read up whenever I could on classical music.

And from the first notes of the piece I was mesmerized; stunned by its beauty and stimulated by its logic. I was, at first, surprised, then gratified, and, ultimately, moved to realize how deeply music could affect me. And that was when I understood, for the first time, that I was capable of love. Profound, meaningful, and complete. My mood changed and, I knew, so had my life. Over the years I'd listened to the Brahms Fourth so often—I bought an LP of it, and I didn't have many recordings back then—that I could hum it to myself practically note for note. And once more, I'd listened to it a few nights before, but then wondered, just as Francine had said, if I'd ever hear it again. I had so many recordings, thousands and thousands, that I concentrated on things I didn't know as well. I was always looking to discover something new. But still, I asked myself if that would be the last time.

*

Walking to our cars, which, it turned out, were parked next to each other, Francine said, "Well, thank you again for a wonderful evening." I didn't look to see if she was smiling, but she sounded convincing enough. "We'll do it again."

"Just not here," I said.

And she laughed. "No," she said. "Just not here." Then, "God, I have a long drive home."

"Me, too," I said. "So let me not keep you."

"Until next time?" she asked.

"Until next time," I said.

And we drove away.

UNANSWERED questions

There comes a time in most people's lives, usually late, I would suppose, when they stop questioning their happiness and learn to appreciate it. The questions are many: Am I *really* happy? Would I be *happier* if I did *something else*? And, most damagingly, are the *right things* making me happy? And all they do is retard our ability to attain satisfaction. Still, we cling to them because we're used to asking them and there's comfort in familiarity. Sometimes we stop asking them because we understand their illogic and know enough to move away, and sometimes we stop asking them because we realize that we're not going to be around for nearly as long as those things that gladden us are, so we'd better appreciate them while we can. But sometimes we never do stop.

When I was growing up, and we were a family of extremely modest means, I used to look at friends' and relatives' houses that were bigger than ours and filled with furniture that was newer and nicer than ours, and think, If only I could have that, I would be happy. What I didn't realize was that the people who had those things were not necessarily, or even usually happy themselves. Because they couldn't appreciate what they had.

To cite an extreme example, one of my parents' friends, an older man named Jackie Day, would buy a new car every year, because he couldn't stand not having "the latest, the greatest, and the best." But what comfort could that have afforded him? He was so busy trying to impress other people that he had no time left to impress himself. And the lucky among us realize, at around the time that we stop asking ourselves those questions, that the only people we can truly impress are ourselves, because no two people's tastes are the same. I could flash a diamond ring at someone, but if he doesn't like the cut of the stone he won't be impressed, and how much better off would I be then?

And that was how, by understanding the nature of happiness, my happiness, I came to understand that what I liked most about Francine, her ability to make me feel good about myself, stemmed from the fact that she made me feel lucky to be who I was. Which is to say, lucky to not be her and lucky to not be like her, because she was someone who would never be happy, never appreciate what she had, and never be satisfied. So now I had to ask myself, did or does or can that make us friends? I don't know. Perhaps that will be answered some other time, and I'm sure that by then I'll have many more questions to ask. And hopefully they'll be good ones.

MEMENTO MORI

It was late. Time to get ready for dinner, as I was meeting Francine in less than an hour. We'd started going back to Roscoe's Diner, so many years after Pano had offended her, because Pano wasn't around anymore. Although he'd left Lake Quaintance High School ten years after she did, I don't think he'd retired, but he never gave any details about what fix he would be getting himself into, and I never heard from or saw him again.

As had become our habit, I would meet Francine at the diner. We never met at her house or mine, and never traveled back to one another's house, either. Whatever needed to be said would be said over dinner, and anything left unsaid would be contemplated then mulled over on the phone the next day. And then one of us would think, God, we've still got so much to say, and we'd tell each other that it wouldn't be long before we got together again, but it always was.

Then what? More lies?

I had to laugh. "I hope I never have to give the eulogy at your funeral," she'd told me once.

"Why?" I'd asked.

"Because I have no idea who you are. Who you *really* are."

And all I could think of was the advice that she'd always given her students. "Take notes," I'd said, and left it at that.

Now I shook my head. Not tonight, I thought. Tomorrow. Maybe I would tell her the truth tomorrow.

Completed March 13, 2020